PRAISE FOR DEBRA WEBB

Deeper Than the Dead

"Expertly plotted and whip smart, *Deeper Than the Dead* is an exceedingly clever crime thriller filled with secrets, betrayals, and complex characters. Webb manages to hit that sweet spot between family drama and police procedural. This one is sure to be a hit in the crime-thriller genre. A wild and massively entertaining ride."

—Christina McDonald, *USA Today* bestselling author

The Last Lie Told

"A complex case fraught with angst and danger ends with surprising revelations."

—*Kirkus Reviews*

"Debra Webb writes the kind of thrillers I love to read. Sure, there is a murder or more. Yes, there's a twisted mystery to be solved. Once again, in *The Last Lie Told*, her characters are fully rendered and reveal themselves authentically as her novel unfolds and careens to its stunning conclusion. *The Last Lie Told* is her best yet. Webb is the queen of smart suspense."

—Gregg Olsen, #1 *New York Times* bestselling author

Can't Go Back

"A complex, exciting mystery."

—*Kirkus Reviews*

"Police procedural fans will be sorry to see the last of Kerri and Luke."

—*Publishers Weekly*

"Threats, violence, and a dramatic climax . . . good for procedural readers."

—*Library Journal*

Gone Too Far

"An intriguing, fast-paced combination of police procedural and thriller."

—*Kirkus Reviews*

"Those who like a lot of family drama in their police procedurals will be satisfied."

—*Publishers Weekly*

Trust No One

"*Trust No One* is Debra Webb at her finest. Political intrigue and dark family secrets will keep readers feverishly turning pages to uncover all the twists in this stunning thriller."

—Melinda Leigh, #1 *Wall Street Journal* bestselling author of *Cross Her Heart*

"A wild, twisting crime thriller filled with secrets, betrayals, and complex characters that will keep you up until you reach the last darkly satisfying page. A five-star beginning to Debra Webb's explosive series!"

—Allison Brennan, *New York Times* bestselling author

"Debra Webb once again delivers with *Trust No One*, a twisty and gritty page-turning procedural with a cast of complex characters and a compelling cop heroine in Detective Kerri Devlin. I look forward to seeing more of Detectives Devlin and Falco."

—Loreth Anne White, *Washington Post* bestselling author of *In the Deep*

"*Trust No One* is a gritty and exciting ride. Webb skillfully weaves together a mystery filled with twists and turns. I was riveted as each layer of the past peeled away, revealing dark secrets. An intriguing cast of complicated characters, led by the compelling Detective Kerri Devlin, had me holding my breath until the last page."

—Brianna Labuskes, *Washington Post* bestselling author of *Girls of Glass*

"Debra Webb's name says it all."

—Karen Rose, *New York Times* bestselling author

WHAT
GOES
AROUND

OTHER TITLES BY DEBRA WEBB

Vera Boyett

Deeper Than the Dead

Closer Than You Know

Secrets You Can't Keep

Finley O'Sullivan

The Last Lie Told

The Nature of Secrets

All the Little Truths

Devlin & Falco

Trust No One

Gone Too Far

Can't Go Back

Standalones

The Devoted Game

The Fatal Confidant

The Ten Year Lie

Deep Dark Truth

The Drowning Season

Lost in the Dark

WHAT GOES AROUND

DEBRA WEBB

Text copyright © 2018, 2026 by Debra Webb
All rights reserved.

Published by Thomas & Mercer, Seattle

www.apub.com

Amazon, the Amazon logo, and Thomas & Mercer are trademarks of Amazon.com, Inc., or its affiliates.

EU product safety contact:
Amazon Media EU S. à r.l.
38, avenue John F. Kennedy, L-1855 Luxembourg
amazonpublishing-gpsr@amazon.com

ISBN-13: 9781662534553 (paperback)
ISBN-13: 9781662534546 (digital)

Cover design by Faceout Studio, Addie Lutzo
Cover image: © Bilanol / Shutterstock; © FrankvandenBergh / Getty; © sakchai vongsasiripat / Getty; © Jose A. Bernat Bacete / Getty

Printed in the United States of America

WHAT
GOES
AROUND

ONE

Tuesday, May 1
Nashville

Positive.

I stare at the pregnancy test stick. My hands shaking, my heart pounding.

Impossible.

Then I look at the other three lined up in a neat row on the marble counter with its double sinks and polished brass hardware. I am pregnant. My eyes close and I move my head from side to side in silent, frantic denial. How could forgetting my pill that one time have culminated in this catastrophic event? In ten years of using birth control products, I have been nothing less than diligent. But after my father's unexpected death, I was a wreck for a few weeks. Then there was the move . . .

The excuses tumble through my brain, all of them irrelevant. None of them change the reality. I'm pregnant.

Only a little, probably. I had a period last month . . . It was light, shorter than usual, but I had one. Does that count? So how pregnant can I be? What the hell am I thinking? You can't be just a little pregnant. You're either pregnant or you're not.

I. Am. Pregnant. The words echo through me like shotgun blasts.

"What the hell have I done?" I mutter to myself as the panic builds.

My cell shudders against my waist before I can start answering myself. A call this early likely means there's no more time to worry about this unexpected development.

"Newhouse," I answer without checking the screen as I reach to gather the test sticks. Can't throw them in the trash. At least, not in the house.

"Hey, Liv."

Walt Duncan, my partner. The gruff sound of his voice makes me smile. He is the one thing in my life at the moment that feels normal, steady.

"Morning. You headed my way already?"

"I am," he says. "We got a call. Over on Twenty-Second. Might be just a missing person, but there's a lot of blood, according to the uniforms on the scene."

I slip the test sticks into the pocket of my khaki jacket as I consider the location, Osage / North Fisk neighborhood. Not exactly the best area when it comes to crime stats. "I'll be waiting on the porch."

"Be there in ten," Walt assures me, then ends the call.

As I tuck my cell away, a knock on the bathroom door jerks my head up.

"Liv, are you going to be a while in there?"

I suck in a sharp breath, then remind myself to stay calm. "Almost done."

I pick up my holstered service weapon and slide it onto my belt, followed by my badge, then check my reflection. Hair in a ponytail, I smooth my hand over a few stray strands. Eyes are clear. No sign of the tears I shed last night. I hate crying. It makes me feel weak. Cheeks are a little pale, but that goes with the territory of being a blue-eyed blonde. *Good enough,* I decide and turn away from the telltale mirror.

Cool, calm, and collected. I cannot deal with another fight this morning. Last night's was bad enough. I haven't had nearly enough sleep or coffee to function properly, much less remind him that there are four other bathrooms in this big-ass house.

Another deep breath. I open the door and brush past him, lips fixed in a fake smile. "It's all yours."

I feel his gaze burning a hole in my back as I hurry across the bedroom and out the door. It's barely six o'clock. Early for him. The man I'm supposed to marry in November is the president of Brentwood's Neighborhood Bank, one of four local banks his family owns. I don't have to look back to know he's still wearing his Ralph Lauren pajama bottoms, that his dark hair is mussed and his green eyes are bleary with sleep. I also know from experience that he'll wait until I'm halfway down the stairs before he decides on an appropriate way to respond to my less-than-cheery disposition.

Everything about him used to make me happy. I have no idea when that changed. Or why. But everything feels different, off somehow. Maybe it's only me who's changed.

"Good morning to you, too!" he calls loudly. Not quite a shout, mind you. Prestons don't shout. They speak firmly, knowledgeably. They stand their ground.

"Morning," I grumble, not caring whether or not he hears me.

He doesn't have to hear me to know that I've responded. He has watched my morning rituals daily for nearly a month now, and two or three times a week for about six months before that. He understands I'm inevitably running behind and that I mutter when I'm annoyed. He recognizes that I am always as tired when I get up as I was when I went to bed because I never, ever manage to get enough sleep. I'm a cop—a homicide detective. I eat, drink, and breathe my work. And sometimes I manage to sleep with the monsters stuck in my head, but not nearly often enough.

And now I'm pregnant.

Charles David Preston II, fondly called David to prevent any confusion with his father, Charles, was well aware of these facts before he pushed me to move in with him. Before he insisted it was time we progressed to the next level in our relationship and became engaged. I agreed to all his demands, however grudgingly, for no other reason than to make him happy—not because I don't want to be with him or I don't love him, and not even that I'm anything less than as committed as he is. The truth is, I'm not good with change. But I took the plunge into all-out rapid-fire commitment . . . for him. Because he wanted to move up the timeline. Because loving him terrifies me on every single level of my being. And because some part of me has suddenly become convinced that I don't deserve him, and I despise the idea that he makes me feel so fragile in that regard.

He dragged me to this new level with his eyes wide open. I am not a morning person. I'm an even worse housemate. I might very well be terrible wife material—I'm certain his parents are still in shock over the announcement.

And I am most assuredly not mother material.

I exhale a ragged breath as I shuffle across the kitchen, with its gleaming white cabinets and shiny black-and-white diamond-patterned floor tiles. From the soaring ceilings to the polished wood floors filling most of the luxurious rooms, this classic two-story is every inch the epitome of his mother's design style. The furnishings alone likely cost more than I make in three or four years of hard work as a detective. Not to mention his top-of-the-line Mercedes parked in the triple-car garage.

This is not my life—it's his, and I am not certain I fit into it. How did I not notice this before now?

I grab a mug and pour coffee into it, then head for the door. Somewhere in the back of my mind, the idea that caffeine is not a good thing while pregnant flits around.

David pauses at the bottom of the stairs, that *caught you* expression on his face. A sigh drains out of me. This—being here, being us—is suddenly, utterly exhausting.

"So you're leaving? Now? No breakfast? Not even a minute or two for quality time with me? I feel like we need to talk about last night."

I am leaving and I cannot eat for fear of vomiting. If I mention the latter, there will only be more questions. "Got a call. I have to go. I don't have a nine-to-five job, David. You know this. I don't understand why my work is suddenly such a sticking point for you, but this is what I do."

His lips compress for a second, then two, while he searches for a different strategy. Christ, I know him so well.

I love so many things about him. Why has everything abruptly changed? Why all at once are we both so determined to torture each other?

Or maybe it's just me. That whole I'm Not Good Enough syndrome.

"What about all these boxes, Liv?" He gestures to the pile a few feet away. "Are you ever going to unpack and actually start living here, or is this nothing more than the new place where you shower and sleep?"

I consider the stack of boxes I reluctantly packed and moved from the farm where I grew up to his stately foyer right here in Belle Meade, where so many of Nashville's rich and famous reside. The boxes do sort of block the view into the dining room. The drab brown color certainly clashes with the elegant decor. I'm sure it drives him crazy.

This morning, however, the boxes are merely something to use as fuel for more unpleasant discourse. He can't really yell at me for doing my job.

Not fair, Liv. You aren't exactly making any of this easy.

I look into his green eyes—the eyes that charmed the pants right off me the first night we met—and remind myself that I love this man. I plan to spend the rest of my life with him. Evidently, I will be bearing his child.

Guilt straddles my shoulders, so I walk over to him, go up on tiptoe, and give him a peck on the cheek. "I'll make it up to you, I promise. And I will unpack the boxes. Soon. See you later. Gotta go."

Then I walk out the door.

He says nothing. He's not happy.

But I'm the one who's pregnant.

A couple minutes later, Walt's Tahoe enters the U-shaped drive and stops in front of the house. I hustle down the steps, leaving my mug on the porch. I have no desire to go back inside and continue the fight that actually started last night—which is exactly what would happen. The issue is that I want to delay the wedding from the day after Thanksgiving until April of next year. I told him I needed more time.

Of course, that was before the pregnancy tests I took this morning, all four of which I tucked inside a trash bag in the bin next to the garage while I waited for Walt. It's not that I don't like kids and don't want any of my own. It's not even that I don't want to get married. I'm just not certain now is the right time. This year has been insane. My father died not even three months ago, the month before I turned thirty. On top of those life-altering events, I agreed to marry the man I love and move into his house—into his life. I feel as if my life is spinning out of control. All I want is to slow things down a bit.

Except now the timeline is completely beyond my ability to manage.

The distant ache in my skull that I woke up with deepens as I climb into the passenger seat and reach for the seat belt. I push away the madness of my personal life and study my partner as he guides his SUV away from the house.

"You look like I feel," I warn.

He glances at me, his eyes bloodshot, his face haggard. "I wouldn't wish that on my worst enemy."

I breathe a laugh. "Me, either."

I continue my scrutiny of him as he drives through the damp streets. Apparently, it rained after I went to bed at about two this morning. Walt left the office a little while before me. I finalized our reports on the now-closed homicide case that had kept us beating the bushes for almost two weeks.

Based on those bloodshot eyes of his, I think maybe Walt's old buddy Jack Daniel's kept him up awhile. That's happened a lot lately—the over-indulging in his preferred whiskey. I don't ask. If he wanted me to know whatever's going on, he would tell me. This is a concept my fiancé doesn't grasp and certainly cannot appreciate. Walt and I—though separated in age by three decades—completely understand each other. We respect each other unconditionally. It doesn't matter to Walt that I'm female or that I'm half his age. We're equal. Of course, I'm well aware he's the experienced detective of thirty-odd years and I'm the newbie with only two under my belt, but he never flaunts that detail. He treats me as a peer in every way.

"Jack can be a real ass kicker the morning after." I turn forward and sink into the seat. Walt's a grown man, turned sixty on his last birthday. If he decides to drink more than usual—far more frequently than is normal for him—it's none of my business. I don't doubt his ability to have my back for a second. He's the best. I just worry about him, that's all. Since his wife died, he's had a hard time dealing with life outside of work.

"What's your excuse?" He flashes me a quick grin.

"Trust me." I fold my arms over my middle as if I fear he might be able to see the answer without me saying a word. "You do not want to go there."

"More trouble in paradise?" He chuckles. "I'm not sure your fiancé knows what he's getting himself into, marrying a dedicated cop like you."

I grunt. I have no desire to discuss my personal life this morning. Way too complicated. "So, what've we got?"

"Uniforms were dispatched for a welfare check. They arrived and found the back door open, nobody home, and a substantial amount of blood in the kitchen, so here we go." He shrugs. "No big surprise, considering the neighborhood. We've worked the area before. Last October, if memory serves."

I remember. Last time it took a week to determine that the wife was the murderer. The diminutive woman hadn't looked like a killer. The vic was a big guy—six four, two hundred plus pounds—a drug dealer. The wife had waited until he was passed out on the couch one night and then put a bullet in the back of his skull with his own backup piece, a .22. Discovering that fact might have been a fairly easy step had she not worn elbow-length rubber gloves to prevent any risk of gunpowder residue on her skin. To be completely certain she covered her tracks, she even went so far as to burn the clothes she'd been wearing at the time. Then she claimed she had spent the entire night at her sister's. The whole family backed up her alibi. But by day seven, she came forward and confessed. Said it was her Catholic guilt. She ended up getting a plea deal for providing information on her husband's drug connections.

I consider Walt's comments about the scene where we're headed. No body at the scene, but lots of blood. "Could be the vic is in the ER after cutting him- or herself with a knife or something." Seems a reasonable possibility. "If the blood's in the kitchen, might be nothing but an accident during meal prep."

"I guess we'll see."

"We will indeed." Nothing takes your mind off your personal problems like a potential homicide.

By the time we reach Twenty-Second, the distant ache in my skull has become a throb on the left side of my brain, and black spots float in front of my eyes. Not a good sign. The shitstorm is coming. My hope is that I can delay the inevitable until we get through this scene.

Migraines can be a raging bitch.

The yard in front of the small gray house is cordoned off with yellow crime scene tape that turns ninety degrees at the far end and continues on around to the back door, I imagine. A police cruiser sits in the driveway behind a rusty Impala that presumably belongs to the vic. The tires on the Impala are flat. The windshield has been shattered. Apparently, someone has been showing the tenant in this rental some love.

A white van sporting the blue Metro Crime Scene Unit logo is parked on the grass at the edge of the street. Along both sides of the block, curious neighbors have ventured out into their yards to watch the evolving show. Probably the Movie of the Week around here—a rerun of last year's classic *Death of a Drug Dealer*.

"Nice place," Walt comments.

I glance around at the trash in the yard, the old, tattered sofa on the porch of the potential vic's place of residence. "Yeah."

A car sits on blocks in a neighboring yard, various parts stripped from the metal carcass. Trash is scattered about and banked against trees and foundations. The power lines sag and the pole nearest the crime scene looks ready to fall over. An empty doghouse sits to the right of the driveway, the bald ground around it suggesting an animal was recently chained there.

I hate when people chain up dogs.

We park on the opposite side of the street. As Walt said, we've been here before. Two houses down is where the drug dealer was murdered the last time we were called to this block. Evidently, someone new lives there now. A little girl with curly brown hair hides behind her mother's legs. I wonder whether the mother realizes that a man was murdered in the house where she now resides. Definitely not the kind of place where you want to raise a kid, if you have a choice. Not that I know one damned thing about raising kids.

I exile the thought.

Officer Sean Little meets us at the yellow perimeter. The starched creases in his inspection-ready uniform make me feel like a dirtbag. My navy trousers and shirt are clean, but they haven't seen a crease since the last time I bothered with a dry cleaner. Like me, Walt wears his favorite jacket; his is navy and matches his trousers. Unlike me, my partner always wears cowboy boots. Not just any boots, either. Lucchese, handmade boots. Over the years, he's become known as the "cowboy detective." Nashville loves Detective Walter Duncan. Me, I'll stick with my flat-heeled, rubber-soled ankle boots. You won't catch me in heels like the detectives on TV or in the movies. Being a cop is rarely glamorous work.

Officer Little nods a greeting and says, "Crime scene investigators just got here."

I don't have to ask if Walt called the CSI guys. He prefers to get them rolling rather than waiting until he's on the scene to make the call. Typically we show up about the same time, which works out for everyone. We have a look and they do their thing, with no delay in the process.

"Any of the neighbors see anything?" Walt asks.

"Just one. It may or may not be relevant. She lives in the next house down. She claims a couple of women who don't live in the neighborhood have been driving by a lot recently. She gave me the color and possible make of the vehicle."

"We'll talk to her when we're done here," Walt says with a glance at me.

I lag behind as we cross the yard and climb the two steps to the front door. I make a face at the ghastly odor there. A quick glance shows a variety of carcasses on the porch. One looks like a possum. Another might be an armadillo. Shit, a raccoon. Just stacked in a stinky pile, waiting for whatever.

Little notices me staring. "No clue," he says. "There are more near the back door. I guess someone was leaving him gifts."

How screwed up is that?

Once inside the small living room, we drag on gloves. I force my sluggish brain to inventory the space. A battered sofa is the only seating in the room. An ancient box-style television is tuned to some morning show, the poor cable or antenna connection making the screen all fuzzy. The television sits on a scarred wooden table. A fake-wood floor is dark enough in color to hide how dirty it likely is. The popcorn ceiling is a dingy yellow, an unpleasant match to the discolored blinds closed tight on the one window in the room.

The headache is raging now. My vision is starting to blur, damn it. I've never had one of these headaches on duty. Why, after all this time, are they back? After years of no migraines, I can't believe another one is happening scarcely forty-eight hours after the last. I close my eyes for a moment and try to slow my plunge toward hell. The dank odor of human filth and the underlying metallic scent of blood have my gut roiling in protest.

"You okay, Liv?"

I snap my eyes open and bring my partner's worried face into focus. "Migraine. I'll muddle through."

"The volume on the TV was turned all the way up when I got here," Little says. "I turned it down. The guy who lives here didn't show up for an appointment with his attorney." He flips to a different page in his field notebook. "One Alexander Cagle. So Cagle called in and asked for a welfare check. Back door was ajar when we arrived. There's a bedroom with nothing but a mattress on the floor and a small bathroom down the hall. Kitchen's straight through that doorway." Little gestures to the cased opening beyond the sofa.

Walt and I enter the kitchen where a crime scene investigator is doing his thing. A sizable pattern of blood has coagulated on the faded blue linoleum. There's a wad of cloth, maybe a washcloth or a hand towel, in the middle of it. No other readily visible signs of a struggle.

"Obvious forced entry at the back door," Little says. "The perp appears to have encountered the victim at the sink. Since none of the neighbors heard a gunshot and we haven't found any indication a weapon was discharged in the room, I'm thinking he used a knife. But we haven't found one so far."

"Could be the perp had a gun," Walt offers. "If the vic was washing dishes, he may have tried to defend himself with a knife or some other sharp object readily available." He gestures to the dishes soaking in the cold, cloudy water in the sink. "Perp didn't want to fire the weapon and risk disturbing the neighbors, so they battled it out. Someone was injured."

As the two discuss the possible scenarios, their words keep time with the pounding in my skull, and the events play out in my brain like snatches of some low-budget slasher film showing in a dark, sketchy theater.

Walt asks, "You have an ID on the possible vic?"

"We're assuming it's the guy who lives here. Just moved in about a month ago. Carl Fanning, that pedophile who was released last month. He was all over the news for a couple of days."

"You should go back to the car," my partner murmurs.

I realize Walt is speaking to me, and I force my eyes open. Hadn't noticed they had closed. "I'm okay." Except I'm not—not really.

In fact, I'm a long-ass way from okay. I'm pretty sure I'm going to puke any second, and the smell of blood isn't helping. Staying vertical is growing more questionable by the second. I can only see half of my partner's face as he stares at me, worry marring his features. The visual disturbances have begun in earnest. There will be no slowing down the inevitable or the momentum now.

"Officer Little, make sure Detective Newhouse gets back to my vehicle. I'll take care of things in here."

If I wasn't afraid the coffee I drank this morning would spew out all over my partner's beloved boots, I would open my mouth and argue with him. Instead, I stumble back outside, puke halfway across the driveway for all the nosy neighbors to see, and then lean against the Tahoe.

A few deep breaths and I feel fractionally better. Enough so that I opt not to abandon my partner. "I need to talk to the neighbor." I say this to Little, who is still watching me. He likely finds this seriously weird, but whatever.

"Well . . . okay," he says with a glance at the crime scene house before leading the way.

I push off the Tahoe and follow him across the lawn and into the next. The neighboring house is about the size of the one we just left, but with a bit of a homier feel. Officer Little knocks on the door while I struggle to focus my vision. I will not let this damned headache win.

The door opens and an elderly woman looks from Little to me.

"Ms. Scoggins, this is Detective Newhouse. She has a few questions for you related to the statement you gave earlier."

The woman eyeballs me. "You ain't sick, are you?"

"No, ma'am. Just a raging headache."

She nods and then backs away to allow me inside. Little follows, evidently concerned I may need his help before this is done.

Once we're seated in the living room, I ask, "Did you know Mr. . . . ?" I look to Little. How the hell could I have forgotten the potential vic's name?

"Fanning. Your missing neighbor," he explains to the woman.

"No." She wags her head side to side. "I saw that news report about him. I don't know him, but I know what he is." Disgust paints a sneer on her lips, but I can see only one side. "We've got little girls in this neighborhood. So I've been watching. That's how come I saw those two women driving by. Every day, sometimes twice. They drive by real slow like they're watching for him to be outside or for something to happen."

"Did they ever stop?" I ask.

She does that side-to-side wag of her head again. "No. Just driving by real slow in that fancy SUV. One of them Land Rovers or Range Rovers."

"Did you get a good look at either of the women?" I glance at Little as I ask this, thankful he's taking notes.

"White women, in their thirties, I guess. Maybe forties. One of them was blond—the one driving. The other one had dark hair."

"But you didn't see them talk to anyone on the street or anything like that?"

"Nope, they just drove by day after day. Most times twice, like I said."

"Did you notice the license plate?" The taste of bile makes me want to puke again.

"I didn't get the numbers, but it was one of those state parks ones. I like those tags."

At least that's something. "You have Ms. Scoggins's details?" I ask Little.

He nods.

I struggle to retrieve a card from my jacket pocket and pass it to the lady. "Please call me if you think of anything else. Or if you hear anything from anyone that might help us figure out what happened here."

She looks at my card, then at me. "I will," she says, "but God knows that monster don't deserve no help from the police or anyone else."

I thank her and manage to walk out of the house on my own. I go straight to Walt's Tahoe and climb in. Little says something to me, but I can't respond.

Instead, I close my eyes and slip into the darkness closing in on me.

Sleep is the only way to escape this hellish nightmare.

TWO

Detective Walter Duncan

By early afternoon, Liv seems more like herself. Damn, I'm glad. I worry about that girl like she's my own daughter.

This case coming right on the heels of the one we just closed adds another layer of stress to both our lives. Fanning, the probable vic, is a newly released pedophile whose victims were mostly little girls. The bastard is a couple years older than me, and the fourteen years he spent in prison weren't nearly enough. God only knows how many children he abused before he got caught. Thirteen that we know of. Personally, I hope someone dragged him out into the woods somewhere and beat the shit out of him before pouring gasoline over his naked body and setting him on fire. Enough said.

Except now he's Metro's problem. No matter that he is a monster, not worthy of the air he breathes; he's entitled to the same protection under the law as anyone else. I roll my eyes and heave a weary breath. It's Liv's and my job to make sure the investigation is handled by the book. The chief already called and warned me that the world will be watching to see that the no-good SOB—my words, not the chief's—gets the same treatment as any other citizen of our fair city.

"I've confirmed," Liv says, dragging my attention from the frustrating thoughts, "the whereabouts of his known victims. Three are dead and two are in prison. One moved to Seattle years ago. The rest still live in this area."

"So we have seven of his victims to check out," I say.

It's possible that someone besides one of his victims broke into Fanning's home, fought with him over drugs or some other unsavory business, and then carried him off, but it's far more likely that the motive is revenge for the bastard's very public sins. Either a victim, or a friend or family member of a victim, is the most realistic scenario.

In my experience, it's always best to start with the things we know. If none of those things pan out, then we delve into the unknowns. None of his neighbors noticed any visitors at Fanning's place—only the somewhat suspicious drive-bys. Of course, he only moved in one month ago, and most of the neighbors prefer not to get involved. No drugs or drug paraphernalia were found on the premises. No alcohol, no firearms. Three pairs of jeans and three shirts in the closet. The same number of T-shirts and boxers, as well as socks, were tucked into a drawer in a single shabby dresser. Cheese and deli meats, along with a carton of milk, were in the fridge. His wallet—cash and ID still inside—was on the bedside table.

I figure if he isn't dead already, he will be very soon.

Unless we can find him first. Which frankly makes me want to slow-walk this shit.

"Right." Liv nods. "Thankfully, it appears most of his known victims were able to pull their lives together."

That's one part of being a victim that just makes the tragedy suck all the more—the aftereffects. The shit that pulls you back over and over to the nightmare you so want to put behind you. Damned PTSD.

"We should pay a visit to Sanchez's mother." I have a feeling about him.

It may be nothing. But in reading the file about Fanning's final victim, Mario Sanchez—the only known male victim—something about the way he escaped gnaws at me. He's twenty-five now. But he was a scrawny ten-year-old at the time of his abduction. He nearly killed Fanning in the process of getting away. Too bad he didn't.

The idea that maybe he wants to finish the job is not an easy one to ignore.

"Wouldn't hurt." Liv stands from her desk and reaches for her jacket. "You thinking he and his pals might not be mountain climbing?"

When I called Sanchez's current cell phone number, it went to voicemail. I located a number for his wife, and she stated that her husband and a couple of his buddies are on a mountain climbing expedition in Mexico. They drove, so they won't be back until Sunday. Cell service is mostly unavailable, so talking to him before he gets back isn't likely.

"Maybe they are," I say. "Maybe they aren't. I just need to know whether or not they chopped up Fanning's body and took it with them."

Liv laughs, the first of the day. "That would be one way to dispose of a body. Maybe Sanchez is a *Dexter* fan."

I grunt an agreement. Sanchez isn't the only one we haven't been able to contact, but I feel as if he's somehow the one we most need to hear from. That said, our one witness claimed to have seen two women casing Fanning's place. There was no mention of a Hispanic man.

But that doesn't mean Sanchez isn't involved, which makes paying his mother a visit a good idea. She lived through the horror of his abduction. I figure she'll have plenty to say. The wife, on the other hand, only knows what her husband decided to share with her.

Sofia Sanchez serves us hot tea. Liv doesn't seem to think this is strange. She adds cream and sugar and appears to savor the disgusting stuff. But I'm too old to think for a minute that hot tea is normal. Tea is made to be poured over ice. So I stare at my dainty cup, pretending I plan to drink it. No need to insult the lady.

"Mario is a good man," his mother says. "A hard worker."

She's already showed us his high school and college graduation photos. He's an engineer now, working toward a second degree in architecture, with a wife and their first child on the way. The wife is visiting her folks in Memphis for a few days while he and his friends are away.

"I'm sure you're very proud of him," Liv says. "We just have a few questions for him. If he can give us a call when he has service again, that would be great."

Mrs. Sanchez looks from Liv to me. "My son has not been near that evil monster—if that's what your question is about." Her voice is stern, almost angry. "He has not even spoken of him. Whatever has happened, Mario had nothing to do with it. Nothing," she repeats.

I give her a nod. "Yes, ma'am, we understand. As my partner said, we just have a couple of questions."

She nods and drinks her tea. The rest of the visit goes pretty much the same way.

As we hit the road, I say, "I don't think Mrs. Sanchez is too happy with us." She didn't have a lot to say after her assertion that her son hadn't gone anywhere near Fanning. I decide not to be suspicious that she jumped immediately to that conclusion regarding our visit. Some folks always see the police in that way first—that we're looking for someone to blame rather than the actual facts in a case.

"Probably not." Liv leans back in the seat and closes her eyes. "Can't blame her."

"True." Though my wife and I never had any children of our own, I get it. A good parent wants to protect their child—even a grown child.

For a while, I drive without saying more. Liv isn't herself today. It's the headache. My wife's sister had migraines. I remember she'd have to go into a dark room for the whole day if one started. I see how hard the headaches are for Liv. Crazy part is that until a few days ago, she hadn't suffered one in at least a year. I hope they aren't back to stay. No one should have to live with that kind of gorilla in the corner, ready to attack at the worst possible moment.

Personally, I think it's the stress. Hell, her daddy died just a couple of months ago. He was the only family she had left. She's damn young to be in the same boat as me, all alone in the world. Well, she has that fiancé, but

I'm not so sure about him. I keep that part to myself, though. She has to make up her own mind about how she wants to spend the rest of her life.

She's noticed that I'm off my game lately. I hope I'm not piling more onto her stress level. I can be a pain in the ass sometimes. She pretends not to notice. I've been a cop for a long time. I have certain routines and ways of doing things. She appreciates my experience, and I appreciate her, period.

"I am still awake, you know." She gives me the side-eye.

I chuckle. "I was just thinking it's been a long time since you've had one of those headaches. Everything okay at home?"

That's as close as I'm getting to asking about the fiancé. Not because I can't talk to Liv about anything, but because I don't want to make her feel worse.

"Same old, same old," she admits. "I guess I'm not paying enough attention to him—to us."

I figured. "I'm taking you home. You need to take care of yourself, kiddo. Make up with him—if it suits you—and we'll dig in again tomorrow."

Now she lifts an eyebrow at me. "It's only four o'clock. We calling it a day already?"

"Yeah. But it's not you," I assure her. Liv is not the type to fall down on the job as long as she is breathing. "It's me. I have a doctor's appointment."

She instantly sits up straighter. "Why? You never go to the doctor. You hate doctors."

"The department is insisting on a physical," I lie.

"Ha!" She relaxes into her seat once more. "I knew you wouldn't be able to put them off forever."

But I damn sure tried.

I hate this place.

It's the same clinic where I brought my wife after she was diagnosed with cancer. The same place I came to again just two weeks ago.

I hate the medicinal smell. Despise the flowery print of the paper on the accent wall in the lobby. Can't get comfortable in the burgundy upholstered chairs that remind me of the endless vials of blood they sucked from my wife's body like vampires. I'll bet they didn't think about blood when they chose the decor theme; they were probably too focused on matching the jewel tones of the accent wall. I wouldn't have known it was called an "accent wall" if my wife hadn't told me. She always wanted an accent wall in our living room, she'd said. Surprised, I told her I didn't recall her ever mentioning such a thing. I would gladly have papered a single wall for her.

By then, there wasn't time for her accent wall.

Maybe that's why I'd rather look at just about anything other than that damn accent wall in this damn lobby. Appointment after appointment, you sit in this lobby, watch the same tired, pain-filled faces until one day you come for an appointment and one of those faces is gone. Next time, it's another one. Then a new face appears. After a while, you come to realize one thing with complete certainty: Soon it will be your face that doesn't show for a scheduled appointment. You'll be the one who died since the last appointment. The one who was planted over at Woodlawn or Spring Hill.

A nurse appears and calls my name. I stand and follow her through the door and then down a long, sterile corridor. She weighs me, checks my blood pressure, then smiles and leaves me waiting in a plastic chair in this all-white room with its cold stainless steel surfaces and wrinkled copies of last year's magazines.

I hate this place.

There are other oncologists in this city. I guess I could have gone somewhere else, but I figure better the devil you know. Besides, this clinic is closer to my house. I know the staff. Know what to expect. I also fully grasp why I've found myself at this place—smoking.

Lung cancer. Terminal, probably. The Pall Malls I smoked for thirty-five years will now claim a second victim.

First it was Stella, my precious wife, who never smoked a cigarette even once in her life. My secondhand smoke killed her. She swore it wasn't me. Her father had smoked, too, she reminded me. Died at the ripe old age of eighty-one still puffing on those unfiltered Camels. Stella insisted her lungs were already damaged before she and I ever met. Between the Camels and the coal the family had used to heat their home when she was a kid, she was doomed from birth, she insisted. None of that changes the fact that I blame myself. I was the one she lived with for thirty-five years of her life. She only lived with her father for twenty-two. I'm the one who killed her. Just like I've probably killed myself as surely as if I stuck my service weapon to my temple and pulled the trigger.

And all this time I thought I was a pretty smart guy.

Next will be the treatments to try to slow down the progression. That was the route my sweet Stella chose. Fury tightens my lips. And for what? The chemo treatments made her so damn sick. Her beautiful hair turned pure white, and then it all fell out. She wasted away to skin and bone. In the end, the treatments didn't slow down the progression one little bit. The only result was the additional misery she suffered the final days of her life. All that extra pain and torment for nothing. She died in three months, just as the doc had speculated when he first gave us the bad news.

Why the hell would I repeat the same steps and expect a different outcome? Isn't that the very definition of insanity?

I think of Liv and feel instantly contrite. But I wouldn't be doing Liv any favors by dragging this out. She would only feel obligated to take care of me. I don't want to put that on her. She has enough on her plate. I remember how she took care of me after Stella died. Liv had just made detective the year before and landed me as a partner. When Stella got sick and then died, I wasn't fit for duty—I recognize that now—but I couldn't stay at home. Liv held me up, covered for my fumbles, and watched my back until I was myself again.

Hell no. I will not shovel more worries onto Liv's back, and I will not be a guinea pig for this clinic's research.

If I'm dying, game over.

No retiring in two years and moving down to Florida to go into the PI business with my former partner. I shake my head. Bob Stack and I were partners for nearly as long as Stella and I were married. God, I miss that woman. Miss Bob, too. Liv is a good partner, though. I just hope she and that fiancé of hers figure things out. He might be rich and from one of Nashville's most prestigious families, but that doesn't make him right for her. The truth is, from what she tells me, they couldn't be more different.

I don't claim to have all the answers, but I do know that when you love someone, you love flaws and all.

I stand, stretch my back, and exhale a blast of impatience. Eventually, I take the three steps across the exam room to stare at the vivid illustration of the human lungs mounted on the wall. Too bad mine no longer look anything like that. More in the range of black tar pits, I imagine.

I check my Timex. Quarter to five. My appointment was at 4:20. Another breath of frustration heaves from my chest. Then I cough until I lose my breath. My heart pounds and my face burns with the rush of blood there. When I can breathe again, I wipe my mouth with my shirtsleeve and struggle to slow my frantic heart.

These episodes are coming more often. The flare-ups of pain are a little worse this week, but I have to be careful of any sort of medication. I can't be impaired on the job. Liv deserves a partner who won't let her down. If it gets to the point where I feel I can't be a good partner, I'll have to go ahead and retire.

Until then, I plan to do my job. I intend to keep this ugly reality to myself. I don't want anyone feeling sorry for me or hovering over me. Work is what I do, it's who I am, and I want to keep doing it until I either die or fall down and can't get back up. Then we'll all know I'm done.

Maybe it's selfish, but it's how I want to do this.

At some point, I will have to tell Liv. I managed to pull off being gone for a day last week for the biopsy. But I can't keep pretending.

The door opens, and I stand a little straighter as Dr. Kingsley rushes in, his nurse right on his heels. Kingsley is around fifty, tall, athletic looking, and always in a hurry. Gray has invaded his hair at the temples. Damn stuff took over mine ages ago.

"Detective Duncan." He glances up from my medical file and smiles. "We have news. You might want to sit down."

Well, shit. Here it comes. I take my seat once more.

The doctor settles onto the wheeled stool and tucks my file under his arm. His hands rest on his thighs and he watches me from behind wire-rimmed glasses. "You do not have cancer."

I open my mouth to tell him that I think we'll just let this thing happen naturally, but no words come out because his take a few extra seconds to assimilate in my brain.

I lean forward. "What did you say?"

"The nodule that had all the earmarks of cancer was benign. We removed it when we did the biopsy, so there's no further concerns there."

I look around, expecting someone to jump out and say, "Just kidding!" Except they don't.

"What about all these symptoms I'm having?" I watched my wife die with lung cancer. I know the damned symptoms.

He nods, his lips compressed. "I've spoken with a colleague, a cardiologist. He's looked at your scans, your lab work. He wants to see you. The symptoms you're having strongly suggest congestive heart failure. The scans show some significant narrowing of the coronary arteries. If you recall, we discussed this."

I nod. I do recall, but I just can't find my voice. I was so damned certain.

"The cardiologist will recommend the steps to take next. They'll set up an appointment for you as you check out." He stands, reaches for my hand. "I'm very glad you no longer need me, Detective Duncan."

I manage to stand and accept the handshake. "So my ticker is giving out on me." Well, hell, how is that much better?

"The cardiologist will advise you on how to proceed, but in my experience, medication and lifestyle changes can make all the difference. You could live a long and productive life if you follow the doctor's orders."

Stunned, I manage a "Thanks."

Kingsley nods once and passes my file to the nurse standing by. He's out the door, and she's ushering me in that direction.

I leave the office with an appointment to see the cardiologist next week.

In the parking lot, still in a bit of shock, my cell vibrates against my hip. I pull it free of my utility belt as I slide behind the wheel of my Tahoe. "Duncan."

"Hey, Walt."

Tim Reynolds from the crime lab. Reynolds is my go-to guy. A couple years younger than me, he has more experience and expertise in his little finger than most have in their entire beings. If there's anything in the collected evidence to help our investigation, he will find it. "What've you got for me, Reynolds?"

It's too early to have a DNA match on the blood. We're operating under the assumption that the blood is Fanning's, but it's always possible it belongs to someone else. Not the sort of news I want to hear, considering what that would likely mean. I want the blood to be his.

"Most of the blood is B positive, Fanning's type. We should have DNA results in a couple of days. The chief put a rush on it."

"Thanks for the update." The idea that he said "most" nudges me, but before I can ask, he says, "Wait, there's more."

I hesitate before backing out of the parking slot. "I'm listening."

"I found a second blood type in the mix, mostly on the hand towel that was in the puddle. This one's O positive. Maybe that blood was already on the towel before whatever happened in his kitchen. Either way, it belongs to someone besides Fanning."

Holy shit. That is not what I wanted to hear. It could simply mean that Fanning's kidnapper injured him- or herself during whatever happened in the house.

Or it could mean Fanning had someone in the house with him. Possibly a victim.

"Thanks, Reynolds. Let me know if you find any DNA matches in the database." I drop my cell phone into the cupholder of the console.

Son of a bitch. I sag in my seat.

Every victim Carl Fanning ever took was a child.

My gut twists. We need to look at any children who've gone missing in the past few days.

This is damned bad news.

THREE

The Child

The bleeding has stopped. I should bandage the wound, but I won't. It's more painful if I leave it gaping open just as it is. Let him suffer.

Most people think I'm a good person, but if they knew the real me, they wouldn't like me very much. They see what I want them to see. They know what I want them to know. They have no idea about the things I've done. Bad things. But, like everything else in life, my actions are relative. Relative to the pain and the fear. Relative to what he did to me for eight long years.

Relative to survival.

I hope they never know how that feels.

The truth is, we all have a then and a now. For some of us, the *then*, our past, is a part of our lives we have no desire to revisit. Sometimes, though, in spite of our best efforts, life forces you back to that ugly past, and you run from it or block it as quickly as possible.

But this is different. My *then* has invaded my now, and I am forced to resurrect a part of me I long ago buried. It is the only way to survive. After what he did to me, revenge is the only possible ending. But first, I want him to remember every depraved moment of our time together. I want him to feel what I felt.

And then I want him to die a slow, agonizing death.

There are those who will completely understand how I feel even without knowing the grisly details. There are others who even if they knew every single horror I suffered would say he is still a human being. All human beings deserve mercy, forgiveness, do they not?

They are wrong. He is not a human being. He is a monster. He is evil. He is going to die soon, but first he is going to suffer.

After all, he started this, then and now.

I was just a child when he took me.

The man's name was Carl Fanning. I didn't comprehend how unfortunate the situation was at the time, but I learned very quickly.

Carl was a very bad man. He pretended to be nice at first. He bought me new clothes and gave me a teddy bear. He had plenty of food in his dumpy little place—even ice cream. I had only tasted ice cream once.

He called me "the child," or "it," never by my name. He said I didn't have a name anymore, and after a while I couldn't remember it anyway. There was a big old trunk in his bedroom, and that's where he put me whenever he had to go out alone. It was dark inside and I always worried that the holes wouldn't let in enough air. At least I had my teddy bear. I gave it a name, but I don't remember now what it was.

Eventually I became too big for the trunk, so he built a box for me. It reminded me of the boxes they put dead people in before they bury them in the ground.

Soon the possibility of death would become very appealing to me.

In the beginning, the things he did to me hurt really badly. I cried a lot, but then he would give me candy or ice cream. The soreness would be bad for a few days, and then I would forget for a while . . . until the next time.

I didn't mind the dress-up playing. But it was the part that came after I didn't like.

During the time I belonged to him, I was the only one he kept. All the others went away after a few hours, but not me. Never me. He said I was special.

Until one day when I wasn't.

I stare at him now. He looks so old. Old and stooped. His hair is gray and thin, his body pale and frail. I've heard what they do to men like him in prison. I hope those things were done to him over and over for the past fourteen years.

He stares at me, his lips smiling despite his current circumstances. I shouldn't have removed the gag. I'll put it back on before I go. Doesn't really matter. There's no one to hear him scream if he does so.

I worry, though, that he's up to something. He is the devil himself. He cannot be trusted. He is capable of anything and completely undeserving of any sort of mercy.

After all, like I said, he started this.

Now I am going to end it.

FOUR

DETECTIVE OLIVIA NEWHOUSE

Wednesday, May 2

I cradle my coffee. Can't get warm. Last night the temperature dropped to almost freezing. It's cold as hell this morning. Blackberry winter or one of those crazy little cold snaps that disturbs the spring warm-up each year. I can definitely do without an encore of last winter's unusually cold temps and all that extra snowfall.

I consider the names on the whiteboard in our joint cubicle. Even a detective as senior as Walt doesn't get an office in the Criminal Investigations Division. Not enough offices. But we do get a larger cubicle, one big enough for our desks to sit face-to-face in the center of the small square. On one side we have a row of filing cabinets with anything else we need to store stacked on top; on the other side of our work area we have a whiteboard and an extra chair for anyone we want to entertain with our scenarios and progress on a given case. The cramped digs aren't such a big deal. We spend most of our time in the field anyway.

"So we can't actually confirm that Sanchez is in Mexico?" I say this knowing my partner is well aware of our current dilemma. What I don't say is that the name is somehow familiar to me. It's a feeling I can't quite put my finger on. A knowing, some small, fleeting flare of recognition that just won't be captured and assimilated. Sanchez doesn't have a criminal record, but somehow I've encountered him before. Or maybe it's only that I've run across someone with that same last name.

Walt shakes his head. "Both of his buddies, Lassiter and Watkins, are single with no significant others that I've been able to locate. I've called all three cell phones and left messages. Lassiter doesn't have any extended family that we know of, so there's no one to reach out to for confirmation on his whereabouts. The other guy, Watkins, has a mother, but she only knows that her son is on vacation in Mexico. She confirmed the trouble with cell service in the area where they're supposed to be."

I glance at my notes. "The three men drove in Sanchez's SUV, so we can't easily corroborate travel."

"Nope." Walt scrubs at his chin. "I've put in a call to the feds to see if we can confirm whether or not their passports show they've left the country."

That could work. "Any ideas on when we'll hear back?"

He shrugs. "Soon, I hope. You never know with the feds."

I can't argue that point. "Moving on." I scan the names on the board. "Considering the second blood type, we can no longer assume Fanning is the vic and not some kid he nabbed off the street." The idea makes me sick. Walt and I don't talk about it too much, but we both hope the scumbag is dead and the second blood type belongs to his killer.

"Based on the report Reynolds faxed over this morning"—Walt passes the single page to me for adding to the case board—"the blood found at the scene was maybe thirty-six hours old, give or take. I checked for any kids who went missing over the weekend. Got two, but they were both found. Checked on missing adults as well. Only one came up, and her body was discovered this morning. Took a bottle of sleeping pills and went to Centennial Park. A jogger noticed her body near the kids' playground. Downed the whole bottle of pills and went night night for the last time. Her baby girl died in her sleep about a year ago. SIDS, according to the report. The husband says she couldn't learn to live with it."

I shake my head. "Damn."

That's another aspect of pregnancy I find terrifying. With my parents gone, I only have me to worry about. I'm an adult and entirely responsible for the steps I take as well as the consequences of those steps. The idea of having a tiny human who depends on me is totally terrifying. If I make a mistake, he or she could pay the price. That's one hell of a scary thought. Like that poor dead woman, how do you live with the death of a child even if it isn't your fault?

Vaguely I wonder whether the fact that I failed to include David in the scenario is an indication that I'm not as committed to him as I should be. That perhaps I don't love him as deeply as I thought. Maybe I'm in love with the idea of being in love. Hitting thirty jarred my reality. Or maybe it was losing my father, the only family I had left, that knocked me over the edge. I don't like the prospect of being alone. And yet lately I seem to be pushing David away more often than pulling him toward me.

I assuage my guilt with the notion that it's hormones. Or maybe this whole moving-in thing has pressed me into some emotional corner. Now that I'm pregnant, perhaps I'm turning on him the way the female black widow will sometimes do her mate.

You are losing it, Liv.

Chalking up the ridiculous thought to yesterday's headache, I force my full attention back to the case. "Since we don't have any other possibilities, for now, I guess we stick with the assumption that Fanning is the vic and move on to the next person of interest on our revenge list." I look to Walt. He's the senior detective. We'll do this whatever way he feels is the best route. The list seems the only logical one to me.

"I don't see a better strategy at this point," he admits. "Let's do it."

I toss my empty Starbucks cup and grab my jacket. Walt gets a call as we cross the bullpen. If we're lucky, it'll be Reynolds with an update that will give us something more to go on.

When the call ends, Walt doesn't say anything, so I guess it wasn't Reynolds.

"The vet," he says in answer to my unspoken question as we push out into the brisk morning air.

"Vet?" My stride lengthens to keep up with my partner's long legs. I'm not exactly short, five seven, but Walt is six two, and when he's distracted, he hustles and forgets all about me. "Is Sandy sick?"

"Nah. It's time for her annual checkup and shots."

"Oh." I smile. "How's she doing?"

Sandy is Walt's yellow Lab. I love that darn dog. As big as she is, she's the most lovable creature. I've never had a dog of my own. Maybe it's time I did. *Dogs can be good for kids,* I think. I dismiss the notion. Way too early to go there.

"Sandy's doing great." We load into his black Tahoe. "What's the address?"

I rattle off the west side address of the elementary school where the next name on our list teaches and then review the few details we have. "Shelley Martin, thirty-two. At nine, she was one of Fanning's first known victims." I pull my seat belt across my lap and snap it into place.

Walt exits the lot, heading across town. He drives for a while without speaking. Whenever he's quiet like this, something is up. Since he's generally an open book when it comes to what's going on in his life, it must be about me. Then again, there's a very good chance I'm being paranoid. In any event, he has something besides the case and Sandy's vet appointment on his mind. He drums his thumbs on the steering wheel, glances repeatedly at me. Oh yeah, it's about me.

"What?" I finally ask, unable to bear the suspense for another second.

"You're feeling better this morning?"

I glance at Walt and wonder why he didn't ask me that question when I arrived at CID this morning, bearing both our favorite coffees from Starbucks. I distinctly recall asking him if he'd had another rough night. His eyes are bloodshot again, and his shirt is wrinkled—the latter is totally out of character for my partner. No matter that we've only been partners for two years, I've known Walt since I started at Metro. Everyone knows Walt. He's top-notch. Always on his A game. One of the most beloved detectives in all of Metro. Whenever there's a particularly sensitive situation that rouses emotion in the community, the chief of police inherently wants Walt on the case. Nashville loves him. Maybe it's the cowboy boots and the extra-heavy Southern drawl or his plainspokenness. Whatever it is, folks adore him. I was damn lucky to be chosen to fill the shoes left by his longtime partner when he retired.

All that said, I'm not ready to spill my guts about the pregnancy or my misgivings about the wedding just yet. I still haven't processed all the confusing emotions myself. Right. I'm kidding myself. What I really am not ready for is to confess that I may have jumped the gun on the decisions in my relationship with David. I made mistakes, and he is the one who's going to be hurt.

I've really screwed up.

"I'm okay." I stare out the window, watch the passing landscape. I also have no desire to talk about how I lost the entire evening and night when that damned headache got its second wind, either. Total amnesia is never a good thing. And if that isn't enough, I certainly feel no urge to discuss how the hangover the headache left me with is determined to try to ruin my day. Instead, I decide to ignore it and hope it'll go away. Very mature.

"You were in pretty bad shape yesterday. Is there something you can take when that happens?"

He slows for a left turn. "Sometimes the pills work, sometimes they don't." This is true, except even if I had the necessary medication, I wouldn't be able to take the pills because I'm pregnant. Last night my only choice was to sleep it off.

"What about Preston? Does he understand and help when this happens?"

Preston. Walt has never called David by his given name. That alone says a lot about how my partner feels on the subject. All the more reason why I can't talk to him about how I'm feeling. "There was nothing David could do. The dark and the quiet are the only things that help."

Walt grunts. "Stella's sister had migraines. She said stress made them worse."

"You think I'm stressed, Walt?" I hide my smile. He and Stella had no children, so he's kind of taken me under his wing. Treats me like a daughter sometimes. I can't exactly say I don't enjoy it. Since I lost my father, my friendship with Walt means more than ever. He's like family.

"Yep, I think that fancy fiancé of yours and the wedding plans have you way too stressed." He parks in front of the elementary school. "I think you both need to take a breath and relax."

Laughter bubbles out of me before I can stop it. "No amount of relaxing makes wedding planning easy."

Another grunt. "There's always the courthouse. Pick a handy judge. That's what Stella and I did."

I can't help it, I laugh even harder now. "David's mother might have a stroke."

He shuts the engine off and turns to me. "You aren't marrying his mother, Liv."

"A mere technicality, partner."

"I guess," Walt offers, "if you're in love him and he's in love with you, that's all that matters."

I reach for the door but Walt doesn't. He is evidently not finished yet. "You love him, right?"

I sigh. "You asked me this before."

"That's not an answer."

I stare forward, thinking about the answer before I give it. Do I say what I should say or what I feel? "I thought I was in love with him," I admit. "But lately I'm having second thoughts." There. I said it out loud. The ground didn't break open and swallow me. The world didn't capsize. The three-carat solitaire at home on my bedside table probably hasn't self-destructed. I don't wear the ring to work. Don't want to risk damaging it or losing it and, besides, the celebrity-size dazzler can be a distraction during an interview.

"It's not until you live with a person that you see who he or she really is," Walt warns. "Maybe that's the problem."

I shake my head. "Actually, I don't think it's him." I drop my head back against the seat. "I think it's me, and I don't know if it's cold feet or what." I can't say what I really feel, like maybe I don't deserve him . . . that I'm not like him and his family. Walt would go ballistic.

"Then you should tell him you need more time."

I have, and until yesterday it would have been that simple. Now everything is complicated.

"I have to think about all this some more."

Walt winks at me. "You'll figure it out. You're way too smart to get yourself trapped in a relationship that isn't right for you."

I smile but inside I want to cry. There was a time when I thought I was smarter than this, that's for sure. The past few weeks, it's as if my ability to think and act with reason and wisdom has deserted me. I've lost my footing, and somehow I can't find it amid all the uncertainty and newness of suddenly being an adult orphan and a bride-to-be. Throw mother-to-be in the mix, and I am totally sinking here.

Focus, Liv. I climb out of the SUV and walk alongside Walt into the school. Work has always been my happy place. I need to stay on task and let the other stuff go. At least for now.

Shelley Martin's principal is more than happy to send an assistant to sit with Martin's class while we speak to her. Walt assured the principal that Mrs. Martin was not in any sort of trouble, that we are hoping she might be able to help us with a case. Still, I doubt the curious principal will let it go. She will want answers. But whatever answers Martin gives are up to her.

We wait in the teacher's lounge. When Martin arrives, she doesn't appear surprised to see us but she does seem nervous. She wears her black hair in a sleek twist. Her cream-colored trousers and blue shirt are modest. She wears only a simple gold band on her ring finger. She was Shelley Jones when the abduction occurred.

Walt explains that we're here to talk about Fanning. She flinches when Walt says the name. Then her cheeks redden and her lips tighten. Hearing his name makes her angry, justifiably so.

"I heard on the news that he's missing." She says this as if it's a confession.

"Mrs. Martin," I begin, "we need to ask you a few questions about him. Is that okay with you?"

She shifts her stern focus to me. "I loathe him. Pray every day that he will die as painfully as possible. He lured me into his car when I was nine years old. I'd gotten lost from my sister at the mall. He took me to the parking lot of an abandoned warehouse and raped me." She swallows hard. "He left me there naked, injured, and terrified. I gave the police his description, but they never found him. There was no evidence because he wore a condom and kept my clothes to ensure nothing from him or his car stuck to what I was wearing. It wasn't until many years later that he was caught. I came forward and testified against him. I hoped he would rot in prison, but apparently that wasn't considered the sort of justice he deserved."

Her words are laced with hatred and bitterness. But who wouldn't feel that way?

"Mrs. Martin," Walt says gently, "we understand your feelings. You have every right to feel betrayed by how the legal system sometimes works. But we're here because it's our job to ensure no one else is harmed by the horrors Fanning carried out against you and so many others. With that in mind, would you tell us if you've seen him since he was released from prison?"

Her eyes round with fear. "I certainly have not. Do you have reason to believe he has been watching the people who testified against him?"

Her reaction is a logical one. No doubt every one of his victims has surely experienced that same thought.

"We don't," Walt admits.

Now for the hard question. My partner and I exchange a glance, and I take the lead. "Ma'am, can you tell us where you were from Saturday night until Monday morning?"

The anger vanishes from her face and shock takes its place. I brace for the blast of outrage that will kick in any second now.

"Are you suggesting I had something to do with his disappearance?"

"No, ma'am," I assure her. "We're only trying to determine who may have seen him or heard from him. Anyone who has may be able to help us figure out what happened."

Fury twists Martin's lips for another moment before she regains her composure. "I was home with my family. We had a big breakfast at home Sunday morning, and after that I took my twin daughters shopping. Sunday was their birthday. The girls, my husband, and I arrived home about nine that evening, and I didn't leave again until I came to school the next morning. I picked up my girls after school on Monday and went home. My family can confirm this."

We already established with the principal that Martin was at school all day on Monday.

"What about Saturday night?" Walt asks. "What did you and your family do Saturday night?"

We're stretching the timeline a little, but so many things can affect the forensic details of a case. There is always something new to learn.

"I had cocktails with a friend."

The fury that rolls off the words warns we've hit a hot button. She is done with the interview. But she also just admitted that she wasn't with her family on Saturday night.

"If you could provide the name and number for you friend," Walt suggests.

Face tight with that building fury, she spouts a name and number. Trina Irvine. I enter the info into the note app of my phone. Walt sticks with the old-fashioned route of a pad and pen. Which is why I generally take the notes.

"Thank you," I say. "We appreciate your cooperation."

She shakes her head. "How dare you come to me—interrupt my day at school—with such ludicrous questions." She jams her thumb into her chest. "I am the victim."

Walt and I share another look. He says, "Mrs. Martin, we haven't released to the public what I'm about to tell you. We would appreciate it if you don't share this part with anyone."

Her anger drains away instantly as fear of the unknown creeps in and takes its place. "You have my word."

"The other person involved with whatever happened to Fanning was injured. We found a second blood type at the scene. Our goal with these questions is to figure out if another person was hurt by Fanning the night he disappeared. If that's the case, we may have someone out there in need of our help and we don't even know it."

"You're saying he may have taken another victim?" The abject horror on her face is palpable.

"We can't say anything for sure," I counter.

"This is why," Walt goes on, "it's extremely important that we ask these hard questions of anyone who is connected in any way to Fanning. For all we know, you may have driven by his place—accidentally or not—and noticed someone who might be relevant to whatever happened there. You may have a friend or family member who—without your knowledge—wants revenge."

She shakes her head. "I do not. I saw on the news that he'd been released, and I tried not to think of him again. Of course it was impossible. Before the trial, I was just an anonymous little girl he picked up at the mall and did bad things to. My name was never released in the news. But then, at the trial, I had to face him. He learned my name; with that, it was easy to find out where my parents and sister lived. I won't lie, I've been looking over my shoulder since the day he was released."

"That's completely understandable," I say. Deep in my skull, the ache begins and I refuse to acknowledge it. I have never had a migraine reoccur so many times in one week. This is really wrong.

We apologize again for disturbing her day and leave the school.

"Somehow I don't think we're going to find out what happened to that bastard through his victims," Walt comments.

"Sure looks that way," I agree. But we have to rule them out nonetheless. We can't skip any steps. This is way too important. Someone's life could depend on what we do. And I damn sure don't mean Fanning's.

When we stop for lunch, I check in with my doctor's office to see if I can manage an appointment later today. They have a cancellation at two. I glance at the clock on the wall of Taco Mama's. It's one now. I take the appointment. I need to know what's going on with my head.

When Walt returns from the men's room, I say, "I need to pick up my car. My doctor can see me at two. Maybe she can give me something to help with these migraines."

"I'll take you," he announces. "I can make some phone calls while I wait."

I want to argue, but I have no desire to beat my head against that particular brick wall. Walt is as stubborn as he is good at being a detective and a friend.

After peeing in a cup and having blood drawn, I sit on the edge of the exam table and wait impatiently while Dr. Raiford goes through the findings listed in my chart. I told her about the pregnancy tests and about the headaches. About the move. She already knew my father died and that I'd gotten engaged. My annual exam was in March, and all was good. How did so much change since then?

Hopefully, she can give me some clue as to why the headaches are back with such a vengeance. I really can't afford to be taking any time off work right now. Walt needs me. And I can't have David hovering over me.

The thought stops me. Part of me feels as if I'm making him the bad guy in all this, but it's more than that. I can't explain these new and intense feelings. Every instinct I possess is sounding an alarm that something bad is coming and I can't stop it. Whatever it is, it somehow involves my relationship with David. The urge to run is strong, but I feel trapped by the promises I've made. Fear of needing to escape is the best way I know to explain it. I have no idea how I'm going to find my way out of this corner.

Bottom line, running away isn't an option. Not that I've ever run from anything.

"Well, everything I can see here looks normal." Dr. Raiford smiles at me. "Of course, some of the tests will take a few days. You are, indeed, pregnant. Based on your last period, I'd say five or six weeks. Considering the fact that your last period was so light, there's a possibility you could be nine or ten. We'll schedule an ultrasound for your next appointment to get a better handle on where you are."

Oh God. This is real.

Smiling just a little at the fear on my face, she goes on. "The wacky hormones you're experiencing right now are quite possibly a major contributor to the headaches. The good news is those hormones usually level out in the second trimester. As you suspect, most likely having recently lost your father, getting engaged, and moving in with your fiancé have your stress level off the charts." She glances at my file again. "Your blood pressure is a little high, but that might just be related to the lack of sleep or the headaches or maybe just because you're nervous or worried. Even tough-as-nails cops like you can get a little nervous and worried sometimes."

I nod. Definitely nervous and worried. I am not ready for this. But it's real and I have to get that way fast. These issues with David have to be worked out. This child will need both of us.

She scans my file once more. "You said this is your first pregnancy?"

I nod and say, "Yes."

She makes some notes on my chart.

"About the headaches, is there anything I can take to help?" I steady my voice and keep going. "They're interfering with work, and it's just not a good time for me to be sick. My partner and I are in the middle of this big case." I don't say as much, but that's not actually unusual.

We're always on a case, and with Walt as a partner, they're generally the most difficult and high-profile ones.

Another smile from the doctor. "Is there ever a good time to be sick?"

I shrug. "True."

She picks up a prescription pad and starts filling in the blanks. "Sadly, there isn't a lot that I would recommend you take. You've had migraines before, you know the triggers. Try to avoid them. Relax as much as you can. This might help." She removes the top page from the pad and passes it to me. "But I'd rather you wait until we have your labs back before filling it."

I stare at the illegible words. It's a good thing cops don't write the way doctors do.

"For now," she goes on, "you need to get started with prenatal vitamins. I'll let you know if there's anything else you should be taking once we have your blood work back. But based on your physical just two months ago, I'd say the headaches are nothing more than stress and hormones. Exercise and meditation are good sources of stress relief during pregnancy. Take long walks in the evenings. Lie down with some hot tea and relax. Put everything else on hold for now. Those are simple things you can do to help."

Except nothing is simple right now. Not in my world.

FIVE

SHELLEY MARTIN

I leave school early. By the beginning of last period, I simply could not bear the tension any longer.

My heart is pounding as I pull into my favorite self-service car wash. There are no other vehicles in any of the bays. Thank God. My hands tremble as I dig for change in my purse.

How can this be happening? I was so careful. They must know something, otherwise why come to my school and ask me all those questions?

Someone had to have seen me. That is the only answer.

But how? I always waited until the wee hours of the morning, two or three o'clock. All the houses, including that sick fuck's, were always dark. I just don't get how anyone could have seen me.

Unless one of the others told.

I close my eyes and fight the descending despair. No. That can't be. Not a single one of us would do that to the others.

Focus on what you have to do, Shelley.

I pop my trunk and get out. At the back of my car, I reach in to remove the spare tire. The odor of death nearly takes my breath. I gag over and over until the job is done. With the spare on the ground and the piece of trunk carpet next to it, I remove the drain plug. I shudder as my fingers encounter specks of blood.

Finally, I walk to the payment console and drop in coins. I select "Wash" and draw in a big breath. I tremble despite my best efforts to steady myself. I should have done this already. It's a miracle they didn't ask to search my car. For all I know, they could show up at my house with a search warrant this very evening.

If my husband or my children find out what I've done . . .

God no. They can't. No one can ever know.

Another big breath and I remove the high-pressure spray gun from its rack and head toward the back of my car once more. I spray the open lid and the interior over and over, then I return to the console and select "Rinse." It takes a while to rinse away all the foam, but I get it done. Then I check for any remaining debris and find nothing. I spray off the tire and carpet before returning both to the trunk.

A voice in my head warns that the carpet will likely mildew before it dries, but I don't care. I only care that any evidence of what I've done has been washed away.

SIX

DETECTIVE WALTER DUNCAN

"That was fast." I open the lobby door for Liv and follow her out of the doctor's office. I'm hoping the doc was able to give her something that will keep the headaches at bay until her life calms down.

Now, that's rich. Since when does a cop's life ever calm down?

When Liv walks straight to the bank of elevators and presses the call button without a word, I trudge after her. I suppose she'll tell me what she wants to tell me in her own time. We've worked together for two years. She's seen the worst of me, and so far she's been open and honest about herself, as have I.

Until recently, anyway.

I can't exactly fault her for holding things close to the vest when I was keeping a whopper of a secret myself. But hey, that one worked out. I don't have cancer. Just gotta get the old ticker looked at. I'm glad, but I don't like being that man—the kind who keeps secrets. The guilt was weighing on me. Stella always said the reason she loved me so much was because I was a good man, an honest man.

When the elevator doors close with us inside, she finally speaks. "She's pretty sure it's not a brain tumor."

Her lips quirk and I smile. "That's always good."

"She did some blood work. Mostly she thinks it's the stress."

"Aha!" I grin and keep the "I told you so" to myself.

"Yeah, yeah." She leans against the back wall. "I need more sleep and less upset in my life. But I'm a cop, and I don't really see how that's possible."

"Speaking of upset," I say, "Reynolds finished most of his preliminary workup on the evidence collected from the Fanning scene. Clean as a whistle, for the most part. Fanning's prints were the only ones he could identify. Whoever else was involved, he or she wasn't in the database or was extremely careful. Didn't leave anything behind except the blood on that hand towel, and for all we know, it may've already been there. Reynolds said there's still some trace evidence to go through, but he's not expecting any game changers."

"This is what television dramas like *CSI* give us," she gripes. "Evidence-free crime scenes."

She rubs at her forehead and my gut clenches. "Did your doc give you anything for the headaches?"

She shakes her head. "For now, she wants to hold off. See what's going on with the blood work."

"Makes sense, I guess." I sure as hell hate for Liv to suffer the way she did yesterday. It was painful just watching.

She glances at the screen on her phone. "We still have time to try and catch Dana Reeves at her office."

The elevator bumps to a stop. "I can handle the next interview if you want to call it a day."

She glares at me before stepping off the car. "No way, this is my case, too."

"Yes, ma'am."

We load up and head to the south side. Dana Reeves is a CPA with her own shop off Powell Avenue in Woodbine. Reeves was eleven when she was picked up by Fanning twenty-two years ago. According to what we could dig up, she never married and has no children. She lives in the same apartment she moved into after college. Never been arrested. No traffic violations. The only hits we got on her name were the registrations for three dogs and a license plate for a Pontiac Grand Am. I imagine all three of the dogs are big, badass guard dogs. Anyone who's been violated, particularly in such a vile way, should get a big old mean dog. My Sandy is far from a badass, but if necessary, she would go down trying to protect me.

Liv studies the file for most of the trip. Usually she talks about what she's reading, bounces thoughts off me. Not today. Today she's oddly quiet. For the most part, she's been that way all week. I wonder again if the doctor said more than she's telling.

"Dana was the only victim from Belle Meade," I say, in the hope of nudging her into the conversation.

Liv closes the file and stares straight ahead. "Her parents still live in Belle Meade. So do her two brothers. But she never went back after she left home for college. If her address is any indication, she lives frugally."

"The Pontiac registered to her is nearly as old as she is." Nothing wrong with that. I hung on to my first car until I was thirty, and it was well on its way to that milestone, too. "You're right, she's either not making a whole lot of money, or she chooses to be tight with what she does make."

"It's possible she and her parents had a falling-out," Liv offers.

"Or maybe she likes to travel and spends all her money on vacations?" I regret that Stella and I didn't travel more. We always put off those plans. Maybe next year, I'd say. She would agree, though I suspected she just went along with whatever I thought. The job always took priority, and the next thing we knew it was too late.

"She has no kids, no husband," Liv remarks, sounding more like herself now.

"She owns her own business," I add.

That out-of-character silence returns, hangs in the air as I take the turn for Powell Avenue. I glance at Liv, but she's staring out the window.

"I find it strange there was no true pattern to Fanning's choice in victims. At least, not one the investigation discovered all those years ago," I say as I slow for a crosswalk. "The age range was unusually broad. Hair and eye color didn't seem to matter." I shrug. "No order to the when or the where he chose to strike. No set MO for how he made the abduction or for what happened after. Well, other than the fact that all his victims were left alive—as far as we know, anyway."

I frown, thinking back to the rabid news coverage of the trial. "Even after he was sentenced, he refused to talk about what drove him, what made him do the things he did. Most of them talk eventually. But not Fanning. He never said a word."

More of that heavy silence crowds in as soon as I stop talking. I glance at Liv to make sure she's still awake.

"He chose what he wanted in the moment," she says, her voice distant, as if her mind is elsewhere. "They were all beautiful to him."

I nod slowly. "Did you read that somewhere in the file?"

She jerks her head toward me, blinks as if she just realized I was in the car with her. "I'm sorry, what did you say?"

"What you said about him thinking they were all beautiful—did you read that in the file somewhere?" I don't remember seeing it.

"I must have."

I brake for the traffic signal, my blinker on for the final turn. A frown lines her face, as if she's trying to recall where she read the conclusion. "This would be a lot easier if I'd worked the case," I admit, "but I was in the hospital having my appendix removed. Stack and Quinn caught the case."

"Detective Quinn," she says. "Maybe I read something to that effect in his notes."

"Maybe so," I agree, though I'm reasonably confident I reviewed all his notes, too. I could have read over that particular comment. After a while, it all blurs together.

Quinn died five years ago, shot at a domestic violence scene. Left a wife and three grown kids behind. I wonder sometimes, if Stella had been able to have children, whether we would have filled the empty rooms of our home. We talked about adopting, but the timing never seemed to be right, and then we were old.

Where the hell did the years go?

Reeves Accounting is open. The Grand Am, with its faded white paint, sits in the lot. Inside, there's no one waiting in the lobby, but the receptionist informs us that Ms. Reeves has a client with her and that it might be a while. I tell her we'll wait.

Liv picks up a magazine and thumbs absently through it. She pretends to look at the pictures, but I know she's not. She's soaking up the vibe of the place. The fresh paint on the walls, the stacks of current magazines on the tables. Newly upholstered chairs, the industrial-style tile polished to a high sheen on the floor. Even the receptionist's desk looks shiny and new. A jungle of plants stands in front of the big plate glass window. The neighborhood might be low rent, but the suite of offices is well done and immaculately maintained.

Twenty minutes later the door opens and the client exits. The receptionist goes into her boss's office for a moment and then returns, leaving the door open.

"Ms. Reeves will see you now."

"Thanks." I give her a nod and follow Liv into the plush office.

The office is carpeted and decked out. Expensive drapes. High-end upholstered wingbacks. The woman, Dana Reeves, is dressed professionally in a gray suit and pink blouse. Her dark hair is cut short. She's gained a considerable amount of weight since she renewed her license four years ago.

"I'm Detective Newhouse," Liv says, "and this is my partner, Detective Duncan. We'd like to ask you a few questions."

Reeves gestures to the chairs in front of her desk. "I'm always happy to help Metro. Please, make yourselves at home. Would you like water or a coffee?"

We both decline.

"Is this about the break-in next door?"

Liv and I exchange a look. I say, "No, ma'am, we're not here about the break-in."

Some cops don't like to do cold interviews unless absolutely necessary. Personally I've decided that folks are far more forthcoming with straight answers if they haven't had time to prepare. No matter if they're completely innocent, they're only human, and most people worry about anything they say making them look guilty. It's better not to give them the opportunity to overanalyze.

Reeves nods slowly, confusion beginning to show on her face.

"Ma'am," Liv kicks off the interview, "we're here about Carl Fanning."

The CPA's eyes flare. "I see."

Her voice is cool, low, and her expression closes instantly.

"I'm sure you're aware," I explain, "he was released last month."

She nods. "I was upset at first, but I've come to terms with the fact that he paid the debt the court required of him, fair or not."

"He hasn't contacted you or shown up at your home or business?" Liv asks.

Fear rounds the older woman's eyes. "No. Has he done that to someone else? Another of his victims?"

"Not that we know of," I assure her. "But there was an incident at his place of residence, and he's missing. We're worried that he may have someone else with him."

"Sweet Jesus." She presses a hand to her chest. "You people should never have let him off so easy with that damned plea deal! What the hell were you thinking? Now he may have hurt someone else?" She shakes her head. "I can't believe this is happening."

Now for the hard part. Before I can ask, Liv does. "Ms. Reeves, can you tell us where you were between Saturday afternoon and Monday afternoon?"

Outrage rushes up her neck and spreads across her plump cheeks, leaving a swath of red. "Why on earth would you ask me such a question?" Her gaze narrows. "Are you accusing me of something?"

"We are not, Ms. Reeves," I say firmly. "We are simply following up with all his victims to determine if he or anyone else involved with him has made any sort of contact with you, particularly over the weekend or on Monday of this week."

The red drains from her face, and she visibly gathers her composure. "I have not seen or heard from him or anyone related to him. I would have called the police if I had. As for my whereabouts, Saturday night I went out to dinner with my wife. On Sunday I was at church until noon, and then we had lunch with my family. My parents can confirm we were there until around four. After that, we went home. I didn't leave my apartment again until I came to work on Monday morning."

"Can any of your neighbors confirm you were home?" Liv asks. "Maybe you walked your dogs?"

"My wife can confirm I was home. She was at home with me. And yes, we walked the dogs Sunday evening, just like we do every evening."

I definitely didn't find a marriage license, so I ask, "May we have your wife's name and a way to contact her?"

"Of course." Reeves jots down a name and number on the back of one of her business cards and passes it to me.

"Thank you, Ms. Reeves," Liv says as she pushes up from her chair. "Please let us know if you hear from Fanning or anyone involved in any way with him."

Liv passes the woman one of her business cards. She stares at it and nods.

We leave. The receptionist watches until we're out the door.

Once we're in the Tahoe, I start the engine and see the receptionist locking the door and turning the Open sign to Closed.

"I guess we ruined her afternoon." Liv fastens her seat belt.

"Guess so." I reach for the gearshift, and a coughing jag hits me. It takes me half a damned minute to get the hacking under control.

Liv passes me her water bottle. "Damn, Walt. You need to get that cough checked out."

I down some water and grunt. My chest feels as if I just hawked up a lung. "Allergies," I lie. I don't know why. Maybe because I want to wait until I talk to the cardiologist before getting into it.

Maybe just because it's easier to lie about it.

Liv reaches for the card from Reeves that I dropped when the coughing started.

"Well, that's interesting."

I clear my throat as I back out of the parking slot. "What?"

"Based on the name Reeves gave us, her wife is another one of Fanning's victims."

SEVEN

DETECTIVE OLIVIA NEWHOUSE

The house is quiet when I arrive. I breathe a little easier as I close the front door and disable the alarm. I couldn't find my garage door opener, so I had to leave my Subaru out front. I think it's against the HOA rules, but whatever.

It's after seven. I can't believe David is not home.

I flip on the light and lean against the closed door. The crystal chandelier sends sparkles over the shiny marble floor and along the polished wood banister that leads up to the second-floor landing.

How can I possibly ever feel like this is home? I should have realized this life was a pipe dream—something meant for a different kind of woman. One who adores the social life, and plans months in advance to ensure no one misses a single one of her parties.

I can't be that person.

My boxes. Eight large moving boxes picked up from a U-Haul store close to the farm sit to the right of the front door, near the grand entrance to the dining room. There are dozens more of these same boxes at the farm—at the only home I've ever known, the only place I've ever felt comfortable—waiting to be filled. At the house I'm supposed to be packing up to sell. How do you pack up a lifetime of living? Not just my life but the lives of my parents? My father bought the farm right after I was born. He and Mom decided they didn't want their only child growing up in the city. I never attended public school. I was homeschooled until I went to college, and even then I lived at home.

I push away from the door and approach the boxes. I packed each one myself. Brought them here jammed into Walt's Tahoe and in my Subaru. David was pleased at first. Happy to see me taking steps toward our future, he professed.

I wonder now if that's what I was doing. Or was I just trying to keep him happy? To be the woman he expected? Either way, I promised him I would deal with the boxes. Since they're well taped, I'll need a box cutter. I blink, inventory my level of exhaustion. Maybe not tonight, I decide. Tonight I'm too tired.

The distant ache in my skull has not evolved into another headache, and for that I am extremely grateful. But I know from experience that my luck won't last. I can't remember the last time I had clusters of migraines like this. The headaches usually came one at a time, with weeks or months in between. This is new and agonizing territory.

But then, I've never been pregnant before. Never been engaged or grieving the loss of the last of my family.

Slowly I climb the stairs. A long, hot shower will help, I hope. I would really love a couple of beers, but that's not an option.

Shit. I forgot to pick up the prenatal vitamins.

I stall on the landing. So, I guess I'm really doing this?

Of course I am. I was raised Catholic. But am I capable of being a mother?

Somehow my feet continue moving toward the bedroom. As always, the bed is made even though I crawled out of the tangle of linens without looking back. The duvet is plump and blinding white, made of the finest cotton and filled with lush down. If I fell onto it now, I would sink into its lavish depths. Pillows, their white cases banded with gold, are arranged three deep against the rich wood headboard. Beneath all those soft white mounds are luxury sheets. Sleeping in this bed is like staying in a five-star hotel.

There are two housekeepers who come in every day. My clothes—generally left in a wad in the hamper—are always laundered and hung in the closet. I walk through the room and into the bathroom, strip off my clothes, and climb into the shower. There is no waiting for the water to get hot; it's instantaneous.

I stand beneath the spray, and the question haunts me again. Am I capable of being a mother?

Drugs have never been a part of my life. I drink too much beer sometimes, but not often. Don't smoke. Though I attended church with my parents growing up, I haven't been in years. Occasionally I swear like the proverbial sailor and am not known for my infinite patience. My housekeeping skills leave something to be desired. But I do eat reasonably healthy foods when I take the time to eat.

I stare at my flat belly. I should be eating regularly now.

However shocking and unexpected this reality, I have an obligation to do the right thing for me and for the baby.

Twenty minutes later, with my hair dried and my favorite T-shirt and lounge pants on, I head downstairs to see what's for dinner. I glance at the clock. Almost eight. Where is David?

I have to admit, I'm enjoying the peace without him—how sad is that?

The sixty-inch built-in fridge is filled with offerings. Leftover pot roast looks good. I guess David had pot roast last night while I was lost to the migraine. That's the other thing about living here. A cook comes most afternoons and prepares dinner, unless we're scheduled to go out.

I place the clear plastic container on the counter and go still. If there is no dinner prepared for tonight, then there was an engagement on the calendar.

"Oh shit."

I drag out my cell, only then noting the four unopened text messages from David. One came late this afternoon.

Don't forget we have dinner with the family tonight.

All the moisture evaporates from my throat. The next one came at five.

I'm sure you're in the middle of something but don't forget about tonight.

There is another of a similar nature at five thirty. The one at six is different.

Never mind. I've told Mother you're working late.

My appetite vanishes in a cloud of frustration and regret. I check my phone's calendar. Yep. The dinner was there. How the hell did I forget? And why the hell hadn't he called me? It's easy to ignore text messages. Usually I don't ignore that many, but after seeing the doctor, I was a little shell-shocked. Taking the home pregnancy tests was one thing, but having my doctor tell me that I'm pregnant, and about all the things I should be doing, was truly life altering.

I could tell David, and all would be forgiven in a burst of astonishment and happiness and celebratory tears. He is the type of man who isn't afraid to show his emotions. I'm the one who keeps things hidden. My father called it a self-protective mechanism.

No one can use what he doesn't know against you.

Despite the missing appetite, I force myself to eat. The television on the kitchen counter is always on, but the sound is muted. Carl Fanning's face flashes on the screen, and I look away. A child could go missing, and he or she wouldn't garner the density of coverage focused on this disgusting pedophile. I banish the frustration that comes with the thought and finish off my dinner. If the media coverage helps us find the scumbag, then I should be glad for it.

A quick rinse of my bowl and I tuck it into the dishwasher. I should leave a note telling the cook, whose name I don't even know, how much I enjoyed the pot roast. I saw her once when she was leaving for the day and I was arriving home. She reminded me of my mother. Red hair pulled back into a neat twist. Petite. She looked to be about the age my mother would be if she were still alive.

I stare at my reflection in the window over the sink, the blond hair, the blue eyes. I didn't get my mother's red hair or my father's brown, or their dark-chocolate-colored eyes. But the sprinkling of freckles across the bridge of my nose is exactly as my mother's was. My father swore I had his mind, and I probably do. As a psychiatrist, his life's work was analyzing people. I suppose as a cop, my work, to some degree, is as well. He and I thought very much alike, that's true. Looking back, I find the idea funny because most of my early years were spent primarily with my mother. She was my mom, my schoolteacher, my riding instructor.

As a young woman, Corrine Newhouse was an award-winning equestrian. Though I competed in my share of local shows early on, they never wanted that notoriety for me. They kept me close, protected me from the world until I was too old to be sheltered any longer. As much as they shielded me, they also prepared me. I had the best private self-defense classes. Knew how to shoot a weapon, how to escape trouble, all before my first day as a freshman at college.

Thinking back on what my father called the MacGyver classes, I smile. He taught me how to take the simplest objects and utilize them as tools for protecting myself and for escaping captivity.

The walls of any prison are only as impenetrable as you allow them to be. Escape is always possible, even if only in your mind.

I never talked about these lessons to my college friends since none of them ever mentioned having been taught such things. My dad took readiness to the next level. He was one of a kind.

My phone vibrates against the granite countertop. Easy to hear in the silent kitchen. I tell myself that if I'd had a moment of silence this afternoon, I would have realized David's texts were waiting.

I pick up my cell, hope it's him wanting to know if I ever made it home. It would be far easier to apologize via text than face-to-face.

Not David. Walt.

A photo of Dana Reeves and Janie Hyatt appears on the screen. The photo appears several years old. The two women look like teenagers. Reeves's dark hair is longer and she is much slimmer. Janie is blond.

Where'd you get this? I reply.

Facebook. LOL. Apparently the two have been together since high school.

Nashville is a large city, but it's not impossible that two of Fanning's victims just happened to end up together after that, whether they attended the same schools or not.

Interesting, I type back. Then I remember the neighbor we interviewed—what was her name? Scoggins. I frantically type this to Walt. The neighbor said the two women surveilling Fanning's place were white, one blond, one brunette.

I watch the ellipsis flash as he responds. My heart is thumping. This could be nothing, but it feels like something.

Holy shit. Hyatt drives a Range Rover.

Here I am knocking around memory lane and Walt has been working. I pull up the Facebook app and search for Reeves and Hyatt. The two went to college together. Hyatt owns a horseback-riding academy in Franklin. There are lots of photos. And, Walt's right, there's a Range Rover in one of them. There are also several photos of them at a cabin. Definitely not the dumpy south side apartment where Reeves lives.

Any ideas about the cabin? I send the question to Walt.

Got a friend looking through property records at this very moment.

That's the thing about being part of Metro for as long as Walt has. He knows everyone. Has serious contacts all over. I hope he introduces me to even half of them before he retires.

Another text appears on my screen.

Bingo. Hyatt inherited a cabin and ten acres way out in the middle of nowhere in Hendersonville. Road trip tomorrow.

Images of Fanning being held by one or more of his victims flash in my head. I close my eyes against the pain that follows. Damn it. Not tonight. Tonight I need to sleep. Tonight I need to make up for my negligence toward David.

I send Walt a thumbs-up and force myself to finish off the glass of milk I'd poured. I give myself a mental pat on the back for eating a decent meal for a change and decide maybe I will tear into those boxes. I search the cabinet drawers for a knife since I have no idea where a box cutter would be.

Knife in hand, I wander to the entry hall and size up the stack. Maybe if I at least get started on one and actually take a few items upstairs, David won't be mad that I forgot dinner.

Yeah, right.

He will be pissed. Once a month his entire family gets together for dinner. The two brothers, the sister, their spouses and offspring descend upon the family home and catch up over the meal prepared by the family's private chef. David's parents have a full-time chef, two housekeepers, and two gardeners. Oh yeah, David has basically the same staff, only the cook is part-time and maybe not an actual chef.

These are things I should be grateful for, and somehow I can only see the waste and self-importance of living so large. Why did I not notice this before? Giving myself grace, I spent more time with David at the farm than at his house until I moved in. Still, I should have done a better job of sizing up the situation the first time I went to dinner at his parents' palatial home.

Is this my way of finding a reason to break up? This sudden need to pick apart every aspect of David's lifestyle? Am I subconsciously looking for a way out?

Pushing the worries aside, I reach for a box, prepared to slice through the tape holding the flaps. But the flaps are already loose on this one. When did I do that?

The security system chimes and announces: *Garage door open.* David's home.

I lay the knife aside and reach for the box. None of them are labeled, so I have no clue what's inside. I've barely pulled one flap open when he appears in the dining room, jacket slung over his shoulder.

"You forgot."

"Sorry. I don't know how I did. It was on my calendar." I shake my head, infusing as much contrition as possible into my voice. I really am sorry. I don't want to embarrass him in front of his family, and I'm certain my inability to show up for their monthly dinners is very awkward for him. "My only excuse is that it has been a crazy week."

"I sent you several texts."

He keeps his voice low and even, but I hear the anger simmering beneath all that control. He's seriously pissed. Hurt, too. I guess I don't blame him.

"I didn't see them until I got home." I reach for another of the flaps.

"What held you up?" He moves closer now. "You realize my niece really wanted to hear some of your competition stories. She's starting her dressage training this summer."

Guilt pings me again. I forgot that as well. "I'm really sorry, but we were interviewing Fanning's victims. We have no choice but to work with their schedules. When I'm in an interview, I have my phone silenced. Sometimes I forget to change the setting after."

"Oh yeah." He glances upward in obvious frustration and then shakes his head. "Interviewing potential suspects is far more important than dinner with my family."

I drop my hands from the box and take a breath. I am not going to fight with him. Clearly, that's what he wants. "Not 'suspects,' 'persons of interest,' and, for the record, I'm a cop," I remind him. "It's my job. We have possibly two missing persons. One or both may be gravely injured or dead. Time is our enemy."

"At least one of them is a pedophile." The words come out a low roar. "Who gives a damn if someone dragged him off somewhere to torture and murder him? He deserves it."

I wish I could say that I don't feel the same way, but I can't allow my personal feelings to interfere with my work. "It's my job. Whatever one or both are, the law protects them as much as it does anyone else."

He stares at me. I'm not sure whether it's disbelief or defeat on his face. Whatever it is, he is far from finished.

"Why did you sleep in the guest room last night?"

I frown, then realize he has no way of knowing the answer. "I had the worst migraine of my life yesterday. When I got home I had to close myself up in a dark room. It was awful."

Sympathy flashes across his face. "I'm sorry to hear that." He shrugs. "Of course, I wouldn't know because we never talk anymore."

"I'm sorry. I told you the other day that I suffered horrible migraines as a teenager." I open my eyes and look directly into his. "I haven't had one for a long time. The reason I didn't hear your first text was because I was at the doctor's office trying to figure out why the hell they're back." My voice rises despite my best efforts to keep it steady. I hesitate, calm myself. "The appointment put us behind, so we had no choice but to work late."

"We?" He raises his eyebrows at me. "You and Walt, right?"

I take a deep breath, hoping it will slow the pounding in my chest. "He is my partner."

"I don't see why you don't marry him. After all, the two of you are always together. He knows all your secrets. Takes you to the doctor. I saw the way he took care of you at your father's funeral. You are more than partners, Olivia. I'd have to be blind not to have seen it."

That part is true. Walt and I are more than partners. We are friends. Good friends. From the day we became partners, he has been a friend and mentor to me. "Walt didn't ask me to marry him," I say. "You did and I said yes."

My words take the fire out of him, at least for a moment.

"Then why doesn't it feel like you want to be with me?"

I hold my breath. Now would be a good time to tell him about the baby. And it is a baby. Not just a pregnancy. There's another human growing inside me. One David and I created together.

I can't. Not yet. He's already crowding me to the point I feel as if I can't breathe.

"I'm sorry about missing dinner with your family. I truly am," I say carefully. "I'm even sorrier that you're having doubts about our relationship. Relationships go through stages, David. It's normal for one or both of us to have the occasional doubt or misgiving."

He scoffs. "Do not try psychoanalyzing me or our relationship, Olivia."

"My father was the shrink, not me." Not just any shrink. The top shrink in the city.

He exhales a big breath. "It feels like you are pulling away from me. I just don't understand."

I mentally grasp for how to reassure him when I can't even reassure myself. "I'm not pulling away. I'm just a little overwhelmed."

Control is everything.

My father's voice echoes in my ears.

The only person who can take it from you is you, Olivia. Do not look back, only forward. What happened in the past is irrelevant. All that matters is what happens now.

David pulls me into his arms. "I'm sorry, baby. I'm not trying to make you more stressed."

"I'm really, really sorry, too." I hug him back, feeling the warmth and promise of his arms. He does love me. And I love him. I don't know what is happening to me. I feel so out of control. "I will call your mother in the morning and apologize. I will make sure I check my phone more frequently in the future so I don't miss your texts. I let you down, and I will do all in my power not to let it happen again."

He draws back and touches my cheek, tracing a tear I didn't realize had fallen. In that instant, staring into his beautiful eyes, I see the man who stole my heart. He is kind and considerate. He will be a good father and a good husband. I want very much to find a way to work this out. To take us back to the way things were before . . . whatever changed. Before, I acknowledge, these self-doubts began.

"Thank you." His hands slide down my arms and take mine. "Forget about the boxes for tonight. Let's go upstairs." He searches my face, worry seizing his once more. "As long as you're feeling up to it."

Rather than answer, I kiss him. I kiss him until we both lose our breath.

He takes me in his arms and carries me upstairs.

He needs this right now. We both do.

EIGHT

Dana Reeves

"They know."

Fear slides through me like icy cut glass. It at once freezes my insides and rips me apart. I stare at Janie and hope to God she is wrong. Really, how could they know? We were so careful. Still, after I told her every detail of the detectives' visit to my office, she says this. As much as I hate to admit it at the moment, she is usually right in her assessments.

"Someone must have seen us," Janie insists. She plants her hands on her hips and swears.

I collapse into the nearest chair. Think of the way the two detectives watched me so closely. Looking for a potential lie, no doubt. "I suppose that's possible." I close my eyes and force the idea away. Why did we do it? It was a ridiculous attempt at doing what the law should have done years ago. But it was obviously a mistake, and now we can't take it back. Dread congeals in my gut.

Still, I admit, it felt like the right thing to do when we all decided. It was a plan. A plan that needed to happen.

Janie lowers onto the chair arm and puts her arm around me. "Whatever they learned, maybe we don't need to worry. No matter what someone may have seen, they can't prove we did anything wrong. We saw the news and we drove by. Big deal. All we have to do is be calm."

"But what if they go to the cabin?"

For a moment she only stares at me. "We say we weren't there. Whatever happened was not our doing."

I stare up at her. She is my lifeline, my one true tether to sanity. I lean into her. Honest to God, I don't know what I would have done without her. By the time I was in high school, I was ready to end it all. My family never understood. They thought I should hold my head up and move on. Not a single one of them had a damned clue. I couldn't bear the dreams anymore. I just wanted to die.

But Janie helped me. We faced our tormented pasts together. We became each other's reason for going on.

She scooches me over and slides down into the big old chair with me. The ragged thing is way past its prime—as is everything in this decrepit apartment. But it's comfortable, and being frugal here allows us to save for the future.

We have so many plans.

But first we have to get through *this*.

"We just have to stick with the plan," she reminds me. "We've all discussed it. We all have our roles. All we have to do is let this play out."

I draw in a deep breath. She's right, but I would have much preferred to know and understand what each of us was doing. We know the expected order of each step but not who carries it out. That way, none of us has to lie to the cops. You can't lie if you don't know.

As for the rest, the agreement was that the plan would go with us to our graves. End of story. Anyone who broke and felt the urge to talk would be just as guilty as all the others. No one could claim innocence regardless of their part in this.

Once the steps were decided upon, they were written individually on pieces of paper and folded carefully before being dropped into a small basket. Then we each took a turn drawing from that basket. We read it, privately, of course, then ate the paper. Literally chewed it up and swallowed it like in some spy novel.

When the step drawn was completed, your part was over.

Janie and I decided to combine ours into one—which should have worked perfectly . . . except it didn't.

Now all we have to do is pray and keep it together until the police finish their investigation. I tell myself this again and again.

Strangely, that's the hardest part.

NINE

DETECTIVE WALTER DUNCAN

It's the holes—the ones that go unrecognized for a little too long—that cause the most trouble in even the best-laid plans.

I sit on the back porch steps, my loyal companion at my side. We both stare out across the lawn for as far as the light will reach through the darkness. I think of Stella's roses and how inept and pathetic I've proven at trying to keep them healthy and blooming. My Stella was a natural with plants. Our yard, front and back, was always a standout in the neighborhood.

Until Stella suddenly got sick, the yard was her domain. Of course, I navigated the lawnmower around the property on Saturdays, kept the grass trimmings up, but the rest was her territory and she had shooed me out of her flowerbeds more than once. She would be horrified if she could see the overgrown mess they have become. I'm glad it's dark and I don't have to look at them.

The funny thing I just realized when I sat down on these steps this evening is that in all my elaborate planning and thorough consideration for my own demise I forgot the most important thing in my life, besides Liv and my work—Sandy. At eighty-five pounds and taller than me when she stands on her hind legs, my yellow Lab should be hard to forget. And yet, I left her completely out of the scenario until that call from the vet.

Back when Stella's final arrangements were made, I made my own. I'm to be buried next to my wife without the bother of a funeral. I told the funeral director to do what he had to do and plant me, no frills, no fuss. My house, everything inside it, and the SUV I bequeathed to Stella's favorite charity. She and I donated her car to the charity before she closed her eyes for the last time. I considered leaving my savings and insurance money to Liv, but she doesn't need it. She would be the first to say her parents left her far more than she will ever need. So I decided to assign it to my favorite charity—the families of wounded and fallen officers. My fellow officers are the only real family I have. Like Liv, I was an only child. Parents are long gone. I was never close to the few distant cousins I met as a kid.

I've been so thorough with all the necessary final arrangements. How in the world did I allow anything—especially something as important as my sweet Sandy—to fall through the cracks in my preparations?

Thank God I don't have to worry about that anymore. At least not for a while. But I do need to make a decision, just in case I get in an accident or have a heart attack or get shot in the line of duty.

Leaving a dog behind is a true dilemma, not like the money or the material possessions. I'm reasonably sure Liv would take her in a heartbeat, but I don't know about the fiancé. Maybe I could bring up the subject of pets with her and get a feel for Preston's take on such things.

"Don't worry, girl." I rub Sandy's back and pull her against me. "I'll make sure you have a good home for when the time comes."

I toss the tennis ball Sandy loves to chase and wait for her to bring it back to me, then I throw it again. At least one of us will get some exercise today. I expect the cardiologist will be taking that issue up with me. Along with diet and such. I'll have to lay off the JD. He and I became a little too well acquainted after Stella died.

A blast of heavy air puffs out of me. Other than the coughing jags and some chest discomfort, I haven't had too much trouble.

I smile. Damn, I can hardly believe it's real. But I don't have cancer, and I might just live a good while longer.

I pitch the ball again. Hell yeah.

My lips fall into a frown as I consider that Liv looked like hell again today. I don't like that those migraines are taking her down so low. In the time we've worked so closely together, I've never known her to look anything but healthy and vibrant. She seems almost withdrawn lately. Distracted and fatigued. The big-ass bags under her eyes underscored by the dark circles have me worried. But she went to the doc. I was there in the waiting room. Her doctor didn't seem overly concerned. These days I'm not sure if that is a good thing or not. Sometimes I think they just run us through like scanning groceries at the supermarket checkout. If you're turned the wrong way, they might not pick up on the real problem. It's all scary as hell and it feels like nothing more than the luck of the draw.

The good news is, Liv is smart. And she's strong. No matter that she's a little off her game right now, she'll pull it together. That's something else I know about her.

"Come on, Sandy." I stand, stretch my back, and lead the way into the house.

I fill her water bowl and move to the fridge to scrounge around for a late snack. For thirty-five years, I came home to a hot meal prepared from scratch, unless we went out, which was rare. I'm spoiled and mostly inept in the kitchen. I round up cheese and crackers and snag a beer.

With my arm full of goodies, I drop into a chair at the table. My working case file lies open on the table. Photos of the known victims of Carl Fanning and a mug shot of the bastard himself stare up at me. I consider Dana Reeves and Janie Hyatt. Is it possible these two average-looking women—neither of whom looks particularly strong—could be holding Fanning for the purposes of torture or could have killed him already?

There's no question they were watching him.

I've mapped out the route to the cabin Hyatt inherited. Maybe we'll get lucky and find Fanning there and wrap this one up tomorrow. I could take Friday off and get a few things done around here. God knows I have an avalanche of leave days built up even after all the time I took off with Stella.

My cell phone vibrates against the countertop. I answer with my usual, "Duncan."

The only sound on the other end is static. I frown. "Hello."

"Detective Walter Duncan?"

The voice is male. Not one I've heard before—that I can recall, anyway. "That's me. What can I do for you?"

"This is Mario Sanchez."

The words break a little, but I still hear and understand that this is the guy on a climbing trip down in Mexico. "Sanchez, thank you for calling."

I stay perfectly still just in case a movement in one direction or the other might cause the connection to drop off. I vividly remember back when most all long-distance phone calls sounded like this.

"My wife and my mother say you've been very adamant about getting in touch with me."

The words crackle across the line in pieces, but I get the gist of it.

"That's right. If you could call me as soon as you return home, I would appreciate it. I have a few questions I'd like to review with you in person. It's very important."

"That's the reason I'm calling. I wanted to confirm that we will return on Sunday and the minute I'm back in Nashville, I will call. Is there anything I can do from here, Detective? I'm a little confused as to what this is about."

It was good to hear such eagerness to cooperate with the police, though I'm not so sure he'll still feel that way when he learns all the fuss is about Fanning.

"Your wife tells me you and your friends left Nashville on Saturday morning and arrived in Mexico City late Sunday evening. Is that correct?"

"Yes, that's correct. We spent Saturday night in Brownsville, Texas, at a Holiday Inn Express."

"Your two friends were with you the whole time and can vouch for your itinerary?"

"Absolutely. This sounds serious, Detective. May I ask what this concerns?"

The static is back, so I wait it out, hoping the call won't drop. "It's about Carl Fanning, Mr. Sanchez."

The long stretch of dead air that follows makes me worry that he's severed the connection, then he says, "I see." He hesitates before going on. "Has he taken another victim?"

That is a tough one to answer. At this point, we still can't say one way or the other. "We're not entirely sure, Mr. Sanchez. You see, he disappeared sometime between late Saturday and midday on Monday. It's very important that we locate him."

More of that tense hush lingers between us; the crackle of static pops again and again. Finally, he speaks. "If the world is lucky, he's dead and buried somewhere."

I can't help wondering whether that somewhere is in Mexico.

"Have a safe trip back, Mr. Sanchez. I look forward to hearing from you as soon as you're home."

The call ends, and I study the photo of ten-year-old Mario Sanchez. He was Fanning's final victim. The one who fought back and won. But was the plea bargain Fanning managed to finagle for owning up to abusing all those victims not what Sanchez had hoped for?

Or is the idea of his own child coming into the same world where Carl Fanning lives too much for him to sit idly by and do nothing?

Would his friends help him take that kind of revenge?

I can't say just yet. I need to sit face-to-face with Sanchez and measure the man he has become. But I have already concluded one thing with absolute certainty: There is no way the boy escaped Carl Fanning without help. Both the detectives who worked the case felt Sanchez wasn't completely forthcoming, but they had the bad guy so they let it go.

Maybe it's time that possibility was revisited.

I turn my attention to Reeves and Hyatt. There's always the chance Fanning is just a few miles up the road in Hendersonville hog-tied in a shed or an old barn awaiting execution.

Somehow I can't muster up any sympathy.

He deserves a lot worse than whatever has happened to him.

TEN

The Child

After the first year, I stopped thinking about who I was before. That life was no longer relevant and the thoughts only made me sad and miserable. I had a choice: I could hope to die or I could hope to survive.

I chose to survive.

The monster became my father, my mother, my world. I had no one else.

When I was older, he started to allow me outside whatever shithole we lived in. Don't get me wrong, it didn't happen often, but when it did it was like going to the circus for a kid who'd spent the past two years as a prisoner. He made sure I looked nice and reminded me to smile. As we left the car and walked into the market or wherever, he held my hand, smiling like a proud daddy. It wasn't like he had to worry that someone would recognize me from a milk carton. I had changed too much.

The first time out in public was the most difficult. Not because I misbehaved but because I was terrified that someone else would take me. I had lived through it once; I didn't want to risk going through it again. I needed the stability. As foolish as it sounds now, at the time, I knew where my next meal would come from and that I would be warm on a cold night. I was well acquainted with the things he would do to me whenever he chose, and though I hated every second of it, I understood that I would survive those awful things. I'd learned to go to my happy place while he took what he wanted, to tune out his sickening grunting and the disgusting things he did to my skinny little body.

It was my new normal. My everyday routine.

Food and warmth and routines . . . those things were all that mattered to a kid who had lost everything and who had been sexually abused in every possible way one can imagine.

You might think it's impossible to do all the things to a small child one can do to an adult, but you're wrong. Trust me when I say he did things to me that I will never share with anyone. Things no one can ever know because I cannot bear the reliving long enough to tell the story.

As I grew older, our relationship began to shift somewhat. He realized he could use me for more than entertainment. No one worried when a child wandered too close to a shopping cart or bumped against the heavy purse hanging from a shoulder or arm. I learned the art of pickpocketing like other kids learn how to ride a bike. It still amazes me the stash of cash most women kept handy in those days. It was as if they feared the need for change or a few dollars while attempting to exit a public parking garage with two sleeping kids in car seats. Or worse, the five bucks they used their debit card for at McDonald's would end up part of a major card security breach that required new debit cards and PIN numbers. Always a pain in the ass.

Since there was inevitably the risk I might be caught by a shopper who wasn't as distracted as I first believed, he taught me how to avoid being trapped into a confession. How to lie like a pro. How to make the same lady I'd just robbed believe perhaps she was wrong after all. When all else failed, there was the ace up my sleeve—the sympathy card. I was hungry. My baby sister needed milk. And then, of course, I learned how to evade capture. I could slip away and hide where no one would find me better than Houdini himself.

But stealing wasn't my only skill. I was also very, very good at begging in a way that didn't actually give the appearance of begging. I would stare, big eyed, at something most kids my age took entirely for granted—like a new pair of sneakers or a new pair of jeans. I never bothered with toys. I had been taught they were pointless. I still had the teddy bear, but it didn't actually count. On those occasions when I set out to get something only I wanted, I wore my most ragged clothes. He didn't teach me this technique; this is one I developed on my own. Even the hardest heart could be melted by a poor, dirty child in need. Children are starving all over the country, and no one wants to hear about it. Put one in front of their faces so they have to look at it, and all bets are off. They can't take it.

Funny thing was, I had no idea at the time that I was learning the skills I would desperately need later.

He still got angry and forced me into the dreaded box from time to time. And he kept me illiterate. He refused to teach me to read or to write. Too afraid, I suppose, that I would turn out smarter than him and then maybe figure out that I didn't really belong to him. The problem was, by then, I didn't remember who I was. I was the child. His child. I belonged to him, body and soul.

During the rare occasion when I had to flee a pickpocket situation, it never once entered my mind to find a police officer or to tell someone I needed help. I was far more afraid of what might happen if I did this than I was of anything else he might do to me. I had survived the worst he could possibly do.

Or, at least, I thought I had.

"I saved you."

My attention jerks to the piece of shit huddled in the darkest corner of his prison. Ah, so he's decided to talk today, has he?

"You saved me?" I scoff at the concept. Obviously his brain was damaged during all those years in prison.

I walk closer to where he huddles. I am not afraid. In addition to having a wide, ugly wound on his upper arm, he's bruised and battered quite thoroughly. As I approach him, he shudders visibly and draws into a tighter ball. How pathetic. I think of all the times he beat me far more brutally than what has been done to him. I think of the endless ways he used my frail, tender body as a child and the need to kill him now—this instant—surges until my heart is thundering in my chest.

"You beat and raped me day after day, week after week, year after year, until they took you. What the hell do you think you saved me from?"

It doesn't matter, really, what he thinks. He is nothing. Less than nothing. I have no idea why I bother interacting with him. Perhaps on some level I am curious how such a monster can believe himself the victim after what he has done. Or more to the point, how could he possibly do the things he did to me or to any other child and believe he deserves anything less than every ounce of pain I am capable of inflicting?

How has he lived with the memories of his grievous acts against the weakest members of society?

And why did he come back to Nashville? He could have gone to Murfreesboro or farther north. I suspect I know the answer to that one, but we'll see.

"I saved you from the people who brought you into this world." Even as he boasts, he braces for my retaliation.

Coward.

I consider kicking him in the side. I've done this numerous times already. Why bother?

"Do you know what today is?" I ask him rather than kick him as I first considered.

He shakes his head, fear filling his pathetic eyes. I do not possess the proper words to articulate how very much that fear pleases me.

"It's day three of our reunion," I say. "I'm surprised you didn't think of this when you were planning this elaborate game you set in motion. Do you remember what you did to me on day three after you took me home with you?"

He shakes his head adamantly at first, and then the movement subsides as the memories flood his wretched brain. The fear tightens around his throat and chest in a choke hold. I hear the change in his respiration. See the growing terror in his eyes.

Oh, how it pleases me.

"But don't worry. I'm sure you were raped plenty of times in prison." I shrug. "Statistics show that men like you were probably raped as children, too. Is that true? Did your daddy or an uncle, maybe a grandpa, rape you as a child? Is that what turned you into the disgusting perv you became?"

He looks away. In all the years we were together, he never spoke of the men in his family. There had to be men. He spoke only of his mother—the one who died of an overdose when he was just eight years old. Before he dies, I'm going to tell him about searching until I found where his mother was buried. I went to her grave in the middle of the night and shit on it. Probably wasn't her fault he turned out the way he did since she died when he was so young, but she was the one who spit him out of her loins. For that, she deserved to be shit on, alive or dead.

"I'll make this a lot easier on you if you just tell me the truth."

After he was taken away to prison, I watched the news. I heard the armchair shrinks create scenarios based on his known history. His father had gotten himself murdered when Fanning was seventeen. His grandfather had been in a nursing home with Alzheimer's. When Fanning was nineteen, somehow his grandfather ended up dead in the shower at the care facility where he was a resident. Strange thing. The staff had no idea how he got out of bed and into the shower, much less fell and bashed his head on the tile. The shrinks speculated that the grandfather had molested Fanning as a child.

The monster remains silent, hovering in that corner like a trapped animal.

"We both know it was your grandfather. That's why you killed him." I experience much pleasure at saying these things to him. I want him to feel the way I felt. The worthlessness, the humiliation, the desolation. The utter uncertainty.

"Then why ask?" he snarls.

I smile. "I just want to hear you say the words, that's all. I want to hear all the terrible things he did to you. Maybe see if you learned those nasty tricks of yours from him."

"Shut up!"

The hoarse shriek gives me another shot of immense pleasure.

I really don't need any answers from him, I know how the story likely went. Does his damaged childhood make me feel the least bit sorry for him?

No.

He chose to continue the vicious cycle of abuse. Since he didn't have children of his own, he abused other people's children.

That is never going to happen again.

Never, ever, ever.

ELEVEN

Detective Olivia Newhouse

Thursday, May 3

"Sounds like she accepted your apology," Walt notes with a quick glance at me before making the turn onto McMurtry Road.

I toss my cell onto the console. What else can I do? I did exactly as I promised David I would. I called his mother. She was, as always, charming and accommodating. "Who knows? You can't ever tell with her."

David's mother would never allow her composure to slip or any sort of improper emotion to show. Not to me. Probably not for anyone. I hesitate, feel bad for half a second for holding this uncomfortable situation against her when I was the no-show at dinner. But then, it's true. I met David's parents not long after we started dating. I've known them for approximately six months, and I still feel like an outsider. My future mother-in-law is one of those people whose social graces are so ingrained that she would smile at the devil himself if he showed up at a function as long as his name was on the guest list. She was probably holding the phone tight enough to crack it as she listened to my feeble excuse for not attending the family dinner. Tracking down a missing pedophile couldn't possibly be more important than one of her scheduled events.

A good future daughter-in-law would be looking for a way to make it up to her. I'm certain she views the situation from that perspective.

I fear I will never be what she considers a good daughter-in-law.

Maybe I'm overreacting. Maybe it's easier to believe they don't like me, and then I don't have to feel guilty when I let them down. David has said this to me frequently since I moved into his house. I wonder whether this is the pattern for the rest of our lives together. I think of this baby growing inside me, and I am suddenly extremely anxious. A child needs a happy home without all this tension and frustration.

"She doesn't like you?"

I push away the thoughts of the future and almost laugh. "I really can't say for sure. I think they're still shocked David and I didn't fizzle out after a few weeks. I'm reasonably certain they had a family meeting and concluded I was a momentary blip on his radar—a rebound adventure after he and his longtime, more appropriate girlfriend ended their relationship."

Walt grunts. He would just as soon see me single and happy again. I shake my head and focus on the landscape as we maneuver onto Hogans Branch Road. It is true that I'm happiest when it's just the work and me. Got that from my dad. I'm not sure I'm capable of changing a part of me so deeply ingrained. Probably embedded in my genes.

First thing this morning, I made up my mind not to mention anything about yet another headache to Walt. He worries about me too much as it is. Besides, how could I explain that not long after David and I made love, the agony woke me up from a dead sleep? That has never happened before. I was sleeping like a baby. I retreated to the guest room and shut out all light and all sound to get through the night. Rather than explain it to David, I left before he came downstairs this morning. I couldn't possibly tell him that after our beautiful lovemaking, I grew immensely ill.

I hope the doctor is right and the hormones go back to normal in the second trimester.

"Here we go." Walt navigates his SUV across a narrow stream that flows over a dip in the long gravel driveway.

The cabin belonging to Janie Hyatt sits about a quarter mile beyond the stream, even farther from the road and surrounded by thick woods. The driveway bends around a small pond with a short dock jutting out over the still surface. A fishing boat floats in the water, one end tied to the dock. From all appearances, it's the typical log cabin with a screened-in front porch overlooking a tranquil pond. The perfect getaway from the noise and stress of city life.

"Nice place," Walt says.

"Yeah." I reach for the door and climb out. No vehicles around. "I wonder if anyone's home?"

"Doesn't look that way," Walt says, mostly to himself. "All my calls to either of these two just go to voicemail."

"They are definitely avoiding us," I say.

I scan the tree line as we move toward the cabin. Leaves flutter with the sudden movement of a bird. I watch it soar across the clear sky and disappear from sight. The quiet reminds me of the farm. Somewhere miles away I hear the sound of a car.

"So I've been looking for a retirement place," Walt announces. He flashes me a grin and a wink.

"Good one." We both know he's planning a move to Florida, but the cover is a solid one. If anyone shows up, we're obviously lost. Just out driving around looking for the cabin we saw on some real estate site. What man wouldn't love his own little fishing hole right off the front porch? Surely this perfect place is for sale.

We separate and move around opposite ends of the cabin. That's when I smell the distinct scent of smoke. Two seconds later I spot the burned structure.

"Walt! We've got something."

He hurries around his end of the cabin. "Well, well, lookie what we have here."

We both approach the burned rubble that was once some sort of structure. A wood door, very much like half the set of double doors to my barn, lies on the ground. The edges are scorched, but it's about the only thing wood that survived the fire. In the expanse of ash that was once the barn are lumps and clumps of things that didn't burn completely, maybe some sort of equipment that could easily conceal human remains.

"I think maybe it was a barn." My comment is unnecessary, but I feel so surprised by the find that I can't hold back the words. This could be where Fanning met his demise. Damn. I blink, feeling oddly disjointed. I can't decide whether to regret the discovery since this means the two vics, Reeves and Hyatt, are in big-ass trouble, or to be jumping for joy that one more piece of shit has been erased from this earth.

"I think you're right," Walt says as he surveys the mess.

Urgency has me venturing around the edges of the debris. Can't disturb or risk corrupting any potential evidence. Not that doing so would be safe even if I dared. There could still be smoldering embers embedded in all that rubble.

"Fanning could have been restrained in the barn," I suggest when Walt doesn't.

"Possibly. But we got nothing that points in that direction." He looks from the cabin to another shedlike structure beyond the burned-out barn. "Looks like they were lucky and there was no breeze to spread the fire."

"Yeah." Another thought occurs to me, this one particularly unpalatable. "Since we haven't been able to contact Hyatt or Reeves since the initial meeting with Reeves, maybe one or both were victims here instead of Fanning."

The fire doesn't appear to have been that long ago. Regret twists in my gut. That would be a damned shame. But the scenario could give us a certain opportunity. I look to Walt.

"You're right, partner. I think we should call in the locals. Get a fire marshal out here to investigate this for us."

"We can look around while we wait. Go inside the cabin." I shrug. "Feels like exigent circumstances to me."

"Absolutely. There could be victims inside—or the perpetrator."

We move back to the cabin. On the east end, the one I round, there's the massive stone chimney. The screened porch wraps around the west end—the end Walt is covering—and comes to a stop just past the back door. Since most of the windows are concealed by the presence of the screened porch, I climb the back steps.

Walt heads back around front. He'll go to the front door. It's our usual routine. One goes to the back door, the other goes to the front. On the porch the flowers in the pewter pitcher standing on the table between two chairs are still alive. I check the water level in the pitcher, half full. Someone has been here recently.

I open the screen door and rap on the wood door behind it. I lean closer and peer through the glass. A small kitchen that leads into the living room. I can see the big fireplace and a couple of comfy-looking chairs flanking it. On a side table in the living room, the screen on the small television is black. I hear Walt knocking on the front door. I should move on to the next window, but instead I pull my sleeve down over my hand and turn the doorknob.

The door opens.

"Hmm." Now that's a surprise. This place may be isolated, but that doesn't mean it's exempt from trouble. Seems odd it wasn't locked.

Going inside without exigent circumstances or a warrant is against the law, but we have that now—at least to my way of thinking. I remind myself of this fact as I cross the threshold.

I drag a pair of latex gloves from my jacket pocket and pull them on as I walk across the uncluttered kitchen. The cabin is small. Can't be more than four rooms. It'll take barely a minute to walk through the floor plan. Fridge is empty except for an opened block of cheese and a half-empty bottle of wine. Stove is cold. No dishes in the sink. I move to the living room. No ash in the fireplace. The temps have been fairly low at night. Anyone staying here would have needed a fire.

Maybe they cleaned up before they left. I pass into a short hall. Three doors, the narrowest one is obviously a closet. I open it first. Shelves loaded with linens and other household goods. The second door is a small bathroom. A good-sized bedroom is behind the final door. Bed is made. No one hiding underneath it. No one in that dinky closet, either.

Walt is in the kitchen when I make my way back there. "Nothing?" he asks.

I shake my head. "You find anything?"

"I opened the door to the crawl space. No hidden basement." He peels off his gloves. "Just the usual. Spiders and crickets."

"We should take a look around beyond the tree line." I survey the main living area one last time. "Make sure there's not an underground storm shelter or a root cellar. Or one of those bugout hidey-holes."

He nods. "Let's do it."

It takes a solid two hours to have a good look around. But it's better than sitting around waiting for the locals to arrive. The Chester County sheriff came first, then the fire marshal. They got started while we carried on with our search of the property.

If there was an underground bunker of some sort, we couldn't find any indication of a fresh-air access or an entrance. No newly turned earth. None of the vegetation appears to have been disturbed. If Hyatt and Reeves killed Fanning, they buried him so deep in the woods we'll never find his body without ground penetrating radar.

Assuming his remains aren't in the rubble from that fire.

Speaking of the fire, in the shed near the tree line, there's a tractor and a number of attachments, like a bushhog. But the most troubling is the two five-gallon metal gas cans—both empty. Based on Walt's sniff of each, one had held gas, the other diesel fuel. Both accelerants.

At the front of the house, I consider the pond. It's possible they dumped him in the water. I walk out onto the small dock; the boards creak and sigh as if no one has disturbed them in a while. I scan the shimmering surface. Doesn't look that deep, but I don't think I want to dive in and find out. The water would be as cold as ice.

"Thinking of taking a swim?" Walt joins me at the dock.

"I'll pass." I turn to him. "We're closing in on the end of our list with nothing to show for it. Maybe we're focused on the wrong victims."

If Fanning took a victim, getting injured in the process, he would be too scared to go back home. That's a given. He would hide until he was found or escaped to someplace far away. The only question is: Where would he hide? He has no living family. No resources to speak of. I can't see him lying low with a friend. Fanning is a loner. Based on his file, he always worked alone and he never ran. According to his own statements, he'd lived in and around Nashville his whole life. The experts agreed that every child he took without getting caught made him braver.

Cocky son of a bitch.

My stomach growls. I turn to my partner. "We should head back. Grab some lunch."

"Sounds good to me," Walt agrees.

I load into the Tahoe while he has a final conversation with the sheriff.

As Walt heads for the Tahoe, he's checking the screen of his phone. "Just got a text from Holland," he says as he climbs behind the wheel.

Detective Renae Holland is part of the Youth Services Division, assigned to the Missing and Runaway Juveniles Unit. This news sets me on edge.

"Two kids were reported missing this morning. A sixteen- and a seventeen-year-old." His face reflects the dread in his voice.

"Damn." Fanning didn't generally hunt in that age group, but he's been in prison a long time. His tastes or his ability to wait out the perfect prey may have changed. "We should eat on the way."

The sooner we talk to the families, the sooner we'll know if this is part of our investigation.

I hope to hell not. No child should ever be touched by a monster like Fanning.

The idea doesn't jibe with our Reeves/Hyatt theory, but for now the possibility that the two former vics nabbed Fanning and burned him to death is just a theory. Even if it proves true, it doesn't exclude the possibility that Fanning could have abducted someone before he was grabbed.

As Walt drives back toward Nashville, I find myself obsessing about David and his family again. I love him. I do. Sometimes I feel completely certain that I want to marry him. Then those doubts creep back in. I can't comprehend why I suddenly feel incapable of relating to his family or beneath them somehow. I've never experienced such a lack of confidence. And if I can't see my way past all that, what about the baby? What do I do from here?

For starters, I don't sell the farm. I may end up needing to go back there to live. It's a good place for kids. Quiet, peaceful. There are no horses anymore, but that can change. I cannot imagine in a million years homeschooling my child as my parents did me, which is okay because the farm is located in a good school district.

Could I be a good mother? My mother was a great mother. She died when I was twenty-three, but my father and I made it a point to speak of her often. Recalled all the fun times. He would not allow her memory to die. He made sure I never forgot no matter how busy I was with work. He reminded me of the family life we shared. Maybe keeping all those memories in front of me was his way of ensuring he never forgot a single moment, either. He was a dedicated, loving husband, father, and doctor.

Though he didn't have an opportunity to get to know David until just a couple of months before his death, he liked him. I had the impression he approved of our fledgling relationship. I wish there had been more time.

I glance at Walt. I wonder whether a man like David can possibly ever be the sort of caring man my father was, that Walt is. I'm not so sure men like them exist anymore. A dying breed.

Walt's gray hair is mussed on one side from our trek through the woods. I smile and resist the urge to reach over and smooth it. I don't want to embarrass him. He'll glance in the mirror and notice eventually.

My thoughts shift back to David. No, he is not like my father or Walt. Chances are, he won't ever be. But then I'm not exactly the storybook picture of a wife. I suppose I'm about as far from a trad-wife as is possible to get and still be a member of the female species. Which begs the question of my nurturing skills.

Too late to worry about that now.

We hit a drive-through and grab sandwiches and drinks.

A few minutes later we're already at the first of the two addresses we need to visit. At the top of our list is Chloe Simone, sixteen years old.

The Simone home is a small white bungalow with green shutters and a wide porch. The houses along the block are shoehorned next to each other with barely a strip of grass between them. It's an older neighborhood with mature trees and no shortage of deferred maintenance. Chloe lives with her grandparents since her parents died in a house fire when she was only ten. She's an honor student at her school and has lots of friends. The girl's grandmother gave her free rein to roam the neighborhood as long as her homework was done and her grades were in order. Brighter than average, Chloe had all the free time in the world to wander to her heart's desire. And now she's missing.

Posters, flowers, and stuffed animals surround a shrine started in Chloe's front yard. "Please send Chloe home!" "Help us find Chloe!" "God will bring Chloe home."

Unfortunately, unless her abductor suddenly grows a conscience and drops her off somewhere or by sheer luck she escapes, the only way she is coming home is if the cops working on her case find her in time or via the morgue. At this point, to believe anything else is wishful thinking. Even the small reward offered for information on the missing girl will likely be futile. Chloe Simone has been missing for twice that critical forty-eight hours. The grandmother mistakenly thought the class trip was this week. It wasn't until one of Chloe's friends showed up looking for her that the grandmother realized her mistake. According to the police report, the poor grandmother is beside herself. She has not laid eyes on the child since Sunday morning and hope is dwindling.

Sadly she has good reason to be afraid. Chloe's odds of being found alive have diminished considerably over the past twenty-four hours. Even Fanning never kept a victim more than a few hours. Thankfully, none of his—as far as we know—were murdered.

Unless his MO has changed this time or some aspect of his strategy has gone terribly, terribly wrong, hopefully he hasn't killed anyone. I think of the blood at his rental house. He's been out of the game for a long while. His abduction skills are no doubt rusty. A fatal accident may have occurred.

Then again, there's always the possibility that he has suddenly decided to keep a victim, hiding in plain sight as he did before. Still, keeping a sixteen- or seventeen-year-old victim compliant wouldn't be an easy task. Add to that the issue of transportation. His vehicle, tires flat and windshield broken, remains in the driveway at his rental house. How did he move a victim?

Lends more credence to the idea that *he* is the victim.

Milton Simone, the grandfather, answers the door. Walt does the introductions and we're promptly invited in. My partner begins with the expected questions. How are they holding up? Is there anything else the police should be doing that they are not? Can we get them anything they might need? Walt knows the manager at the local Kroger. He can have anything they need delivered at no charge.

The elderly couple assures us they're fine and that they have everything they need, except their granddaughter. A framed photo of Chloe sits on the coffee table surrounded by lit prayer candles and the family's Bible. The book is dog-eared and visibly worn from use.

"Mr. and Mrs. Simone," I ask, "have any of Chloe's friends mentioned seeing her with an older man?"

Chloe's friends and classmates, as well as the neighbors, will all be questioned endlessly about any strangers who might have been lurking in the neighborhood or around the school. Only time will tell if anything will emerge in all the questioning. Did Chloe have any enemies? Any trouble at school, or at home? Is she happy? Has she adjusted well to living with her grandparents since her parents' deaths? All these questions will be asked and analyzed. Detectives have already been at the house and combed through the place. Her cell phone and laptop are now at Metro's crime lab for processing. Her room and this home have been searched. A friend last saw her on Sunday evening just before dark in the parking lot of the apartment building at the end of the block. Several of her classmates live in those apartments.

It's all just beginning and there is no way to forecast how it will end.

Mrs. Simone shakes her head adamantly. "Chloe would never let herself be fooled by offers of gifts or money. We taught her to beware of strangers. If she got into a car with a stranger, then she did so unconscious or kicking and screaming. There is zero chance it happened any other way."

Her voice wavers on the last word.

I nod, summon an encouraging smile that I in no way feel. "You taught her well."

The Simones were shown a photo of Fanning by the other detectives. Walt requested that any situation related to the missing be treated as if Fanning might be involved. The grandparents stated they had never seen him before.

"The police still think it might be related to that man—this Fanning?" Mr. Simone asks.

"We're following up on every possible avenue," Walt explains. "The fact that Fanning disappeared at approximately the same time gives us reason to believe there might be a connection, but that is the only related thread we have. No other evidence or statements suggest he was seen with your granddaughter."

"There was that one girl," Mr. Simone says to his wife. "You know the one who told you she thought an old man had been hanging around the apartments. She said he was watching her and Chloe."

Mrs. Simone shakes her head. "You're thinking about the janitor they used to have at the school. He's retired now. They got a new one," she reminded him. "The detectives who came by this morning promised to check him out."

We go through the relevant questions, the same ones they have no doubt already answered, and we get nothing that actually helps. Sadly that's the way this usually goes.

Walt places his business card on the table. "Please call the detectives you spoke with this morning or us if you think of anything else or if one of Chloe's friends comes to you with any new information. We're all working together to find her."

The Simones promise to do so and we leave. I glance around the run-down neighborhood. The Simones are clinging to their optimism about their granddaughter, but I have a bad feeling this will not end well. So often it does not.

"You said Sanchez will be back on Sunday," I comment as we climb into the Tahoe. "You going to call me when he calls you?"

Walt starts the engine and shifts into Drive. "You know it, partner."

Frankly, it seems like a bit of a moot effort since Sanchez appears to have been out of town since before Fanning went missing. But Walt doesn't want to mark him off the list until he's interviewed him face-to-face.

That's because Walt is a good cop.

A damned good cop.

Whether Sanchez is involved or not, I guess we'd find out on Sunday.

At the end of the day, I am spent.

Walt and I drove by Dana Reeves's office, and it was closed. Janie Hyatt owns a training facility for horseback riding and horsemanship in Franklin. The receptionist at the facility informed us that Hyatt was on vacation this week. Something is definitely up with those two. I feel it all the way to my bones. That fire at their barn has to be related to Fanning.

We also interviewed the parents of the other missing teenager, Suzy Eldridge, and then caught up with one more name on our list of Fanning's past victims, Patricia Shelby. The latter was yet another harrowing account of the worst that one human can do to another. Shelby had an airtight alibi. She went into labor on Saturday evening and had her baby—a girl, Lily—on Sunday. Watching her take care of her newborn was unnerving. I cannot even imagine handling such a fragile human. I am so in over my head.

Her Fanning story only reiterates how absurd it is that the bastard got off with a few months shy of fourteen years in prison. Plea bargains save the courts money, ensure a conviction. I understand this. Still, it's a travesty. One, I suspect, is being amended. I push away the images of torture that instantly come to mind.

As a cop, I'm disappointed at the prospect that someone has taken the law—justice—into his or her own hands. Conversely, as a human, I'm thrilled that anyone had the balls not to let this go. My father would say it's the universal issue of civilized society. Our basic instinct is survival and self-protection. The rules of society push us to forgive, to turn the other cheek . . . to give a slap on the wrist to the evil among us and carry on. All will be well.

But evil doesn't live by society's rules. Evil lives for one simple purpose: to fulfill its selfish desires, whatever the cost to others.

Carl Fanning is pure evil. Regardless, society's rules dictate that Walt and I must find him and protect him if need be or arrest him if he's committed some crime. We are no closer to accomplishing one or the other than we were seventy-odd hours ago when this case landed in our laps.

No matter that I've been late every night for days. No matter that David will be home soon, instead of going to his house, I go to the farm where I was raised. Half an hour commute from Nashville into the horse country of Franklin.

Am I avoiding the man I love? The man I'm supposed to marry? Yes. If I avoid him, I don't have to reveal my fears and uncertainty about us, about the baby. I can pretend I'm too busy to go into such a profoundly life-changing discussion at the moment. Life will be calmer when this case is solved and David and I can discuss and plan for this new reality.

He wants children. We haven't discussed the when, but that's irrelevant now.

I unlock the house, step inside, and disarm the security system, then close my eyes and inhale deeply the scent of home. I'm not sure how many years it will take for me to see anyplace else as home. I know it happens. People marry and leave home and start their own homes. But some part of where you came from is always home, I think.

David is intent on me selling this place. The house is so big, and there's more than forty acres of woods and pastures. Someone who has horses should have the place, he reminds me. Someone who has the time to appreciate the property and all its natural majesty. He's right, I suppose, but I can't imagine not having this place to escape to whenever I feel the need.

Like now.

Walt suggested I lease the land and keep the house for a getaway from the city. Lots of Nashvillians have country houses or lake houses. No reason I can't keep it. It's mine. It's paid for. I open my eyes and survey the massive great room that serves as the centerpiece of this house. Any way I look at it, this is home. Large and airy but not the slightest bit ostentatious.

I lock the door behind me and wander through the room. Those damn packing boxes are scattered everywhere. I feel ashamed that I even started the process of packing up my parents' things. It's too soon. I shouldn't have listened to David. Since I didn't argue with him on the subject, I can't blame him. If I don't want to sell the house or pack up their things, all I have to do is say so.

The past is the past, Liv. Living there can sometimes be a futile and harmful thing.

My father reminded me often that though it was perfectly fine to feel wistful about the past, particularly lost loved ones, it was never smart to linger there unless it was in the good memories. "The past is the past for a reason," he would say. "It's behind you. Move toward what's in front of you, Liv."

But it's the past that has drawn me back here today. Right after my father's death, it was necessary to pull out his will and other essential papers and to go through his office. He'd had a number of those necessary documents laid out on his desk already. I don't know whether he was feeling ill and just didn't tell me or if he was merely doing an annual update to his paperwork. Some financial records and insurance documents were out of their folders. A sealed envelope that contained a letter of instruction, reminding me where important documents were stored, the names of insurance companies, passwords for bank accounts and other online accounts, had been right on top. He made sure the instructions were as easy to follow as a detailed road map.

I walk beyond the cavernous great room and into the side hall that leads to his home office and on to the principal suite. My father loved his office. It looks out over the rolling green pastures of the property. Those pastures spill out around the front and west side of the house's perch on a rise. Behind the house are acres and acres of woods. I loved exploring those woods when I was younger.

I round his desk, pull out his Herman Miller chair, and sit. Memories of him turning me around and around in this beloved chair flash in my mind. I have a life full of memories here, how could I possibly sell my history?

Pulling myself back to the present, I set to the task of reviewing what's in front of me. The files are neatly arranged. Most are personal files related to his finances and the property and all that it entails. All but a few I pulled from where they were stored as I prepared for settling the estate. I've been through those repeatedly. Across the room the row of steel cabinets house his professional case files. There are certain steps that need to be taken on those files. He left specific instructions. Just something else I need to get around to. I open the center drawer of his desk and retrieve the notes I stuffed there after removing them from the trash bin under his desk. The day he had the heart attack, he'd been right here at this desk, cleaning out some of his drawers apparently.

I didn't find out until after the funeral that he had been having some heart issues. I found the prescriptions and visited his doctor, a family friend. He hadn't said anything at the funeral because he assumed I knew. But my father never told me. Didn't want to worry me, I suppose. He was always far too concerned with ensuring I was happy to tell me bad news. I could never understand why he viewed me as so fragile. I'm strong. I'm a cop—a homicide detective.

Even if these migraines have kicked my butt recently.

So far, so good today. Any aches I've suffered have been a distant twinge. I mentally cross my fingers.

My intention is to go through everything—eventually—and burn all the papers that were related to his work or finances that he appeared not to want or need—which is what he wanted according to the letter of instruction. Discounting, of course, the official patient files. Those are the ones with the precise instructions regarding disposition. Anything else I deem simple rubbish I will toss in the burn barrel out back and destroy. I probably would have burned the pages of notes I found in the bin under his desk if I hadn't noticed a name. At the time the name wasn't one I recognized, but I worried that it was either a patient or a work-related associate. It wasn't until Walt mentioned that Sanchez would be home from Mexico on Sunday that the memory finally clicked. I knew that name was familiar to me.

So maybe I didn't come here after work to avoid David. Maybe I came in search of some truth that will help us solve this case. Only, this doesn't feel like a simple, unexpectedly discovered truth. This feels like a stumbled-upon, well-hidden secret.

I open the papers and confirm that nagging worry: The name on my father's tossed handwritten notes is "Mario Sanchez." Under normal circumstances, this wouldn't exactly be a stunning revelation. He treated hundreds of patients in the Nashville area over the course of his long and prestigious career. But this is not just any name, this is a name on Walt's and my list of persons of interest.

I skim through the notes once more in search of any other names I might have overlooked. I reach the last page and my gaze stalls. Letters—initials possibly. Two simple bits of the alphabet that were jotted next to each other shock the breath out of me.

CF.

Carl Fanning.

I have to tell Walt.

TWELVE

PATRICIA SHELBY

They know. They know. They know.

I pace back and forth in the nursery. I glance at the bassinet, where my sweet baby sleeps. I have to protect her. No one else can. No one else understands. *No one else knows.*

This is *my* burden.

The police came to our house. Spoke to me and my husband. They wanted my story, when I am certain the entire event was in the case file. Still, they made me relive it. Made me speak of him. Asked dozens of questions. This is how I recognized they know something.

Why ask me all those questions if they didn't suspect something . . . something I did?

I have not been able to rest properly since he was released. On Saturday it became unbearable. I cannot close my eyes without seeing his face. I cannot eat for my stomach will not accept it.

I understood from the moment I heard he would be released that I had to do something. There was no other alternative. As long as Carl Fanning was breathing, my baby would never be safe.

The need expanded inside me until there was no room for air . . . for anything.

I will not allow that bastard or anyone like him to get close to my little girl.

With my arms hugged around me, I keep pacing. I am so tired. My body needs to sleep, but I cannot permit myself to indulge in that luxury. I cannot risk letting down my guard.

My thoughts rush back to the moment *he* and I came face-to-face five days ago. To that exact instant when I saw him watching me.

Old, sick, frail looking. I wanted to kill him then and there.

I wanted to charge him . . . like a bear protecting its cub.

He stared at my swollen belly, and that lurid grin detonated something hard and scorching inside me. My fingers itched to rip into him . . . to claw out the very veins and arteries that allowed blood to pulse through him.

In my mind, there was no other choice. He had to die.

For that to happen, I had to do my part.

THIRTEEN

DETECTIVE WALTER DUNCAN

I rap on the open door to Reynolds's office. He didn't call or text saying he had anything, but I just can't let the day end without being sure. I need something to give Liv and me some definitive direction.

The burned-out barn is something, but unless remains are found, it could just be a sad accident. A coincidence. But I never have believed in coincidences.

Whatever the case, we have to keep digging and looking for Fanning and other potential scenarios to explain his disappearance.

"Walt." Reynolds motions for me to come on in.

He appears to be doing paperwork, probably in an effort to get out of here. I doubt he's happy to see someone like me at his door.

I take a seat in front of his desk. "I was about to head home and thought I'd check in to see if there's anything back on the Fanning crime scene."

"I wish." He closes the manila folder in front of him. "The lab is running behind. Hopefully tomorrow. Nothing on that trace evidence, either. I know it's frustrating, but we're going as fast as we can."

I nod. I figured this would be a waste of time. Beyond the DNA, the rest probably isn't anything that will help. White cotton, potentially from a sheet or other piece of linen. A hair that likely belonged to

Fanning. Some animal fecal matter that could have gotten tracked in on Fanning's or the perp's/vic's shoes.

"I understand." I get up. "I'll check in with you tomorrow."

The folks up in Chester County will likely be just as slow with answers about the burned-out barn. It's the nature of the beast. These things take time.

Reynolds pushes to his feet, gives me a thorough once-over. "You're looking a little more haggard than usual, Walt. Everything okay?"

No point lying to this guy. "Gotta see a cardiologist. The old ticker is misbehaving."

He touches his chest. "I feel ya. Mine has me on a strict diet and exercise regimen. It's no fun, but if it keeps me alive, I can deal with it."

"No kidding."

After living for a couple of weeks with the idea that I might have lung cancer, this is a piece of cake.

Outside, I climb into my Tahoe and kick aside the frustration with the case.

The worst part is that we still can't be certain Fanning is even the victim. He could be the perpetrator of whatever took place in that dump he calls home as well as in that barn belonging to Hyatt and Reeves. What started out as two vics taking revenge may have turned into two women becoming victims all over again, considering we haven't been able to reconnect with either of the two. Either way, someone—two someones, actually—were injured, and we need to figure out what happened in Fanning's rental. And in that damned barn. Hopefully while we can still make a difference.

My cell vibrates with a text from Liv.

You need to come to the farm now.

I shoot off an answer: On my way.

I'm hoping she's not sick or been in a fight with the fiancé.

I don't want to have to kick the guy's ass.

I park next to Liv's Subaru. She waits at the front door of the house, leaning against the jamb, arms crossed over her chest.

She knows before I get out of the car the things I'll ask first, and she's ready to defend her feelings and choices. You feeling okay? "I'm fine," she would say. "You don't need to worry about me. A little headache isn't going to keep me down." Have you been home? Aghast, she would demand, "How is that relevant? I'll get there when I get there. I called you here for an important reason, Walt."

I know her almost as well as I know myself. I'll bet she hasn't been home yet. It's almost seven. The fact that she's still wearing the gray jacket and black trousers she wore to work today tells me I would win that bet. I wonder whether she's even called him. As much as I dislike the guy—and really, I don't even know him—I know she loves him. I just can't figure out why she's working so hard to push him away. Even when I play devil's advocate, she won't exactly say she doesn't love him or that she wants to end the relationship. She's confused and feeling uncertain.

If Stella were here, she'd tell me to mind my own business.

"But she's like a daughter to me," I mumble.

Stella would say, "I know."

I climb out of the Tahoe and amble across the yard. "Traffic was murder." As I take the steps up the porch, I ask the expected question, "You okay?"

Before she can even answer, a weariness washes over me and I resist the urge to sit down right there and just lean against the railing. I am tired. More tired than I have felt since those all-night vigils with Stella. I'd work all day while the nurse sat with her, and then I'd spend the night entertaining her or just watching her breathe. I was terrified that if I closed my eyes, I'd wake up and she'd be gone.

"I don't know," Liv admits. "'Okay' is suddenly complicated."

These words surprise me. Liv isn't one to bemoan her lot in life. If she's having a bad day, she usually pretends it's merely challenging or that she has no idea what I'm talking about. She keeps her chin up. Always. Even, I've learned lately, when one of those headaches kicks her butt.

"How complicated?" I pause at the door as she steps aside to let me in.

"You should have a drink."

"Oh." I groan. "That complicated."

Liv is not a drinker. The occasional glass of wine or beer, but she's way too levelheaded to go overboard with either. Never smoked. Runs and works out. Eats all those natural, colorful veggies they say are good for you. The list of healthy stuff she does makes me exhausted just thinking about it.

I lower myself onto Dr. Newhouse's leather sofa. Liv rounds the bar and pours me a scotch. My mouth waters. This won't be the cheap stuff. Her daddy bought only the best. She returns to where I wait, but she's carrying only one drink.

"What about you?" I accept the glass she offers.

"That's part of the complication."

I knock back a slug of the scotch, clear my throat. "All right. I'm listening."

Liv sits down on the coffee table, her chin in her hands, elbows on her knees. "All these migraines and feeling utterly exhausted all the time really had me worried. And I was late." She glances up at me, and I nod in understanding. "So I took a pregnancy test and it was positive. That's really why I went to the doctor. With all the headaches, I thought something might be wrong."

The wind goes right out of my sails. I'm nodding again, like a cheap bobblehead doll. "What does your fiancé have to say about this?"

I recognize my tone is accusing as if the man has done something bad and needs taking down a couple of notches. When she smiles, some of the heaviness lifts from my chest.

"You're the only person besides my doctor who knows."

My smile turns into a grin. "He won't like that you told me first."

She rolls her eyes. "That's the least of my worries. I don't know if I'm properly equipped to be a mother, Walt. This is seriously complicated."

I reach out, take her hand in mine. "First, yes, it's complicated, but it's also amazing and crazy wonderful. Stella and I wanted children so badly. It's a blessing. After losing your father, it's a miracle. That's what it is. Second, you'll be an incredible mother. The best. No question."

"I wish I could feel as sure as you do."

My mind goes back to the logistics of all this. "So is the pregnancy causing the headaches?"

I'm hoping the answer is yes and that there isn't some other underlying issue.

"Dr. Raiford said it's a combination of the pregnancy hormones and all the loss and stress I've experienced lately. She thinks it'll pass or at least ease up in the next few weeks as I move into the second trimester."

Anticipation has me asking, "So when is this baby due? I have to start making plans, kid."

"December fourteenth, give or take a few days. We'll know more after an ultrasound." She shakes her head. "Merry Christmas to me."

The pages of the calendar—the days, weeks, months—whirl in my head. I have to get to that cardiologist and get my act together. I need to be here for Liv . . . for the baby.

I square my shoulders and do the fatherly thing. "You have to talk to Preston about this. It's not right to leave him out."

"I know." She nods. "I will talk to him, I promise. I just need to get used to the idea myself before I go there. He'll want to tell his parents, and, well, you understand. Particularly right now, with this case. I just can't handle all that."

I do understand. Which is part of why I haven't told her about my own complications. No matter that the latest twist in the story is better than the previous one, her father died of a heart attack. I don't want her looking at me and worrying about the same fate. After I see the cardiologist, I will tell her.

"So, how does he feel about dogs?"

I can't exactly ask her to take Sandy if something were to happen to me without telling her the reason I started worrying about the issue. For now, feeling out how her future husband might react to having a pet around the house will have to do.

When she looks confused, I add, "You know, they say men who like animals make better fathers." I have no idea if this is true, but it seems reasonable.

"He loves dogs." She says this as if she finds the answer surprising herself. "He had a border collie for twelve years, she died just before he and I met. He hasn't had the heart to get another one." A smile tugs at her lips. "So I guess that's a good sign."

I nod, relieved. "Definitely a good sign."

"There's more." She stands. "This is complicated in a different way. I need you to look at something for me."

"Okay." This does sound ominous. I stand, leaving my glass on the coffee table, and follow her across the room and down the hall. In her father's office, she crosses to the desk and picks up a few pages of paper that look as if they've been crumpled and then smoothed out.

"You starting with your father's office on your packing, or was he doing some housekeeping before he passed?" Doesn't take a crystal ball to see either scenario is possible. There are a couple packing boxes taped and ready to fill on the floor. Several file folders lay in a neat stack on the desk.

"A little of both." She hands me the pages. "There are several notes about a man he spoke with or treated." She shrugs. "Or had some sort of dealings with."

I scan the first page but don't see a name until I reach the second. My gaze crashes into hers. "Mario Sanchez?"

"Yeah. The notes don't make a lot of sense. It's mostly dates and locations. But there are initials noted on that last page. I think he was referring to Fanning."

I scan the third page again, more slowly this time. I see what she means. *CF.* "Okay, I see it. The rest of the notations are mostly dates."

The realization of what I'm looking at suddenly sinks in, and I tap the page. "These are dates from the time period of Fanning's trial." The bastard was arrested in June, but he didn't go to trial until the next year.

"Maybe my father evaluated the victims, assessed their reliability. Something like that."

"Have you found any files related to Fanning or Sanchez or any of the others?" I don't have to tell her that Dr. Newhouse's name is not in the official case file. If he was officially involved in any capacity, it was for the defense and was never revealed. Not something Liv will want to discover, I'm sure.

"Not so far." She turns to the row of filing cabinets on the far wall. "I've been through all those, and there are no names from our list—unless the patients were listed under aliases. I suppose that's possible, in which case, I wouldn't know where to begin."

Before I can pull together a reasonable theory, she warns, "It gets worse. While I was waiting for you to get here, I did a little more looking around." She picks up the leather-bound calendar from her father's desk. As she shuffles through to find whatever she's looking for, I see numerous notes on page after page. Like me, her father preferred making notes the old-fashioned way.

"Have a look at this." She passes me the calendar.

I stare at January twentieth. Just over two weeks before her father died. *C. F. Riverbend.*

"Why in the world would my father visit Carl Fanning in prison?"

Although, knowing her father, I'm certain there is a perfectly logical explanation, I can't for the life of me think what it would be.

"The *CF* on his calendar and on that page might not be Carl Fanning," I offer.

She cocks her head and gives me a look. "Get real, Walt. I guess the Mario Sanchez in those notations isn't the same one climbing mountains down in Mexico, either."

"I guess we need to find out."

Maybe Liv and I aren't the only ones keeping secrets.

FOURTEEN

The Child

I watch him sleep the sleep of sheer exhaustion—the sort that comes after endless hours of pain. The adrenaline of fear or pain will keep one wide awake for long hours. It would be so easy for a victim to simply pass out, and that does sometimes happen. But a true artist of pain knows just how far to go before that particular defense mechanism kicks in. If you fail, there's always the dash of cold water to get things going again. These things I learned from the master. Now the tables are turned. I wonder what he will learn from me?

I smile. I have only begun to hurt him. Before he takes his final breath, he will know all the pain and fear I knew.

The pain, the fear, the uncertainty. It was ruthless in the beginning. But I adapted. Like all things, with the passage of months and years, the child I was when he first took me began to change. Time waits for no one, as they say. The changes in the human body as adolescence kicks in can be startling to those unprepared. I hated it. Hated every part of how I looked . . . of how my body was developing. I wanted to stay a child. The world looks at a child as an innocent—no matter the things that happen behind closed doors. A child is revered in many ways. A child is forgiven for their trespasses.

A child is the universal symbol of hope for mankind.

However hard I tried to stop it, my childhood was abandoning me, leaving me like the skin of a snake being sloughed off because it couldn't stretch any farther. I was becoming an "it." Not a child, not an adult. An it, *his* it.

Ultimately I became whatever he wanted me to be, whenever he wanted. That was my sole mission in life. He warned that no matter how much I changed, I would always be his. Until the end of time, I would belong to him. Strangely, this warning included the most comforting words he ever said to me.

Some changes presented a problem for his plans as well. A child could easily pick the pockets of unsuspecting shoppers and pedestrians. People were far more likely to toss money to a child. I hated myself. Hated him for allowing these changes to happen. He was, after all, all powerful, the ruler of my universe. He should have been able to stop this disaster before it changed everything.

Except he couldn't. And one day another change occurred. One even more terrifying than the last. I screamed and cried. He laughed at me, allowed me to huddle in fear for hours before he explained that this, too, was a natural progression of aging. He didn't actually explain why it was happening just that it was and that I could expect more.

I lived in new, abject fear of what might occur because of these changes. He still took my body whenever he wanted. That had not changed. Suddenly, his grunting and disgusting actions became reassuring. This was my normal. Routine. Everything was okay no matter that I was changing. I needed him to still want me, to do with me as he pleased. It was the only gauge by which I could measure my worth to him. I was terrified at the idea that he might decide he no longer wanted or needed me. What would I do then?

How would I survive?

My newest secondhand clothes quickly became too small. Shoes grew too tight almost overnight.

The more I changed, the angrier he became.

My fear expanded and undulated inside me, eating away at any semblance of confidence I had developed. I was frantic to please him, to ensure my relevance in his shitty little world. Not only did I do whatever he asked, I begged him to tell me more ways I could be useful. That was when he started to use me to lure in the other children he wanted to play with. I hated that part most of all. I hated that he turned to another child for what he had always taken from me. I hated that they were cuter, fresher, and sweeter than me. He told me this over and over, so it must have been true.

I hated him, hated the other children . . . hated me.

As the days dragged on, his frustration and anger with the changes happening to my body began to amuse me to some degree. I was his, he'd said so a million times. I would always be his. So, as far as I could see, he was stuck with this new me.

Inside my head where he couldn't see or hear, I would laugh when he struggled to make me look more childlike. I just stood there letting him fight the battle to conceal the changes as if I were a life-size doll.

I even heard other men ask him about me. How much did I cost for an hour? This seemed to outrage him. He would growl and make threats at these men for saying such things about his child. Then he would take me home and rut into me until he wasn't angry anymore.

My belief that his taking of my body and keeping me fed and warm meant that he loved me solidified each time he acted out his claim of possession. We were a family. Slowly but surely I learned again to trust this illusion without question. I had watched mothers and fathers with their children, and even though he was never as kind and gentle as those people, he took care of me, and for a child who knew nothing better, that was important. No one else would do so. As if his confidence was the one slipping now, he reminded me over and over that no one would ever want me. I was ugly with pimples popping out all over my skin.

Who would want such an ugly it?

He was right. I was grateful he wanted me.

Ultimately I learned something from the changes and his reactions to those changes. I didn't need to be scared anymore. He wasn't going to give me to anyone else. He wasn't going to sell me or leave me no matter how many other children he played with. In fact, since he had already done all those bad and hurtful things to me, there was really no reason at all for me to fear what he might do next.

Over the years I had survived the worst he could possibly do to me . . . or, at least, I thought I had.

FIFTEEN

DETECTIVE OLIVIA NEWHOUSE

Friday, May 4

I'm waiting for David when he comes down for his first cup of coffee. I'm dressed and ready for work, and on my second cup of caffeine-infused brew. Still forgot to Google whether or not it's possible to consume too much caffeine during pregnancy. I did remember to pick up the prenatal vitamins. Took my first one this morning. I really have to do better than this. Just because I'm screwing up my own health by not eating as I should and not getting nearly enough sleep doesn't mean I want to screw up this kid's chances at normal.

The word gives me pause. What is "normal"?

Images and voices filter through my mind, make my stomach churn.

"Morning," he says as he shuffles to the coffee maker.

"Morning."

I really had intended to talk to him when I made it home last night, but he'd already gone to bed. It wasn't even midnight. That was early for him. Unless he had some sort of big bankers meeting and was mentally wiped out. Judging by his bloodshot eyes, I'm thinking he went a couple of rounds with something stronger than beer and it took him out. David isn't generally a heavy drinker. I suppose I've sent him down that dark path. Apparently I can't do anything right anymore.

Last night got away from me. I hadn't meant to be so late, but after Walt left, I just passed out for a few hours. I woke up face down on my father's desk, drooling all over his blotter pad. I need to ask the doctor about that, too. I went down for the count and slept the sleep of the dead for at least two hours. I guess I needed the rest.

Exhaustion can do strange things to you.

"We need to talk," I announce. My throat goes instantly dry and my heart starts to pound. Walt is right in that I need to tell David about the baby and somehow slow down this lunge toward disaster that our relationship appears to be caught up in. We're here and I've had some decent sleep. This is as good a time as any.

David waits until the final drops of coffee have plopped into his mug from the machine, picks it up, and swallows a mouthful, then flinches from the burn. "I have my own ideas about that, but what is it you think we have to talk about, Liv?"

"All we do lately is argue," I say, weary of this battle. He clearly went to bed angry with me and now he's awakened still irritated. How are we supposed to get past this unhappy place if he's unwilling to move beyond it? I really have no idea how to begin.

He props a pajama-clad hip against the counter. "I suppose that's my fault, too."

Perfect example of why we can't get past this rut. "I apologized to your mother."

He sips his coffee, nods. "She told me. I appreciate that you made the effort."

"So you're still angry with me about missing dinner, even though I've apologized repeatedly."

"No, Olivia. I'm frustrated because you're never home for dinner anymore. For anything, really. It's like you don't want to be here."

I can't tell him that he might be more right than he knows. "It's this case." I shake my head. "It's different . . ." *Horrifying*, I don't say.

"So you were working last night?" He looks directly at me as he asks this question. The accusation is stark in his beautiful eyes.

"Yes. You know this without asking." I hold my own mug of coffee so tightly, I fear it may crack at any second. "When I came home, you were already in bed."

"You were at the farm."

For a moment I'm rattled that he somehow knows this when we haven't talked about exactly where I was. What the hell? "First, what difference does that make, and second, how can you know this? Do you have some sort of tracker on my phone?"

"First," he echoes, an edge in his tone, "you just said you were working, which was apparently not entirely true. Second, your iPad dinged with a notification that the security system at the farm had been disarmed. Is there anyone else who would be there?"

Okay. He has me there. I hesitate for a moment. Do I want to tell him about what I found? If I don't, he's never going to trust me, but to tell him feels like a betrayal of my father.

Stop, Liv. This is the man to whom you've said yes to spending the rest of your life. This is the father of the child you're carrying. Why the hesitation?

"I found some notes my father made regarding a victim in the Fanning case—the one I'm working on. I'm sure there's a perfectly logical reason for him being involved in any way, but I have to know what that reason was."

"So your father is a person of interest in your investigation now?"

I think about that for a moment. It was a smart-ass remark, but a valid point. "In a manner of speaking. We haven't found anything that concretely ties him to the case, but we have to look into whatever part he played."

"'We' meaning you and Walt?"

The sarcasm in his tone leaves me both baffled and angry. "He is my partner. How many times do I have to point out that fact?"

"So you and Walt were at the farm, together."

Somehow he makes the detail sound lascivious. "When I found the notes, I called him immediately. Making a judgment one way or the other about something my father did or didn't do in this situation would be the wrong thing to do. I'm personally involved, my objectivity is compromised."

"Aren't you and Walt personally involved?"

"What?" Obviously David really is only interested in fighting. "We're partners."

"And friends. Good friends. Isn't that personal?"

I slam my mug down on the counter. Coffee splatters. "I don't even know why I try. You want to fight. You don't want to understand what's happening with me right now."

He walks slowly toward me. Any other time I would have considered this sexy, but right now I just want to run away from the frustration and uncertainties. But I can't. I owe it to him—to our child—to figure this out. What in the world is happening between the two of us?

"Why didn't you let me know? Text? Call? Something?"

"There are rules about evidence." He knows this, too. "I can't always openly share my work with you. What I've told you this morning is already skirting the fringes of breaking those rules."

He nods. Places his own mug next to mine and then stares directly into my eyes. "You could have let me know where you were and that you would be late. Would that be breaking the rules? Either way, you didn't. What's happening to us, Liv?"

I search his eyes for a long moment, looking for the glimpses of the man I fell in love with, but all I see is anger and frustration. "I wish I knew. I can't seem to do anything right anymore. And you have a valid point, I should have called or at least sent a text, but I was so upset, so confused, I couldn't think."

"I suppose Walt comforted you?"

"What?" I don't believe this. "We discussed what my father's notes could possibly mean. Trust me, it was all very clinical."

"You said yes when I asked you to marry me, Liv. You made a commitment to me." His tone hardens with each word. "Walt gets your days. Your nights should belong to me."

"You're twisting everything I say! Walt and I are partners—and friends. That's all. If anything, he's like a father to me."

David leans closer, stares into my eyes until I blink. "Why don't I believe you? It feels like you're keeping things from me. Like I can't trust anything you say anymore."

The words echo in my brain as familiar as if I'd said them myself. I drown out the voices that seem to be a replay of the fight we just had. Have we had this fight before? I can't remember. The hours and days are blurring together. The headaches, the fatigue. I don't know how much more I can take. I am so, so tired. So confused. I feel completely out of control.

I summon my resolve and say what needs to be said. "I honestly don't know what your deal is with Walt. It's like you're suddenly jealous of him. The idea is absurd . . . it's totally outrageous."

He laughs. "You can't remember anything about our lives anymore, and I'm the outrageous one?" He flings an arm outward, toward the wall that separates the kitchen and dining room. "Your stuff still sits in boxes in the foyer. You haven't unpacked a damn one of them. Do you even want to be here, Liv?"

A distant throb starts in the back of my skull. I can't do this.

I slide from between him and the counter. "I have to get to work."

"There's the answer!" he shouts at my back. "Walk away."

I stop, turn to face him. "I'm not walking away, David. You're pushing me away."

He smiles, but there is no amusement in the expression, then he bangs a fist into his chest. "I'm pushing you away? From where I'm standing, you're the one who can't wait to get away."

This time I turn my back and I keep walking.

I guess I'll just have to wait for a better time to tell him he's going to be a father.

Or maybe I won't tell him at all.

Doesn't matter. I'm out of time. I'm meeting Walt, and we're going to talk to the warden at the prison where Fanning spent the better part of the past fourteen years. I need to know if my father visited him there. More importantly, why.

The street that leads onto the compound of Riverbend Maximum Security Institution could be the driveway to a large estate. As Walt navigates the long stretch, I survey the landscape. Trees and lampposts line the way. Freshly cut grass spreads out for as far as the eye can see. Beyond the meticulously maintained landscape, the Cumberland River encircles the vast property. But as you round the bend in the drive, you see the wire fence and the institutional boxes that make up the prison. This is no estate, no spa resort; this is a maximum-security prison that houses several hundred prisoners, including the state's male death row offenders.

The sky is overcast, threatening, as I climb out of the Tahoe. I draw in a deep breath heavy with the smell and taste of rain. The air crackles with the potential of the coming storm. The forecast is rain today and possible thunderstorms late tomorrow.

I've always had a thing for thunderstorms. They make me feel alive. The crashes and booms of thunder and the steady drum of rain are soothing to my soul somehow. It's weird, I know.

"You should try talking to him again tonight."

I glance at Walt. He could see that I was upset the moment I hopped into his passenger seat, so I told him the latest with David. "I will. I really don't know why he's got such a bug up his ass. Maybe he's the one having second thoughts."

Walt pauses to look at me. "If that's the case, he's a damn fool."

I refuse to tell Walt about David's jealousy where our relationship is concerned. No way would I do that to him. I will not allow David's insecurities to become Walt's guilt. Or mine, for that matter.

"Are you thinking of holding back until you see how things go from here?"

"Honestly?" I exhale a weary breath. "Yes, I am. I don't want the baby to be the only reason that we follow through with our wedding plans. If we're not supposed to do this, then we don't need to do this."

We stare at each other for a moment, then carry on toward the prison entrance. What else is there to say? My relationship with David is unraveling at breakneck speed. The best I can do is brace for whatever comes next and hope we can find our way beyond this rocky place that has suddenly consumed our lives. There are so many things I should be telling him; then maybe he would understand. But I can't bring myself to do that—to expose this . . . whatever it is . . . that's happening to me.

Can a person have a midlife crisis at thirty?

"Hyatt and Reeves are still avoiding us," Walt says, dragging my attention back to the here and now. "I called each one and then each of their places of business. The only person who answered any of the four was the same woman at the riding school who said Hyatt was on vacation. She has not heard from her since our last call. I think I annoyed her."

"No question they're avoiding us," I agree. "The reason is the issue. Are they the reason Fanning is missing, or is it the other way around? Problem is, we don't have anything that justifies taking the next step to locate them." BOLOs and the like require justification. Until we have more than an elderly witness's account of seeing two unknown women in an SUV driving by and a burned-out barn at a secondary residence, we can't do more than keep trying to reach one or the other. If remains are found in the barn rubble, that would give us the needed impetus. Until then, we keep looking the old-fashioned way.

So we're moving on to the next name on the list, Andrea Donnelly, as soon as this prison visit is over. *This* makes my heart hurt.

Inside, we sign in and are escorted to the warden's office. Walt informed Warden Scott Tennison what we needed when he called and made the appointment. Hopefully, Tennison will have taken the time to look into his request.

Tennison is a short, heavy man who looks closer to seventy than sixty. He stands behind a government-issue executive desk surrounded by government-issue filing cabinets and cheaply upholstered chairs. The view out the window behind him is of the quad between buildings. There are a few trees and picnic tables and more of that well-done landscaping.

Walt shakes the hand Tennison extends. "Walt Duncan," he says. "And this is my partner, Olivia."

I shake the warden's hand as well. Walt left off my surname to prevent the inevitable questions of how I might be connected to the deceased psychiatrist we're here to discuss.

"Please, have a seat," Tennison says.

We settle into the stiff chairs. Tennison resumes his seat in the high-back leather executive's chair—definitely not government issue.

"I had one of my assistants pull the records on Fanning's visitors," Tennison begins. "Besides his attorney, he had only one during his final months with us."

The warden places four different photos across his desk, all of my father signing in at security. My heart thumps hard against my sternum. I ask, "There were four visits in all?"

Tennison meets my gaze. "Yes, one in December of last year, two in January of this year, and then a final visit on February second."

I struggle to conceal my surprise at the number of times my father visited, particularly that last one mere days before he died. "Fanning had no other visitors?" He has answered this question already, but I suddenly need confirmation that I heard right.

Tennison shrugs. "The only other person was his attorney. He visited once in January and then again on February ninth."

It's not surprising that the attorney would visit, considering Fanning was coming up on his release date. Why in the world would my father visit the son of a bitch four times? This makes no sense whatsoever. I wasn't aware my father even knew Fanning beyond what was seen in the news leading up to his release.

This is wrong somehow. My head is spinning and every breath is a struggle.

"In what capacity was Dr. Newhouse visiting Fanning?" Walt asks.

My heart practically stumbles to a stop.

"Newhouse listed himself as Fanning's therapist. I was under the impression he was helping him to prepare for being released back into society, which is why I granted extended visitations."

A chill leaches into my bones. "These visits weren't recorded?" I know the answer before I ask, but I had to be sure.

"Certainly not," Tennison assures me.

"Thank you, Warden." Walt stands and thrusts out his hand.

I do the same, my knees feeling weak with this ground-shaking news. Why would my father hide this from me? We discussed Fanning's upcoming release. I remember distinctly telling him I could not believe, even with the plea deal, that his sentence wasn't at least a decade longer.

"You know," Tennison says as we prepare to go, "it's not unusual for an inmate to seek help from a therapist or a man of God prior to release. They all leave here hoping never to return. Generally, they seek counsel from one of our staff therapists. I don't know how Fanning landed himself a prestigious doctor like Newhouse."

"Maybe if we find Fanning alive, we'll learn the answer to that question," Walt replies.

I'm grateful my partner responded, because I couldn't have spoken if my life depended upon it. I feel as if I'm in a dream—a nightmare—that keeps dragging me deeper and deeper into this place I don't recognize.

"The really strange part is, Newhouse's last visit was quite volatile," Tennison goes on. "The guards said Fanning demanded to be taken back to his cell and that the two men were still shouting at each other when Fanning was escorted away. It didn't sound like any therapy session I've ever heard of."

Walt hesitates. "Any chance either one of those guards is on duty today?"

Air rushes into my starving lungs.

"I believe one of them is," Tennison says. "Would you want to speak with him?"

Before I can shout yes, Walt says calmly, "If possible. We understand you have a prison to run here, and we've already taken up a great deal of your time."

"I do have a meeting," Tennison says, "so I'll have the two of you wait in my conference room. I'll see that Officer Winslow joins you as soon as he can."

Walt and I wait in the conference room, both of us looking rattled. We know better than to discuss our concerns until we're outside these prison walls. You never know when you're being recorded, particularly since we're not attorneys or doctors.

Seventeen endless minutes later, a tall, thin man in his mid-forties enters the room. "Ricky Winslow," he announces.

He stands at attention, awaiting our questions. My money's on him being former military. Maybe a marine.

"Have a seat," I suggest, grateful my voice is steady once more.

Winslow pulls out the chair at the end of the table and settles into it.

Walt kicks off the questions. "Warden Tennison tells us you overheard what sounded like an argument between former inmate Carl Fanning and Dr. Lewis Newhouse back in February."

"That's correct, sir," Winslow confirms. "We heard shouting in the interview room. Fanning's voice was particularly loud. He was calling for us. He wanted to return to his cell."

Walt appears to consider his answer for a moment. "Do you recall anything else he or Newhouse said? Think carefully," Walt urges. "This could be very important."

A frown furrows Winslow's brow as if he is doing exactly as Walt asked and concentrating hard to remember any little detail. "The doctor appeared visibly upset. I remember that in particular. He told

Fanning he'd better remember his warning or there would be severe consequences."

I swallow with effort and throw out the next question. "Did Fanning say anything in response to my—to Dr. Newhouse or to you as you escorted him back to his cell?"

Winslow shakes his head, then frowns. "Wait. He kept muttering something like: We all got bones buried somewhere. Didn't make any sense at the time." He shrugs. "To tell you the truth, I think the man was crazy. I mean, crazier than we already knew. We all thought he got off way too light for what he did, if you know what I mean."

When I say nothing more, Walt presses, "That's all Fanning said?"

Winslow nods. "'We all got bones buried somewhere.' That's it."

The image of a shovel sliding into dirt slams into my brain with such force that I flinch.

The rest of the exchange between Walt and the guard is nothing more than a jumbled hum of syllables.

This can't be—none of it. My father would never have been involved with a man like Fanning, and he sure as hell didn't have any bones buried anywhere.

Nothing about any of this makes sense.

There has to be some mistake.

Poor Walt. He spent the drive from Riverbend to the next address on our list trying to reassure me that I had nothing to worry about despite what we learned from the warden and the guard. I'm a really lousy partner right now. I feel terrible that he has to deal with all these personal issues of mine on top of this perplexing case. This is not me. This is not my life. And yet, it is.

I feel like I'm coming apart from the inside out.

With every ounce of courage I possess, I focus on moving forward to the next step in the investigation. I can't look at these personal issues—my father's involvement with Fanning, and David, and the baby—for even a second longer.

Andrea Donnelly is the next name on the list of Fanning's victims. She was eleven when he picked her up from the movie theater. An ER nurse now, Andrea is petite and pale, but her voice is steady and there is strength in her eyes as she explains what happened to her nineteen years ago.

"My friends Sunny and Ellen were making fun of me because I'd told them about my secret crush on a boy in our class." She shakes her head. "It was silly." A sad smile tugs at her lips. "They didn't mean any harm, but at that age, you take everything to heart. I'd gotten my period earlier than them, and I guess they were jealous. God only knows why, but it was a big deal at the time."

When she hesitates, I nod my understanding. "Girls can be cruel at that age."

She exhales a big breath. "I have two of my own now, and I remind them every day that adolescence is the hardest time they'll face in their lives."

"You were angry with your friends, so you went outside," Walt prompts.

Andrea nods. "It was so foolish. I should've stayed inside." She closes her eyes for a long moment. "But I didn't. He spotted me on the sidewalk half a block from the theater. I was headed home. He offered me a ride. I said no, of course. But then I saw those mean boys from the high school. I was far more afraid of them than of a stranger who was old enough to be my father. And I was pretty sure I'd seen him at the theater dropping off a girl I thought was his daughter, which turned out to be a mistake. Carl Fanning never had a daughter." She shakes her head. "I don't know. I was stupid. Stupid and naive."

Andrea shares how terrified she was when she realized he wasn't taking her home and how he pulled over, yanked her out of the front seat, and stuffed her into the trunk. Her throat works with the remembered fear. He took her to the rear parking lot of an abandoned factory, raped her, and left her naked and unconscious on the cracked and faded asphalt.

As she speaks, the images flash through my mind as if I were there. I can smell the sweat from the bastard's physical exertion. Can hear his raspy panting. I can see her lying on the ground like a discarded rag doll.

The black dots float across my field of vision, and I know I have to get out of this house soon or I will vomit on the woman's beautiful Persian rug.

I touch the phone at my waist and say, "I have a call."

I rush out of the house so fast I almost stumble over the dog.

SIXTEEN

Andrea Donnelly

I step up to the window and watch as the older detective walks toward his SUV, where the other one, the woman, waits.

My heart is thundering. I don't know why I didn't see this coming, but somehow I didn't. From the second I saw the news that the bastard was officially missing, I should have realized this would happen. Of course the investigation would include all the victims. Each one would be questioned, maybe even considered a suspect.

The remembered sound of shattering glass has me squeezing my eyes shut. I was so certain no one saw me that morning. It was very early. The neighborhood was dead silent. And still, except for my movements.

I wore all black, even a ski mask, and of course gloves. The baseball bat I used did the trick quickly and fairly easily. Slicing the tires was a little harder than I expected. But I managed.

Then I saw him. My heart almost stopped. Does the same thing now. I force myself to breathe. He stood in the doorway that I hadn't even heard open. He watched me. Just stood there watching me. He couldn't possibly know who I was, and yet somehow I felt utterly naked in front of him.

I felt as if I were that little girl again and he could see all of me.

I wanted to kill him right then, right there.

But I had to be smart . . . for my kids.

So I finished what I had come to do. *My part.*

No matter what happens, I will never regret what I did. I would do it again in a heartbeat.

SEVENTEEN

Detective Walter Duncan

I finished the interview as quickly as I could. I climb behind the wheel of the Tahoe and glance at Liv, who has her eyes closed. Damn.

"Andrea Donnelly was home Saturday night. She says her best friend can confirm it, since they were together making margaritas. She pulled a twelve-hour shift on Sunday night and spent Monday at home with a sick daughter," I say.

Liv grunts. "I guess we can check her off the list, then." She says all this without opening her eyes.

I start the vehicle without agreeing or disagreeing.

There is only one more victim on the list that we haven't had some sort of contact with: Melanie Hardeman. We still haven't been able to interview Janie Hyatt, but her partner spoke for her, sort of. Admittedly, the two's alleged surveilling activity of Fanning is suspect. As is the burned-out barn, but we haven't found anything more to take our suspicions to the next level. And we can't get a call back.

But I'm fairly convinced that something went down related to Fanning with those two, Reeves and Hyatt.

Sanchez is still a potential actor in all this despite being away. His alibi regarding the road trip to Mexico has checked out. He used his passport to cross the border into Mexico, as did his friends. But that doesn't mean they didn't have a body with them. The timing is the suspicious part for me. Not to mention that I just can't get past this story of him as a skinny little kid taking down Fanning all by himself. He had to have help. I simply cannot see it otherwise.

In the end, I am growing more and more convinced that we're beating a dead horse.

Even if all seven prove to have firm alibis, we're left with a family member or friend or maybe a totally unrelated vigilante who could be responsible for Fanning's disappearance. The fact that he hasn't shown up at a hospital or in a morgue leaves no doubt that he is missing, conceivably dead.

Then again, it's possible he has taken off and plans to set up a new identity someplace. But that takes money, which makes the option unlikely.

The only reasonable alternative makes my heart ache. I do not want to find out that Fanning has hurt another person and is holed up somewhere.

Damn him. He should have died in prison. He should be in hell, where he belongs. How is it good people like my Stella can suffer such horrific, slow deaths and that bastard is still breathing?

Well, he might not still be breathing. But then again, if he is and he took a victim—considering that victim has not shown up anywhere—the victim is likely dead by now. Dammit all to hell. It's a vicious fucking circle of possibilities without a single one that stands out a little more than the other.

Fury quakes through me as I drive away. I glance at my partner again. She's still slumped in the passenger seat. "You okay? You don't look okay, Liv."

"I am definitely not okay." She scrubs a hand over her face. "Sorry about running out on you in there. It was either that or puke on her carpet."

"We're going to lunch. You need something in your stomach." I pull away from the curb.

"Chances are, I'll just puke it up," she says. "I can't decide if it's related to the migraines or if it's plain old morning sickness." She untwists the lid on her bottle of water and sips gingerly.

"Is that normal either way?" I am worried sick about her. If it's the migraines, that can't be good for the baby. If it's morning sickness, that can't be good for Liv. Hell, I don't know. I've never been in this situation before. My fingers tighten on the steering wheel. Damn, I wish I knew what to do.

"It can be normal either way, yeah."

She sounds so weak. "What about soup? That bread place you like has killer chicken noodle soup. You're always saying that. I'll bet soup would help."

She sighs. "Maybe. I'll give it a try."

The weight on my chest eases a little. "I kind of like that broccoli-cheddar soup, and I'm not usually a soup man." No one can make soup the way my Stella did. I don't have to say as much. Liv knows. Stella sent soup to her plenty of times.

"Stella spoiled you for anybody else's soup." She laughs.

I'm glad. The sound is weary but it's a laugh nonetheless. I'll take it.

I decide to lighten things up. "You been thinking about baby names?"

"Are you kidding? I'm still dealing with the concept that I'm pregnant."

I hit my blinker for the next turn. "Bullshit. Baby names have crossed your mind. That's just normal."

"Maybe I'm not normal." She smiles.

I grin. "Normal enough."

"I'll get around to names eventually."

At least she smiled and sort of laughed again. That's something.

"You want to go inside and eat?"

"We probably should. That way I can make a run for the bathroom as necessary. I don't want to puke in your car."

At half past one, the biggest lunch rush is over, so we're served and seated fairly quickly.

"You want to talk about what the warden said?" I talked her down from the edges of hysteria as we left Riverbend. Then she moved straight to the next name on the list. I took her cue and let it ride. But Riverbend is the elephant in the room. There's no avoiding it for long.

She shrugs. "I'm thinking maybe my father spoke to Fanning on Sanchez's behalf. So far, those are the only two names related to the case that I've found in his notes or files. Sanchez may have been his patient, and he may have asked my father to talk to Fanning. It seems a bit unorthodox, but there has to be some reason, and that one sounds more logical than any other I can come up with. I don't believe for a second that my father was acting as Fanning's therapist. I'm certain that was a ruse to gain access to him."

"We can drop by Fanning's lawyer's office and feel him out. If Fanning had his own therapist, the lawyer should have a record of the name and any visits before and after his release."

"But we both know he's not going to tell us either way."

I drink down the last of my soup, not bothering with the spoon, and offer, "No harm in asking."

Liv sips at her soup for a while longer, then pushes it away. She didn't eat much, but at least she ate something. The few crackers she nibbled on should help as well.

Once in the Tahoe, she reaches into the back seat and grabs a Walmart bag, dumps the dog shampoo out, and pokes the bag into one of the cupholders in the console.

Our gazes meet. "Just in case," she explains.

I nod. "To the lawyer's office, then?"

"Let's drop by the Hyatt Riding Academy first," Liv suggests. "It's probably pointless to hope we'll find Hyatt, but maybe the receptionist will let us have a look around."

"Can't hurt."

"Can't hurt," Liv echoes.

The riding academy sits on one hundred exclusive and valuable acres in Franklin. Part of the property is wooded, but most is covered in beautifully manicured pastures and high-end barns. The place is very fancy. It's also not for beginners looking to have their first experience with a horse. This is the place you go when you want to learn to compete. Where someone who wants to be like Liv's mom, God rest her soul, would start out.

The main office is large, with a lobby that exhibits photos and pamphlets showing off their award-winning former students and the teachers who once went home with the trophies and ribbons. Said trophies and ribbons stand proudly in glass cases. Two customers—a mother and daughter, I figure—are perusing the stuff meant to encourage application.

Liv walks up to the counter and displays her badge. "We're here to see Janie Hyatt."

The woman, receptionist or whatever, glances at me, then back to Liv. "As I've already told you, Ms. Hyatt is on vacation this week. She and her wife are in the Smokies for a long weekend."

I move up next to Liv. Show my badge as well. This is the same woman I've spoken to twice, and she wants me to know it. Well, I want her to know that we're tired of waiting. "I'm wondering," I say, "why she hasn't at least called back, since I'm confident you've passed along the messages that we need to speak with her."

The receptionist blinks, takes a moment to consider how to respond. "I can't say. I've passed along your messages. That's all I can tell you."

I put my badge away. "Well, maybe we'll just have a look around."

The woman blinks again, hesitates once more. "I'm afraid we don't allow that sort of thing. We do have weekly tours of the facility on

Mondays. If you'd like to come back then, you'll get a very good look at our facility and what we do here."

"We really need to do this today," Liv presses. "We're not looking to sign up for classes. This is police business."

Without hesitation and with a big smile, the receptionist leans forward and lowers her voice for our ears only. "Then I'm afraid you'll need a warrant."

"Is that what Ms. Hyatt told you to say?" I ask.

Her full attention lands on me once more. "No. That's standard operating procedure."

Now I'm just pissed off, but before I can say something I shouldn't, Liv speaks up. "We'll need any associated phone numbers and the exact address of that vacation location."

She stares at Liv for a long moment, then scratches something onto a notepad. She tears off the page and hands it to Liv. "Good day, Detectives."

Frustration has me gritting my teeth on the way out the door.

When we're back in the Tahoe, I sputter, "Damn it."

"It was a long shot," Liv points out.

As I back out of the parking slot, I mutter another curse.

"I'll call Gatlinburg PD," she says, "and have them knock on the door at this location." She eyeballs the info provided by the receptionist. "There's no phone number, just an address."

"But this," I say with a nod toward the property we're about to drive away from, "would be a great place to hide the bastard if they didn't barbecue him in that barn in the woods." Our gazes meet. "If we don't reach one or the other of these two by morning, we're going to go for that BOLO on account."

Liv makes a funny face. "On account of what?"

"On account of"—I shift into Drive—"they're pissing me off."

Her laughter makes me feel like maybe, just maybe, she's getting back to her old self.

My cell vibrates and I take the call. "Duncan."

It's the Chester County sheriff. I listen to his update and then thank him. When the call ends, I give Liv the news. "No remains found in the burned-out barn. But the fire marshal says definitely accelerants were involved."

No surprise there . . . the question is why.

The lawyer's office is on the west side of town in a sketchy strip mall. Not too far from the Reeves Accounting firm, in fact. Reeves's office is still locked up tighter than a drum. But, like I told Liv, we're not going to let those two get away with their evasion tactics for another twenty-four hours.

This has gone on long enough.

We park in the lot and eye the two remaining businesses still operating in the strip mall. A nail salon and the lawyer's office. The other three shops are for lease. Considering the faded signs and the peeling paint, they've been empty for a good long while.

Liv sits up straighter and asks, "We doing the good cop / bad cop routine?"

"I get to be the good cop this time," I say.

"Suits me. Right now, I feel a lot more like a bad cop than a good one anyway."

I chuckle like she's joking, but I have a feeling she's not kidding.

We climb out and cross the lot. The traffic on Powell is heavier than I would have expected for this time of day. There are two cars parked in front of the nail salon. One of the technicians or whatever they're called stands in the open door. She shouts a two-for-one deal at us as we move past.

Liv waves her off and goes for the lawyer's door. The door as well as the plate glass windows on either side of it are covered with iron bars. There are no vehicles parked in front of this office. I imagine most of his business scurries in on foot and well after dark.

Inside, the place smells of roses, compliments of the candle burning on the receptionist's desk. The chair behind the desk is empty.

The sound of rain draws my gaze to the ironclad windows. A torrential downpour has started. Damn. That was fast. One minute the sun was shining, and now, this. The weatherman said it was going to rain. I guess he got it right this time. "Looks like we walked in just in time."

Liv nods. "Hopefully, it'll pass before we're done here."

"Can I help you?"

The man—Alexander Cagle—is standing in the doorway of what I presume to be his office. "My secretary is at lunch." He gestures to the empty desk.

I flick the lapel of my jacket aside and reveal my badge. "Detective Walt Duncan." I hitch my head toward Liv. "My partner. Olivia. We need to ask you a few questions about a client of yours—Carl Fanning."

Cagle's expression closes instantly. "I'm sure you know that—particularly in light of your ongoing investigation—I can't answer any of your questions, Detective."

"Your client is missing," Liv says. "If you expect us to find him, I suggest you hear us out."

Reluctantly he leads us into his office. As soon as we're seated, he picks up his cell and appears to answer a text.

While the reception area was as plain as hell with its seventies-style paneling and the utilitarian tile floor like you see in hospitals, his office is as lavish as any I've encountered in the high-end law firms downtown. Mahogany desk and matching credenza. Lush carpet. Richly painted walls adorned with elegant artwork and the framed accolades that herald his right to practice law. His chair is as big as a throne and every bit as ostentatious. The two chairs flanking the front of his desk are overstuffed and clad in a classic paisley fabric.

"Sorry for the interruption, my secretary needed to confirm my order for lunch. So, what can I do to help?" He looks from me to Liv and back.

I go first. "Have you spoken with your client since his release from Riverbend?"

"I have, yes." He braces his elbows on his desk and steeples his fingers. "Of course, our conversation is privileged."

Liv throws the next punch. "Did he at any time mention feeling as if he was being watched or followed?"

"He did not. In fact, he insisted he was settling in well. I can tell you that he accepted part-time employment to supplement his social security."

"Where?" Liv asks. This is news to us.

"Dawson's Detail Shop just off Dickerson Pike. I can give you the specific address, but you cannot harass the owner."

"We get that part," I remind him. Then I ask again, "Have you heard from him by any means since he disappeared?" Lawyers can be tricky. Being more specific is sometimes necessary.

"As I said, I have not. If I had, I would have urged him to turn himself in so as not to waste taxpayer dollars."

How nice. The two-bit, ambulance-chasing lawyer is concerned about waste in government spending. I wish I had a nickel for every sign plastered around the city with his face and stupid logo on it. Not to mention the television and radio commercials. I resist the urge to roll my eyes. The man has no class whatsoever beyond the paisley fabric he chose for these fancy chairs. Stella always loved paisley, said it was classic.

"Do you have any theories on what may have happened to him?" This from Liv.

"I believe a vigilante has taken him somewhere and murdered him. I don't think we'll ever hear from Carl Fanning again unless his body is found."

Funny, he doesn't sound too torn up about it at all. I inquire, "Are you speaking from firsthand knowledge about some aspect in his disappearance that we don't know about or are you simply theorizing?"

"She asked for a theory." He turns his hands up, his face smug. "I gave her what she asked for."

When Liv doesn't take her turn, I move on to another avenue. "Does Fanning have any friends or relatives we don't know about who might be hiding him?"

"He has no family and certainly no friends."

Liv doesn't say a word about her father. I decide to follow her cue. Maybe she's changed her mind.

She stands. I do the same. "Well, thank you, Mr. Cagle. I hope you'll call us if you think of anything that might help us find your client."

The attorney pushes up from his elegant chair and gives me a nod. "I certainly will. I am just as interested in finding my client as you."

I keep the chuckle to myself. Yeah, right.

We're almost to the door when Liv turns around. "Mr. Cagle, did you hire on Mr. Fanning's behalf a private psychiatrist to help him with transitioning back into society?"

The lawyer's flinch is almost imperceptible, but I spot it. Good move, Liv!

"He mentioned wanting one," Cagle says, "but I think he found one on his own."

She tilts her head. "I'm sure you remember the therapist's name."

Cagle shakes his head. "Actually, I don't." He reaches for a file on his desk, a cue that he's done answering questions. "I'll call if I think of anything else."

I follow Liv across the lobby. We stall at the door. The rain has stopped, but half a dozen news vans are waiting outside right next to my Tahoe.

Son of a bitch. Cagle wasn't ordering lunch. He was ordering publicity.

EIGHTEEN

"Detective Duncan!" a reporter shouts.

"Detective Duncan," another fires, "is it true you're treating Fanning's case as a potential homicide?"

"Detective Duncan, just one comment, please!" the first one entreaties.

Both women rush forward, blocking our path to Walt's Tahoe.

I freeze. Tell myself to go around them, but somehow I can't. I feel exactly like a deer caught in the headlights.

"No comment." Walt grabs me by the arm and starts ushering me toward the passenger side as if I'm a victim or a witness and not a cop.

I abruptly pull away from him and storm through the line of vultures on my own. I will not allow being pregnant or confused or upset or whatever the hell else is wrong with me to rule my existence.

Walt ignores the shouts and opens the driver's side door. The reporters and their camera people crowd up to his door.

"You should give them something," I say, my heart pumping faster and faster. "We both know they will make it up if you don't. Or worse, take this deadbeat lawyer's word for why we were here."

"I hate this part," he grumbles as he lowers his window. "Lowery," he calls out to one of the reporters he knows fairly well. The brunette rushes forward, elbows past the blond. "Like the chief said at the press conference earlier this week, we are treating this case like any other where foul play is potentially involved. We have nothing new to share. But we are hoping to have this case resolved very soon."

He powers up the window, blocking out more urgent questions.

"Good job," I say, eyes forward. "You sounded just like a politician, talking without actually saying anything."

He chuckles. "I believe I've just been insulted."

As the Tahoe reverses slowly out of the parking space, a body slams against my door. I jump. Walt hits the brakes.

The man whose face is plastered against my glass is another reporter. Don't know where this one came from or why the hell he would ram the door. He shouts at me through the glass. "Detective Newhouse, is it true Carl Fanning was one of your father's patients?"

"Son of a bitch."

I hear the words Walt mutters, feel the SUV rolling once more, see the reporter's mouth moving as he continues shouting questions, but I suddenly feel a million miles away. Somehow still looking on yet unable to participate in what's happening around me.

As soon as Walt is clear of the reporters, he twists the steering wheel and guns the engine. We barrel out of the parking lot.

"He knew," I say. The fucking lawyer knew my father went to see Fanning. "He told that reporter."

It's not until we hit a red light and Walt stops that he speaks. "Looks like we stirred a hornet's nest. This is day four of our investigation. The chief mentioned both our names on day two. Why hasn't the lawyer said anything before now?"

Good question. "What do you know about the warden? Is it possible he leaked our visit?" No one else was aware of my and Walt's discussion about my father's involvement. Well, no one else except David, and he would never do such a thing. And maybe Officer Winslow. As annoyed as I am just now at his behavior, I know he would never hurt me that way.

The light turns green, and Walt removes his foot from the brake and hits the gas. "I know basically nothing about the man. But I'll remedy that ASAP."

The ache in my brain is still distant, but the black dots hanging around my vision warn that I may not be able to ward off the inevitable for long. I need to do everything I can before then.

"Take me to my car. I'll go out to the farm and start looking for any hidden files." Even as I say the words, I do not believe any of this is possible. My father would never have kept a secret like this from me. Never. He was not that kind of man. Yet, how else can what we've learned be explained? "You talk to the warden again and keep me informed."

"I don't think that's a good idea." Walt shakes his head. "You need to take this slow and easy, Liv. I'm really worried about how these revelations are affecting you."

This is the one thing I did not want: to be treated as if I'm incapable or weak. "I'll be at home, Walt. At the farm. I have the best security system on the market, and it's where I feel the most relaxed these days."

When he still hesitates, I say, "We need to head this off before the connection to my father becomes the bigger issue in the media. The chief will take me off the case." I don't have to say how this thing going public would seriously jack up my stress level.

"Point taken. We'll do this your way, but you're taking some food with you."

By the time I'm in my Subaru, I have a six-pack of bottled water, a box of crackers, individual cheese sticks, apples, and grapes. Walt ordered me to eat while I work and to drink plenty of water. Just outside Nashville, I ran through another rain shower, but it passed by the time I reached Franklin.

As I maneuver along the driveway that extends deep into the woods before hitting the clearing that is the family farm, one of the bags falls out of the seat and bottles of water roll around in the floorboard. I can't help but smile. Walt really does want to take care of me whether I like it or not. He cares about me. I think it's safe to say he loves me like a daughter. He really has been there for me, before and since my dad died. David is right about one thing: Walt is more than a partner. He's family.

I wish David could understand our relationship. This abrupt jealousy is so uncharacteristic. Despite his hurtful words this morning, I sent him a text explaining where I'd be for a few hours. I even double-checked my calendar to make sure the two of us had nothing planned. Of course, I didn't tell him what I would be looking for at the farm. I told him I was going to pack a few more boxes.

I am certain neither he nor his family would want to hear that there is a chance my father was treating a patient named Carl Fanning. I don't want to hear it myself. Still refuse to believe it.

But I'm not a fool. He did visit the prison. He did pass himself off as Fanning's therapist. I also understand my father may have done those things as a way to cover his real reason for visiting the scumbag. He may have done those things to help his patient Mario Sanchez. There is no other reasonable explanation.

A face-to-face interview with Sanchez is growing more and more important. With only a couple other names whose alibis we can't confirm on the list of victims besides Sanchez, his is becoming increasingly more relevant. Maybe the three have been working together. Hyatt and Reeves may be the planned distraction from what Sanchez is actually doing.

After Walt checks in with the warden, he will interview the next person on our list, Melanie Hardeman, before he calls it a day. I feel guilty about not going with him, but I need to do this. He agreed. Like me, he understands on some level that neither of us can explain how we know, but we do. Time is running out. Something bad is coming.

I emerge from the trees, and my gaze sweeps across the open pastures, where horses once grazed and trotted. My mother had so many trophies from her horseback-riding competitions. She and my father had high hopes that I would be the one to reach the Olympics, but an injury at thirteen ended that goal. I didn't really miss the competition part of the horses. I think that was more my mother's dream than mine. Still, horses or no, I love this place. I absolutely cannot sell it. David will just have to deal with the idea.

The big horse barn sits a good distance from the house. It, too, is beautiful. Classic. From the outside, one would think the house is the typical farmhouse. Two stories. Wraparound porch on the first level. Salvaged brick foundation and classic white siding with wood storm shutters that actually work painted in a deep black. Topped with a metal roof, the house was built about fifty years ago, but the architect went to great lengths to ensure it looked as if it had sat on this hillside overlooking the green pastures for centuries.

I consider that the barn and other buildings in the distance remind me of Hyatt's riding academy we just visited. My mother could have had a place like that here. I shake off the thought.

Inside the house is a different story from the exterior. There are plenty of original features like wide plank flooring and a massive stone fireplace that resembles something from the eighteenth century, but in the center of the house, the ceilings soar to the roofline. The second-floor landing circles around this area, the railing open to the central living space below. Four bedrooms, each with an en suite bath, wreathe the upper floor. On the main level, the centerpiece of the floor plan is the vast open space that includes the living room, kitchen, and dining areas. On one end of the first floor is a massive library and workout room, while my parents' bedroom suite and my father's office are on the other end.

It's almost four when I park in front of the house and get out. The peace and quiet envelops me instantly. There's a chill in the air, but according to the news, this cold spell is almost behind us. By tomorrow we should be back into average temperatures for May. Thunderstorms are supposed to usher in the warmer temps. I grab the bag of snacks, gather the bottles of water, and head for the front door.

Inside I lock the door and reset the security system. I've never been afraid here, but the last thing I want is some reporter walking in while I'm digging around in old files. Though I haven't experienced a reporter invasion, Walt has. He told me about one joining him and his wife in the backyard on a Sunday afternoon. Walt was grilling steaks. His wife was setting the table on the patio, and all of a sudden a reporter from Nashville's biggest newspaper strolls around the end of the house and shouts a hello as if he'd been invited to lunch.

On top of not wanting a reporter to bully into my house, Fanning is still missing. If he had some relationship with my father, he could show up here. As much as I consider him the scum of the earth and not worth the cost of a bullet to his head to stop him, I don't want to have to deal with an Internal Affairs investigation about my father's potential involvement with the man and me shooting him.

I put the snacks away, grab myself a stick of cheese and a bottle of water, before I head to my father's office. I sit in his chair and consider his desk. Might as well start at the top and work my way down. Putting aside my disbelief and dragging my objectivity back to front and center, I start with his calendar notebook for this year. Since he died on February 6, there's not a whole lot to look at. I find the dates the warden mentioned. All are marked with *CF.*

I shake my head. "What in the world were you doing, Dad?"

I round up an organizing bin, one of the many lining the shelves in the credenza behind his desk, and place the calendar there. Whatever I find that is relevant in some way to the investigation, I'll put in the bin for Walt and me to dissect. Part of me feels guilty for looking through my father's things with the intent of finding evidence. But that's not exactly what I'm doing. My goal is to find *no* evidence. I need to discover that this was some sort of step taken in support of Sanchez. My father doing what he always did, being the man who saves the day.

There are no other notes on his desk. I open his laptop and scroll through the files there. My father wasn't big on electronic files. He preferred the old-fashioned way, so most of his files are paper. I peruse his contacts list, his sent and received emails. Nothing jumps out at me. No exchanges between him, the warden, the lowlife attorney, or any other representative of Carl Fanning or his victims.

I close the laptop and move on to the desk drawers. I find a bag of my father's favorite snack—Reese's candy. I open one and pop it in my mouth. The combination of chocolate and peanut butter is instantly soothing. A smile touches my lips as I think of all the times as a kid that I came into his office and shared a Reese's with him.

My continued search reveals no notes or business cards or anything else in the drawers that suggest collusion with the enemy in this case. I stand, stretch my back after being hunkered over the desk for so long. I stare at the row of steel five-drawer filing cabinets—the kind that are supposed to withstand the typical house fire for an extended period of time. I've fingered through the rows of file folders already. Didn't spot a single name on our list.

No matter, I walk over to the cabinets and open the top drawer on cabinet number one. Another look can't hurt. I begin with the first name on the list and go through it once more. Drawer after drawer, I drag it open and search. Then move on to the next cabinet. Nothing. Not a single file related to one of Fanning's victims from before he went to prison is here. I double check for Sanchez, even check the files on either side of where Sanchez would be. Nada. Finally, I open each file and read the name there to ensure it's not some variation or alias that was used. Nothing.

This makes no sense.

I scour the credenza and the rows of bookshelves and find the same. Not one thing. Then I go to my parents' bedroom.

"This is a true low point, Liv," I mutter.

Guilt piling higher and higher on my shoulders, I search my parents' things. I go through all my father's clothes, check pockets, look under stacks of neatly folded clothes. I find a few coins and a gum wrapper but nothing else.

Finally, I collapse on the carpeted floor of the massive walk-in closet. I close my eyes and inhale the scent of my father. My mother's scent faded years ago. Unless I open one of the boxes with her favorite handbags tucked neatly inside, then I can smell her perfume.

She always carried a tiny bottle in her handbag, along with breath mints and tissues.

I miss them both so much.

That distant ache is building. I haven't seen the dots in the last hour or so, but I fear they're coming. I need to finish before the headache hits. There is only one other place my father might store files. Searching his bedroom for clues of a meeting with Fanning, the warden, or the lawyer was a logical step. He might have left a card in a jacket pocket, or perhaps even a sticky note. But my father would never, ever conceal sensitive files any place someone else might easily access. Like his bedroom or the library.

No way. Any patient files would be under lock and key, which leads me to the only other place where he kept any sort of files. I walk down the hall from my parents' bedroom toward his office. I enter the laundry room across the hall. The laundry room is quite large. There's a door to the portico that leads out to the detached garage, and there's another door, this one hidden behind a tall cabinet. I open the double cabinet doors and step into the empty space. Before me is the steel door and keypad that lead to the panic room. I enter the code and the steel door slides away. It doesn't open out or into the room but disappears into a slot in the wall.

The panic room has its own heating and cooling system as well as a fresh-air input of some sort. A two-piece bathroom. The main part of the room is ten by twelve. The small bathroom and an equally small storage room stand side by side at the farthest end. There's a set of pull-down beds against one wall. The lower one works as a sofa as well as a bed. On the wall above it is a second pull-down twin-size bed that serves as an upper bunk. There's a small table surrounded by four narrow chairs. A refrigerator, microwave, and a television. The electricity in the room is powered by thermal and solar energy. If the grid goes down, this room will operate.

Another filing cabinet stands in the storage room. This one doesn't have the typical lock. It's biometric. I place my thumb there and listen to the locks release. Inside are the most private files of the Newhouse family. The deed to the property is here. My parents' last will and testament was stored here until I retrieved it for settling the estate. Birth certificates, social security cards, passports, and a handful of files related to upgrades and maintenance to the property. The six most recent tax year files. All of this I find in the top drawer.

I pull open the bottom drawer. Inside, I find another row of files. I lower onto the floor, folding my legs into a comfortable sitting position, and pull out the first file from the bottom drawer. The folder is marked only as "The Child." There is no name, just a long history of abuse and neglect about a young child. The words, written by my father, are disturbing. I shudder and reach for the next file. As I read the name on the tab, those damned black dots appear in my line of vision. My pulse trips with disbelief. I toss the file aside and move to the next one, and the pain in my skull ramps up, rising to a crescendo.

Shelley Martin, Melanie Hardeman, Janie Hyatt, Dana Reeves, Patricia Shelby, Andrea Donnelly, and Mario Sanchez, as well as a half dozen others. They are all here.

Every single known victim, dead or alive, of Carl Fanning.

NINETEEN

Detective Walter Duncan

I'm just walking into the lobby of Vanderbilt University Medical Center when I get the call from Warden Tennison.

I step to one side, out of the path of visitors going in and out. Vanderbilt is a large facility. The same one where Stella had so many tests and procedures.

Being here makes me sad . . . reminds me of the worst time in my life.

"Duncan," I say, rather than hello.

"You have more questions for me, Detective?"

Warden Tennison's voice is tense. He knows he's done wrong. "Did you give Fanning's attorney a heads-up about our visit?" Before he can respond, I tack on, "Think carefully before you answer, Tennison. I'd hate to see you charged with impeding an investigation."

He exhales a big breath. "It's not what you think."

Somehow I doubt this. My instincts are humming with anticipation.

"I called Cagle to demand to know why Newhouse wasn't listed as a therapist Fanning was consulting with. I don't like being caught with my pants down as I was when you visited."

"Which put you in a position to have to tell the man about our visit." It's not a question. Bastard.

"What choice did I have? I need answers the same as you do."

Not the same at all. "We'll see what the chief has to say about that. You know he plays golf with Commissioner Straton." Straton is the top dog in the Tennessee Department of Corrections. In other words, Tennison's boss.

I end the call before the asshole can respond. There is nothing I despise more than self-serving public servants.

At the bank of elevators, I select the proper floor and wait. I had to put off my cold visit to Melanie Hardeman. The husband of Patricia Shelby called with a rather odd story about his wife. His repeated mention of Fanning in the account pushed a visit to him above all else. The whole story sounded strange, but the fact is that everything about this case is strange.

I didn't call Liv. She's doing what she has to do at the farm. I'll talk to her tomorrow. Let her work through this business with her father without interference.

Liam Shelby waits for me in the small lobby of the Maternal Special Care Unit. Since his wife has so recently given birth, any illness potentially connected to that event assures she is admitted to this unit for care. I have no idea what her rehospitalization has to do with Fanning or the case, but the whole situation sounded far too bizarre to ignore.

"Detective Walt Duncan," I say as I extend my hand toward the man, who looks harried and exhausted.

He barely brushes my palm with his. "I wasn't sure if I needed to call you but, to tell you the truth, I didn't know what else to do."

Since we have the lobby to ourselves, I gesture to the row of chairs. "Why don't we sit and you can tell me what's going on."

We settle and he scrubs his hands over his face before he begins. "Patricia had just put the baby down yesterday afternoon. This was after you and your partner interviewed her. I had noticed she, Patricia," he notes, "hasn't been sleeping. Like at all. For days. So I urge her to take a nap while the baby is sleeping." He shakes his head. "I mean, the whole point in my taking this time off is so I can help her. But she acts like no one can touch the baby or watch the baby but her."

Though I have no experience on the matter if new human mothers are anything like the mothers of any other living creature, I can see how they would feel extra protective of a newborn.

I say nothing, just listen.

"For the next hour," he goes on, "she just walked the floor. Like she was trying to prevent herself from falling asleep. She kept going over to the bassinet and checking on Lily." He flashes a pitiful attempt at a smile. "That's our baby. Lily."

"Pretty name," I offer even though his wife told us this yesterday. The poor guy is way out of sorts.

"When Lily started to rouse, I went over to pick her up. Patricia had stalled at the front window and was just staring out like she'd fallen asleep with her eyes open."

Not impossible. I've seen people do it.

"Suddenly, she whirled around." Horror creeps over his face. "She started screaming and ran at me. She snatched the baby from me and just kept screaming. Stuff like, 'You cannot have her!' And 'Stay away from my baby!' I was stunned. I tried to make her see that it was me. But it took like ten minutes for her to calm down enough to stop screaming at me."

Again, I don't really have any experience in the area, but in the early days of my career, I did respond to a domestic disturbance or two involving postpartum depression, where the new mother had a bit of a psychotic episode.

"Postpartum psychosis, they called it," Shelby says as if he'd read my mind.

"How is she now?" I hope like hell our interview didn't have any part in this.

"She's getting back to normal. She's still agitated. Nervous. Afraid like. But she recognizes that she flipped out and has apologized over and over. She wants to go home to Lily. Her mother is taking care of the baby while we're here."

"Would it be all right if I spoke to her?" I have a feeling about this. Might be nothing, but I need to see it through.

"Please do," the husband urges. "It was after those questions about what she did over the weekend that this situation escalated. I mean, I'm not suggesting it's your fault. I just think it's about the bastard who hurt her. Maybe she needs some extra reassurance from you—the police. This Fanning thing has pushed her over an edge. Really, I think she started going downhill the minute he was released."

Shelby gets up and I follow. At the door to the room, he hesitates. "I hope this is the right thing to do."

I nod. "I'll make sure she understands we've got this."

He opens the door and we step inside. Patricia Shelby's attention shoots our way. She looks from me to her husband but says nothing.

I approach the foot of her bed, keeping a bit of distance. Her husband moves to stand at her side. She takes his hand, hers shaking as she does so. Damn, I hate she's feeling this kind of vulnerability.

"Ma'am, I'm Detective Walt Duncan. You remember me? My partner and I spoke to you yesterday. We're working the Fanning case."

His name causes a wince, and I wish I hadn't needed to say it.

"Your husband tells me you have some concerns regarding the situation."

She looks to her husband then, and tears slip down her cheeks. "I'm so sorry for all this."

He brushes at her cheeks, his face lined with concern. "Honey, you do not need to be sorry for anything."

"He's right," I say. "You did nothing wrong. If our interview had any part in this, I am truly sorry."

She shifts her attention to me. "No. It wasn't you. It was me. And I did. Do something wrong, I mean."

The unexpected statement brings the moment to a standstill with no one blinking or even breathing.

"Saturday morning," she says, shattering the odd stillness, "I went to Dawson's Detail Shop on Dickerson where *he* works."

The husband's face pales. "Oh my God, baby, what were you thinking?"

I want to tell him to be quiet, but I ignore him instead. "Where Fanning works?" Liv and I only just learned from the lawyer that the bastard has a job. In fact, Dawson's was another of the calls I made after leaving Liv at her Subaru. No one there has seen Fanning since Saturday around noon.

"Yes," Patricia says. When her husband starts to say something else, she holds up a hand to stop him. "That was my part. The thing I was supposed to do."

No matter that my instincts go on point, I don't ask what that means. She's talking. I want her to keep doing that until she's finished. The clarification that she is talking about Fanning is all I need at this point.

"I was supposed to go early, before the place opened, and spray paint the words 'sick fuck' on the front of the building."

Her husband's expression shows shock now, but thankfully he says nothing.

When a couple of beats pass with her saying nothing more, I prompt her with, "Were you able to accomplish this?"

She blinks and sets her gaze on me once more. "No. He was there already. Before anyone else. Almost like he knew I was coming."

Shit. "Fanning?"

She nods. "He told me that I should go home and be a good girl or he'd be coming for my little girl next."

"Oh my God." The words come from the husband, who now looks aghast. "How did he know we were having a little girl?"

She shrugs listlessly. "Social media, I guess. We posted the gender reveal party months ago. It's the only way he could have known."

My chest hurts with the effort to breathe. This means he was keeping tabs on his victims via social media. The idea tears at my gut.

Not really surprising but damned infuriating. "What happened next, Patricia?"

"I ran back to my car and rushed away." More tears are streaming down her cheeks. "But look what I did." She stares at me with such worry and fear, it makes my heart ache all the more. "He could come for our baby. And it'll be all my fault."

"First," I say, "I'm putting a surveillance detail on your home. He is not going to get your baby or you." I turn to her husband. "Call home and let the grandmother know that an officer will be there soon." Then I shift back to Patricia. "I understand why you felt compelled to do this. Really, I do. And you have every right to hate this man and want to force others to see what he is."

She swipes at her damp cheeks. Her husband has moved to the other side of the room to make the call.

"I wish he was dead," she admits, her voice quavering.

That makes two of us, but I don't say this.

"I have one more question, Patricia." I approach this cautiously. I don't want to spook her or have her guard going up.

She nods as if she understands.

"What did you mean when you said that was your part, the thing you were supposed to do?"

She moistens her lips and takes a halting breath. "We all got together and decided something had to be done. Painting those words on the building where he works was my part. It was what I had to do."

I struggle to stay calm on the outside. This is the break we've been waiting for. "What were the other parts, and who was supposed to do them?"

"I don't know who was supposed to do what. I mean, it was all really secretive. I just know that the goal was to make it look like someone was warning him, and then he would disappear. The police would believe some vigilante took care of him."

Oh hell. I hesitate, feel almost compelled to suggest we talk about her rights before going on. But I can't. I have to know the rest. "Who else was involved?"

She looks to her husband. He is back at her bedside and has reached for her hand.

"All of us." She bites her lip for a moment. "His victims."

"Mario Sanchez?" I ask.

"Detective," the husband interrupts before his wife can answer. "I think my wife has said all she needs to say without a lawyer present."

"Thank you," I say, rather than argue. I have what I need for now. "You've been more help than you realize."

On the way out, I make the call for a surveillance detail on the Shelby home. Then I head home myself.

I won't call Liv about this. Let her do what she must.

I have to find Hyatt and Reeves. With the two unreachable for so long, there's no question in my mind that they have either taken Fanning or are his victims . . . again.

Either way, this is not going to end well.

TWENTY

The Child

By my next birthday, something new was happening to my body.

I decided I no longer disliked the boobs—that's what he called them—I grew. My wide hips and long legs no longer made me mad. I noticed how other girls looked, and I decided I liked my look. I was no longer "the child" or an "it," and I knew it.

No matter what he called me, I was a girl, a young woman.

This made me very happy. At least for a while. I don't know when my real birthday is, but he chose one for me. May fifth. On May fifth of that year, I was fourteen, he told me.

We had started a different method for getting money. I was still very good at pickpocketing. But it was harder to get close to the unsuspecting old ladies and the distracted mothers. I had to work harder to grab a few bucks here and there. We never took credit cards. Too much risk of getting caught, he claimed, with all the authority of a man who had mooched off others his whole life. A lot of stores have cameras now, he told me. They could look back and see who used the credit card. So we stuck with cash rather than take the risk.

The new method of making money involved me pretending to be one of those girls who haunted the street corners. It was easy, really. All I had to do was flirt with the guy and lure him into the alley where he was waiting. Sometimes I worried about how hard he hit the guys, but none of them died as far as I know. We didn't have to worry about any one of them looking for us because we always went to another part of town or even to a nearby town. Never shit where you eat, he said.

One of the things I hated most about the changes to my body was when the blood came between my thighs. The first time, I thought I was dying. About the time I started to get used to it, it stopped. I was really, really glad.

I hoped it never came back. I didn't tell him this. I didn't like talking about it.

Then I started to get sick. I felt really bad all the time. If I ate, I puked it up. And I was so tired. He eyed me suspiciously, but he didn't say why. I begged him to take me to the doctor, but he refused. He said I would live as if he knew all things.

Pretty soon the sickness passed and I felt better. Not tired anymore. We kept running the scam on the guys who wanted to buy me for a few hours of disgusting pleasure. Until my belly started to swell like I had swallowed a ball or something. That was when things went to hell for me. He screamed and ranted and kicked at me. I cried and cried, begged him to tell me what was wrong. Finally, he said I was pregnant. I was having a baby. But I shouldn't be pregnant since I didn't have a husband or a boyfriend. All I had was him. Then I realized he was the one who got me that way.

I had no idea how those things worked.

I stared at my belly. I had a baby growing inside me? He started to cuss and scream about the time he got drunk and forgot to use a condom. I didn't completely understand, but I eventually figured out it had something to do with the stuff that came out of him when he was grunting and rutting into me.

The angrier he got, the more terrified I became. What were we going to do? How did I get it out? What did we do with it? At first he wouldn't answer me. He just stared at me as if I was a pile of dog shit in his path. Then he told me he was going to fix it. Over the next few days, he forced me to drink nasty black medicine. When the only thing that accomplished was to make me shit myself to death, he punched me in the belly and beat me up worse than he ever had before.

That didn't work, either.

My belly just kept growing.

Then he told me we would wait until it was ready to come out and take care of it then. The way he said this made me worry, but I had no clue what I could do about it. He made all the decisions. I just did what I was told.

This was my life, my normal.

The first time I felt it moving around inside me, I screamed. I was like, what the hell is that? I was afraid to ask him about it, so I just waited and finally figured out it was the baby. For some reason, it made me happy. Really happy. I had never had any toys except for that ratty old bear. Now I was going to have a baby of my very own. I could play with it and take care of it. It would look at me the way I looked at him. We would be a family.

Except that isn't what happened.

When the labor pains began, I thought I was dying for sure. I screamed and cried and screamed some more. He went and got this old woman who lived down the block. She claimed she had brought dozens of babies into the world. The pain went on for hours. It felt as if my body had a mind of its own and was going to pop open any second. The pressure. The need to push. I couldn't stop it. I had no control. I thought I was going to split in half for sure. All I could do was keep screaming.

Late that night, it finally happened. The woman used her hands and fingers to help the baby come out. She said I was real lucky that she was able to help the baby come out without a lot of tearing and extra bleeding. I was still hurting like hell, but mostly I just wanted to hold my baby. It was a boy. She cut the cord with scissors, then clamped it with a clothespin. She cleaned him up, wrapped him in a towel, and handed him to me. He was the most beautiful thing I had ever seen.

No other baby had ever been as beautiful as him. And he was mine.

She told me to let him suck at my breast. It hurt like hell, but I did it. Later I fell asleep. When I woke up, the old woman was gone and so was my baby.

I stare at the disgusting shell of a man collapsed into a heap in the corner. Even as he sleeps, his chest rises and falls with the rattle of the dying. The wound on his arm is infected. Yellow pus leaks from it. I am certain it hurts like a son of a bitch. I stand, walk over to him, and kick him in the arm, ensuring the toe of my boot goes into the wound.

He awakens instantly, howls and writhes in pain.

I smile and wonder how much longer his black heart can hold out. Long enough to keep the misery going for a day or two more, I suspect. Long enough for me to block out the memories of what he did to me with the howls of his agony. I squat down and watch as he shudders and quakes and cries.

When he has calmed himself and the pain has subsided to a tolerable level, I'll kick him again.

Oh, what fun we're going to have. I find it so amusing how his carefully laid plan to get back at me has backfired on him.

TWENTY-ONE

DETECTIVE OLIVIA NEWHOUSE

Saturday, May 5

"You're saying they all got together and set up this plan." It's stunning, really. I can hardly wrap my head around it. We were concerned one of the victims might have started this thing, but all of them?

"She wouldn't confirm who all was involved," Walt points out. "But she did say 'we all' before her husband decided she needed to lawyer up. So last night I did some more research, particularly into Hyatt and Reeves. With those two MIA, I feel like Fanning is either with them or they are with him."

"Damn," I say. "Not really a good thing either way."

Walt glances at me as he slows for the coming four-way stop. "Exactly."

My gut is in knots. We have the Melanie Hardeman interview this morning. She wasn't at the salon where she works as a stylist, so we're headed to her residence. Maybe she will give us more.

However slowly, it's all coming together now. The news Walt learned from Patricia Shelby helps tremendously. "So this is why Reeves and Hyatt were cruising past his place. They were the ones who were supposed to make him disappear." I pump my fist in the air. "I knew that receptionist at the riding academy was not giving us straight answers."

"Agreed," he says. "Which is why I had a BOLO issued for the two of them and their vehicles, including a '69 blue Ford pickup we didn't know about."

"It wasn't listed in the first search we did." A frown tugs at my brow. I don't know how we would have missed it. The Grand Am was the only vehicle registered to Reeves and the Range Rover to Hyatt.

"It was listed as belonging to the riding academy." Walt shakes his head. "Along with a commercial-size van used for competition road trips."

"Speaking of road trips," I remember to tell him, "Gatlinburg PD called. No answer at the address we gave them. No vehicle, no sign of anyone staying there. Either that receptionist flat-out lied or she was lied to."

"Someone is lying, that's for sure. Maybe they have him stashed in one of the barns at that place—the riding academy," Walt suggests.

"Unless he's in Mexico with Sanchez," I counter.

Walt chuckles. "Unless he's in Mexico, yes."

"This is about the wildest thing we've encountered." I feel giddy at the idea that these victims banded together to make this bastard pay. I can't help but respect the hell out of them for it.

"Movie of the week," Walt says.

"No kidding."

I shake my head at the other info Walt shared. Warden Tennison did give the lawyer a heads-up about our questions. Scumbag.

I feel terrible not telling Walt first thing about the files I found at the farm. But I can't. Not yet. Not until I figure this out, at least to some degree, myself. As much as I adore Walt, love him, really, it truly would be like betraying my father.

Besides, Walt had big news and I let him go first.

My cop instincts warn that I'm allowing emotion—my allegiance to my father—to get in the way of the job, of the law. But I just can't do it. Not yet. We still have another victim to interview. Not to mention Sanchez is coming back in to Nashville tomorrow. There's time to talk about the files later. Maybe Sanchez will shed new light on that part of the puzzle.

I heard my father's name mentioned on the news this morning. The reporter apparently did a piece on the late news last night that was picked up on all the networks this morning. The chief has already called Walt, which he downplayed when telling me. I expect a call from David any second.

Walt glances at me. "You okay, kid? You still don't look rested."

I open my mouth to tell him I didn't sleep well, but he reaches for his cell. I'm grateful for the reprieve. Gives me a minute to figure out what I am going to say.

By the time I flipped through the files on Fanning's victims last night, my vision had blurred to the point that I could no longer read the words on the pages. The new headache consumed my ability to think, pain exploding over and over in my skull. I crawled to the lower bunk in the panic room, and that's where I woke up this morning.

There was dried vomit on the floor, so at some point I threw up. The bad taste in my mouth was more than sufficient evidence that it had come from me. Not that there was anyone else around, only me.

I rinsed my mouth and made a pot of coffee, then checked my cell for the first time since I went unconscious. David had called three times during the night. The problem is I left my cell in my father's office. No way could I have heard it through the foot of concrete that makes up the walls of the panic room.

I called him back this morning. He didn't answer, so I left him a voicemail telling him I had worked so late packing at the farm that I'd fallen asleep. When I woke up in the middle of the night, I just decided to stay the night. There was a nugget of truth in the story. With all that's happened, I don't know how he and I will ever get back to each other. The gap between us widens a little more each day.

My mind goes back to the files. There was nothing there that suggested my father had done anything other than conduct background research on each of the victims. There were no notes from meetings or sessions. No conclusions. No summaries from telephone conversations. But why would he need background information on Fanning's victims? Since Sanchez's name is the only one I found in his office, I have a feeling it begins and ends with him.

Sanchez has to know what my father was doing. I refuse to believe he was gathering information for Fanning prior to his release. No way he would do that.

"That was Reynolds."

I force those dark worries away and turn to my partner. "He got the DNA results?"

Walt nodded. "Only on the B positive. The analysis confirms that it came from Fanning."

I blow out a breath. "Well, we knew that was coming. What's the holdup on the second type?"

"Just the timeline. We ordered the first test the day before the second. Those results will probably pop up in his system by tomorrow or Monday."

"That's something, I guess." Not that we doubted Fanning was one of the people who had been injured in whatever went down in his house. There wasn't enough blood at the scene to believe he'd died there, but there was a sufficient amount to conclude that he had sustained a serious injury.

Walt reaches for his cell again. I wait, hoping it's Patricia Shelby and that she has decided to tell the rest of the story.

"Thanks for the heads-up," Walt says before putting his phone away. "That was Holland."

Renae Holland is the detective working the two missing person cases we added to our list of potential trouble with Fanning. I brace for the news.

"Suzy Eldridge was found over in Knoxville with her boyfriend's sister." He brakes for a traffic light. "Chloe Simone is dead. They found her body this morning."

Not what I wanted to hear but not a surprise, either. "Any chance her murder is connected to Fanning?"

Walt shakes his head. "They got the killer. The old janitor who used to work at the school. He'd been watching her for months. Bastard finally worked up the nerve to go after her. I guess he had too much time on his hands after he retired."

I close my eyes and shake my head. "Sick fuck."

"My thoughts exactly."

I can only imagine what the Simones are going through. How in the world can a sane person bring a child into this screwed-up world? I think of the child developing inside me, and I wonder whether I'm making the biggest mistake of my life. Will he or she blame me for dragging him or her into this shitty place?

Too late to worry about that now. It's done.

Walt parks a few yards from the front of Melanie Hardeman's home. It's a modest brick on Second Street in Cleveland Park. The neighborhood is up and coming. Lots of hipsters moving in, jazzing things up. Melanie is my age, thirty. Single. No kids.

I scan the street as we wander up the walk to the front door. An Amazon package sits on the small porch. Since there's no garage and no driveway, street parking only, I'm thinking Melanie uses the front door. With the package untouched, it's possible she isn't home. Her car certainly isn't anywhere near the house. She's not at work, so maybe she's visiting a friend or shopping.

Walt knocks on the door.

No television or other sounds beyond the closed door. Blinds are shut tight, so there's no looking in through the windows.

"Looks like we'll have to give the lady a call."

There's a good chance once she learns what we want that she'll blow us off. Even putting aside Patricia Shelby's statements, all too often victims don't want to talk about what happened. It's too painful, too humiliating. I can understand how they feel. At this point reliving the nightmare won't change anything about what happened to them. But it's our job to convince them that the details of their nightmare might prevent the same thing from happening to someone else.

In the end, what we really need is whatever we can get on this let's-get-Fanning plan the victims were involved in.

Walt reaches for his phone at the same time a silver Corolla pulls to the curb in front of the house. I elbow him and nod toward the street. A woman—tall, brunette, dressed in leggings and a long tee—emerges from the car. Shopping bags in her arms, she is around the hood and headed up the walk before she looks up and spots us.

I smile.

Walt says, "Good morning, Ms. Hardeman. I'm Detective—"

The bags hit the ground and Melanie runs.

"Well, shit," Walt grumbles.

I take off, dodging the apples and oranges rolling across the sidewalk.

Walt is right behind me.

"Ms. Hardeman," I shout, "we only have a few questions for you. You are not in any kind of trouble."

She keeps running.

We didn't find a criminal record. What's up with this reaction to a visit from the cops? So maybe Patricia Shelby has already called the others and warned them that she spilled at least part of the beans.

My heart is pounding as I grow closer and closer to her. The woman clearly runs regularly. I have been ignoring my workout routine lately, and it shows.

Just as I draw within reach of her, she apparently runs out of steam and slows to a stop.

We both bend over and struggle to catch our breath.

"You're not in trouble," I repeat between gasps for air.

Walt trudges up to where we are huddled. "No offense, ma'am," he complains breathlessly, "what the hell was that about?"

"I did it, okay?"

Walt and I exchange a look, then stare at her. Is the woman admitting that she kidnapped Carl Fanning? Or only that she took whatever step she was supposed to take?

"What did you do, Ms. Hardeman?" I ask.

She flops down on her butt on the ground, puts her knees up, and wraps her arms around them. "I followed him around. Harassed him. I'm not ashamed of what I did."

Not exactly a confession to murder.

"At any time did you touch him?" Walt asks, his voice still breathy.

"I didn't lay a hand on that son of a bitch. I just heckled him. I made sure that the customers at every store he went into knew what he was. I followed him through each department, shouting to all who would listen until he left the store empty-handed. I hoped he would starve to death."

It's hard to shame a woman for heckling the man who raped her as a child. "Did he ever speak to you?" I ask.

Walt goes down on one knee, his forearm braced on his thigh. He's obviously struggling to catch his breath. His face is pale, and beads of sweat slip down his forehead. I drop into a crouch as if to catch my breath as well, but mostly I just want to be at his level so I can better assess his condition.

"He wouldn't even look at me," Melanie says, drawing my attention back to her. "No matter how often I showed up, he tried to ignore me. He pushed his cart around, reaching for whatever was on his list. Eventually he couldn't take it anymore, and he abandoned his cart and left. I never followed him outside. I wasn't quite that brave."

"Did you ever see him with anyone?"

She shakes her head at Walt's question. "He was always alone."

"Did you notice anyone else following him or watching him?" Walt pulls a handkerchief from his pocket and scrubs it over his face. If possible, it's even whiter than it was before.

I start to ask him if he's okay but figure I better wait until we're finished here. Men don't like to have their weaknesses pointed out. Not even smart guys like Walt.

Melanie appears to consider his question. "I can't remember anyone, but I was always so angry and focused on him that I can't be sure I was really looking, either."

"Did he ever show up at your house?" I ask. "Try to turn the tables on you?"

She shakes her head. "I thought about that later, after I'd already harassed him a couple of times. But thank God he never came around."

"Are you certain he recognized you?" Walt asks.

Good point. If he thought she was someone else, he might have gone after the wrong person.

"I told him who I was." She raises her chin in defiance. "I wanted him to know I was no longer afraid of him."

"This," I say, "was your part?" The startled look on her face warns she wasn't aware we knew about their little plan. "We'd like you to tell us about when and how you got together with the others to make this plan." Before she can respond, I explain, "We already have statements from other victims. We know there was a plan." This might be a slight exaggeration, but if it works, it's worth it.

She exhales a big breath. Almost looks relieved. "As soon as the news broke about his release, we got together. Janie Hyatt set up the meeting. We were all there." A shrug and then she goes on. "Except for the ones who moved away or are dead or in prison."

"Why don't you list the names just so we're clear," Walt suggests, his voice hoarse. He still looks as if he's struggling for air.

I pull out my phone. This is a bit unorthodox, but I set it to record. "We'll record this as part of your official statement." Not exactly by the book. I state her name as well as ours, and the time and date for the recording.

"Janie Hyatt, Dana Reeves, Patricia Shelby, Andrea Donnelly, Shelley Martin, and I met at that steakhouse over on Eighth to discuss the news."

Walt and I exchange a look. No Sanchez?

"What did you decide?" I ask.

"We decided unanimously that we wanted to do something. Something to see that real justice was done."

As much as I hate to do this, I can't ignore where this is going. "Ms. Hardeman, before you say more, it would be better if I explain your rights."

"I know my rights." She shakes her head. "I don't need you to explain them to me. I waive my rights or whatever."

I look to Walt and he nods. "All right, go on then."

"A week later we met again. There was a list of steps that needed to be taken. Surveil him. Harass him. Make his work life miserable. Stuff like that. The final step was to make him disappear. All the steps were written down, folded up, and put into a basket. Then we all drew one. We were to look at it, remember it, and eat the paper. No one was ever to tell who got what step."

Again I consider this is all so very spy novelish.

"I notice," Walt says, "you didn't mention Mario Sanchez."

She nods. "He wasn't at the first meeting, but he was at the second."

"He drew from the basket," I inquire, "just like the rest of you?"

She nods. "But I can't tell you what part he got."

Another look between me and Walt. The idea that Fanning's remains are now somewhere in Mexico feels all the more likely.

"What other steps do you recall?" Walt is breathing a bit easier now.

"There was one about damaging his car. You know, flatten the tires, crack the windshield. Another that involved trying to run him off the road."

Damn. These folks were not playing.

"Oh, and to leave dead things at his door. You know, like you see driving down the road. Roadkill."

Well, that explained the carcasses at his house.

"Have you been in contact with the others since that meeting?" Walt asks.

She shakes her head. "There were rules. We would all draw a step. We would do it. We would never speak of it again. We would never speak to each other again."

I stop the recording. "Thank you, Ms. Hardeman," I say. "This has been very helpful. I would advise you to be watchful since Fanning remains unaccounted for. Keep your doors locked. We'll be contacting you again, but until then, if you need to speak with anyone about what you've just told us, make it an attorney."

She nods. "Is that what happened?" She looks from me to Walt and back. "Did one of us take him?"

"We don't know the answer yet," Walt tells her.

I stand, offer her my hand.

She pulls up, dusts off her bottom. "Sorry I ran. I guess I got scared and panicked. But I'm not sorry for what I did."

I smile but keep my thoughts on that one to myself. No matter that Fanning doesn't deserve any better than whatever he gets, there are laws. I'm supposed to uphold those laws.

I offer Walt my hand next, but he waves me off and pops up like a man half his age. He reaches into his pocket for a business card and hands it to Melanie. "Sorry you felt compelled to run and then we scared you with our chase." He chuckles and swabs at his face again. "The way you ran, we were worried you had a kilo of blow or something in that bag of yours."

Melanie's expression freezes.

Oh hell. I shake my head.

She shrugs. "It's only a gram."

TWENTY-TWO

Melanie Hardeman

The detectives drive away. I relax as best I can, regather my bags and carry them to my house. I really shouldn't have overreacted to their appearance. We were all warned to expect interviews at the very least.

I plop my bags on the porch and dig for the house key. My hand shakes so badly I can scarcely get the damned thing in the slot. Finally, the key slides in and I give it a twist.

It's okay. I'm okay. They believed me. I have nothing to worry about.

They don't know what happened yet.

I close my eyes and think of how I'm going to celebrate. That bastard has to be dead. It's the only explanation.

Maybe his body will never be found.

I hope he's burning in hell the way he deserves.

TWENTY-THREE

DETECTIVE WALTER DUNCAN

Sometimes as a cop, the best thing to do is walk away. Since Melanie Hardeman was never arrested before, never been in any kind of trouble, we let the confession about the gram go. We didn't see the drugs. We had no reason to search her purse, the bags of groceries, or her car. We came to ask her questions about Fanning, and she answered those.

End of story.

We've driven less than three blocks away from the woman's house when the coughing starts.

I try to get it under control, but the spasms won't stop. The pain shears through my body, twists inside me like barbed wire.

I can't catch my breath.

"Walt, you okay?"

I whip over to the curb, push the gearshift into Park, and shove open the door.

I'm on my hands and knees on the pavement when Liv reaches me.

"Can you breathe?"

I nod jerkily, dragging in a short breath before I start coughing again.

"Should I call 911?"

I grab her arm with one hand and shake my head. Tears and snot flow down my face as I try to regain control of my respiratory system.

The coughing gets nastier for half a minute. Son of a bitch, this is the worst one yet. I hack and hack and hack until I feel like my lungs will burst out through my throat.

Liv hovers next to me, her face cluttered with worry and fear.

Finally, things start to calm down to a mere wheeze. I sit back on my heels.

"Let me get you some water."

She dashes away. I fumble in my pocket for a handkerchief and swab at my face. My chest heaves, but the air just won't come in fast enough. My heart thuds wildly, trying hard to push enough oxygenated blood through my veins.

As the coughing spasms subside, the pain gets worse. Sharp, jagged shards of searing pain fire through me. Hell, maybe I'm having a heart attack. But this has happened before and passed. I'm hoping it will this time.

My hand shaking, I shove the handkerchief back into my pocket and dig for the small vial of pain pills I was given when we all thought I had cancer. I try to open it. Can't. The damned pharmacy put a childproof top on the damned thing. I've never had a childproof top before! Why start now? God dammit!

"Let me try." Liv takes the vial of pills from my hand and places the water bottle there in its place.

The top is already off the bottle of water, so I sip it slowly, let it soothe my raw throat. This is by far the worst coughing jag I've had. My whole body shakes.

Liv doesn't read the label on the vial. She simply opens it. "One or two?"

"Just one." I spit the words. I'm not even sure I should still be taking these with this new potential diagnosis.

"Open your mouth."

I don't argue. I comply. She pops the pill into my mouth, and I swallow. Follow with a swig of water. My eyes close in blessed hope. It takes a few minutes, maybe twenty, but relief will come.

"I'm taking you one of two places," she says firmly. "To your doctor's office or the ER. Which will it be?"

"Home." I grab my open vehicle door and pull myself up. My body trembles. "Please, Liv, don't argue with me."

Her face says she needs an explanation now. I shake my head. "I just need to get home. I'll tell you everything then."

"Can you drive?"

"Better not," I confess.

She doesn't attempt to lead me like a crippled old man. Instead she walks next to me all the way around the vehicle, opens the passenger side door, and waits for me to climb inside. Once I'm seated, she closes the door and returns to the driver's side.

While she climbs in and adjusts the seat, I shove the bottle of water into a cupholder in the console and fidget with my seat belt. I can breathe fairly easily now. The pain spike is leveling off, not gone by a long shot but not worsening.

Liv puts the Tahoe in Drive and rolls away from the curb. I sit in silence and wait for her questions. I didn't want to talk about this until the case was closed, but I'm confident there will be no escaping the coming interrogation.

"You want to talk about it now?" she asks.

"Nope."

"Okay."

She drives. I slump in the seat, waiting for the painkiller to kick in fully.

The car stops and I open my eyes to mere slits. They feel too heavy to open wider, and besides, pushing the issue might banish the fog I've drifted into.

"I'll be right back," she says.

Through the narrow slits, I watch Liv go to the front door, unlock it, and push it open. Sandy rushes out to greet her, then follows her back to my side of the Tahoe. I try to unfasten my seat belt, but my hands aren't working so well. Liv opens the door, steps up on the running board, and reaches across me to unfasten the damn thing.

"Take it slow," she says as she steps away.

Sandy dances from side to side. Even she looks worried about me. Probably remembering me bringing Stella home looking like this.

I practically fall out again, but this time Liv keeps me from hitting the ground. She leads me away from the door, shoves it closed with her hip, and then guides me to the house. Sandy sniffs at my right hand, where it dangles at my side. I scrub at her head and make soothing sounds.

Liv doesn't stop in the living room, she takes me straight through to my bedroom. She visited Stella there plenty of times.

I sit on the side of the bed, shoulders slumped forward, as she kneels before me and tugs off my boots.

"I can do that," I say, my tongue thick. Oh hell. I sound like a drunk.

"You just take it easy," she says as one boot pulls free. "I got this."

Once my boots are off, she peels away my jacket next. I hear the rattle of pills as she places the small vial on the table next to the bed. She removes my side arm and clip as well as my badge, places both next to the pain meds.

She urges me to lie back, then lifts my legs onto the bed. She covers me with the big old afghan at the foot of the bed. Stella made that afghan a million years ago. It has lain draped across the foot of our bed for as long as I can remember.

Stella. I wish she were here. I blink back the damn emotion. As long as she was well, of course. I wouldn't wish the other on her for anything.

I hear the water running in the bathroom that connects to our bedroom. Liv brings a glass of water and places it on the bedside table, then perches on the edge of the bed next to me. For a long time she just sits there, holding my hand. I close my eyes. Can't ignore the pull of the drugs.

"Tell me what's going on, Walt."

Her words nudge my eyes open a crack. I lick my lips.

"You want a drink of water?"

"Nah." I drag in a big breath, thankful my lungs and heart are working properly again. "At first we thought it was cancer. Like Stella."

Fear flashes in Liv's eyes. "But?"

"The thing in my lung turned out to be nothing. But the chest scan and the symptoms couldn't be dismissed. There's a good bit of blockage in the arteries." I tap my chest. "And the oncologist, after speaking with the cardiologist, thinks it's a heart issue."

"How bad?" Her face is lined with worry.

"Don't know for sure. I see the cardiologist next week. The oncologist says, based on what he sees, there's reason to believe medicine and lifestyle changes will make all the difference. I should live long and well." That might be a slight exaggeration.

Her soft fingers tighten on my hand. "Okay. I'm going with you to that cardiology appointment, and we're going to get whatever changes he recommends going."

I knew this was what she would say.

"If you insist."

She smiles a little. "I do."

"Just so you know"—I need to tell her this—"it was a wake-up call. I realized I needed to get my affairs in order. I've taken care of most everything. My final arrangements, the house. I just don't know what to do with Sandy if she's still around when I go. I want her in a good home."

"You don't need to worry about anything. I'll take her." Liv's fingers give mine another squeeze. "I'll take good care of her and love her just the same as you do. You have my word."

"Are you sure? Preston might not want a dog."

"Tough." She shrugs. "The truth is, I'm thinking about moving back to the farm. I think David and I need to slow things down."

I frown. "And the baby?"

She shrugs again. "I don't know. I haven't gotten to that yet."

"You'll figure it out." I reach up and tug at a wisp of hair that's fallen loose from her ponytail. "You're good people, Liv. Preston is . . . I think he might be okay, too. But take your time. Talk to him. Make sure. If he's the one, work it out. Don't hold back over things misunderstood or unsaid." I feel my lips grinning. "You both should work a little harder at solving the issues between you. I don't want you to be alone. It sucks. But I also don't want you to be with the wrong person. That sucks worse."

She laughs. "I can do that—work harder, I mean."

I sigh. Feeling utterly calm and relaxed now. Before I pass out entirely, we need to talk about work. "What do you think about these victims rallying together and coming up with this coup?"

Liv shakes her head. "I have to admit, I'm surprised. I wouldn't have expected any of them to have the guts, frankly."

"We've confirmed what's going on with all the players but three," I consider aloud. "Sanchez, Hyatt, and Reeves."

"Whatever has happened to Fanning," she says, "it may be one or all of those three. At least, it's looking that way." She lets go a big breath. "I haven't told you about my find last night."

I struggle to hold my eyes open. "I'm listening."

"My father was investigating Fanning or digging around in his past. It's far more than his visits to Fanning in prison."

I wait for her to go on. She won't look at me. I get it. Whatever she's discovered is confusing, maybe even disappointing.

"I found a file on each of Fanning's victims." Her brow furrows with mounting concern. "They were hidden in the panic room in the cabinet where he kept the personal files, like the deed to the farm and stuff like that." She swipes back a tear from one cheek. "I don't understand it. He never mentioned Fanning or anything about his victims."

"Are they case files? Was he treating any of them?" Seems like that's what she's saying, but I don't see how we got through all these interviews without one of them having mentioned seeing a shrink with the same name as the detective doing the questioning. Doesn't make a whole lot of sense.

"I don't think he was treating them—at least, not anyone but Sanchez. The files are more like background information taken from various sources. I don't understand why he would have wanted this information unless he gathered it for Sanchez or, worst case, for Fanning. That's the part that really worries me. I can't believe he would do that."

"You're worried he was working for Fanning?"

Another big breath heaves out of her weary body. "Yeah. I don't want to believe it, but there was obviously something going on that involved Fanning."

"But maybe not in the way you think," I counter. "Whatever Dr. Newhouse was doing, it wasn't to help a man like Fanning. We both know better than that. The only way he would have been working with a piece of shit like that was if the court ordered him to, and since he was retired, you know that can't be the case. At this point, we don't know what any of this means."

She nods, some of the worry disappearing. "You're right. It would just be nice to understand, the sooner the better."

"Sanchez will be back tomorrow. Maybe he can tell us what was going on. Maybe the BOLO will locate Hyatt and Reeves. I have a feeling this ends with those three." I squeeze her hand. "Go home. Get some rest. I'll be as good as new tomorrow. I promise."

"No way, partner. I'm staying until I know you're good for the night, then I'll get a cab back to my car."

I'd argue but Liv is as hardheaded as I am. "Fine. Then make yourself useful and feed Sandy."

Sandy barks as if she knows exactly what I said.

I watch her prance out of the room at Liv's side.

A frown nags at my forehead again.

This damned case is eating that girl alive. We need more answers. Soon.

TWENTY-FOUR

The Child

I have no idea how many months passed with me in a daze. I didn't care if I lived or died. I thought of my baby all the time. I begged him to tell me what he'd done with him, but he just laughed at me.

I made up my mind then and there that he would never hurt me again. I was no longer going to allow him to rule my world. I was old enough to begin to see that I didn't need him to survive anymore. I could take care of myself.

The way I saw it, the biggest drawback to my situation was the fact that I couldn't read. Couldn't write. Didn't understand math. I was illiterate. But he refused to teach me to read. No way was he going to teach me to write and to do math. I wasn't entirely sure he could do either of those things very well himself.

So I bided my time. There were always times when he disappeared for a few hours. I had no idea what he was doing since he refused to include me anymore. Since he had stopped rutting into me very often, I figured he might be out finding other girls to stick his nasty thing into. The idea made me jealous a little. I belonged to him. He was my family. Then I thought of the baby, and I knew all that I had believed was a lie.

He was not my family. I did not belong to him. I belonged to me. The baby was the only real family I would ever have, and he was gone.

The next time he went out for a while, I sneaked to a neighbor's house. She wasn't the old lady who helped get the baby out of me, she had moved away. This one was a younger woman. She worked a street corner. I had seen her a couple of times back when we used to pretend I was one of those girls to fool old men and get their money. But I didn't care what she was as long as she could read and write, that was all that mattered.

When I asked her to teach me to read, she laughed. She thought I was kidding. "You can't read? What the hell? You stupid or something?"

Angry tears burned my eyes, but I refused to cry. "No one ever taught me," I snarled. "I've never been to school."

The look on her face told me she suddenly felt bad about what she said. When she agreed to teach me, I made her promise never to tell him. We had to do it in secret. She seemed to like that part most of all. We agreed she would call me "girl" since I didn't know my name. I didn't want her to call me "it."

Learning was slow at first, and I started to think maybe I was stupid. But then the words began to click in my brain. The letters and the sounds they made when put together fused in my memory. Pretty soon I could read. I have never been so happy about anything in my life except for those few minutes when I held my baby.

Writing was harder, but I got it. My handwriting was really pathetic, but I could do it. When I had a good handle on the reading and the writing, she started with the basic math concepts: addition and subtraction. Then she made me memorize the multiplication table. She said her mother had made her do that when she was a kid. Once I knew the multiplication table by heart, she taught me about division.

One day she looked at me and said she'd never realized how much she'd taken for granted her whole life. She'd learned all this stuff as a little kid. Everyone she knew had learned it. To run into someone so young like me who hadn't had the opportunity, who couldn't read or write or do math in this day and time, was just weird, she said.

It was weird. I was weird.

I realized for the first time since I was seven years old that he was not my father or mother or family or friend. He became my whole world because I was his prisoner for all those years. I hadn't understood that profound fact because I never had a real family. I had no idea what one was supposed to be like. Think about when someone asks you to describe what chocolate tastes like or what closing your eyes and spinning around and around feels like, telling them should be easy, right? But if you've never tasted chocolate or never spun around, it's not so easy.

At that moment I realized that I might never know what it felt like to have a real family, but I was going to make sure I was smart and strong and that I could take care of myself. No one—especially not him—would ever hurt or control me again.

That was the day I stopped being his "it."

TWENTY-FIVE

DETECTIVE OLIVIA NEWHOUSE

A nightmare wakes me.

I sit straight up in the bed, struggle to gain my bearings. The darkness crushes me. I take a deep breath. Remind myself to breathe slow and deep. Thunder booms and a streak of lightning flashes, brightening the darkness for an instant. Rain beats against the roof. What the hell was I dreaming? Something about that child I read about in my father's file. I shudder.

David sleeps soundly next to me. The soft rumble of his snoring should be comforting, but it makes me shiver again, reminds me of the nightmare.

What the hell was the dream about, anyway? Beyond the girl in the file, I mean.

I can't remember the details, only snippets. Fear . . . running. She was lost, and then the dream was suddenly about me and I was in my father's arms. My father morphed into Walt.

Walt.

Jesus Christ. Walt has heart issues, too. He could die suddenly just like Dad.

Tears flood my eyes and rush down my cheeks. How can I lose him, too?

I push back the covers and climb out of the bed, careful not to wake David. Dinner was less awkward than I feared it would be. I rattled on about all the packing I had done at the farm. I promised to unpack the boxes I'd already brought to his house within the next few days. I assured him the news reports about my father were twisted and blown out of proportion. Mostly I lied with every breath, saying the things I knew he wanted to hear.

He smiled at all the right times. Said "great" and other reassuring comments as I spoke.

What I didn't do was tell him about the pregnancy . . . the baby.

I slip from the room and move more quickly along the hall, down the stairs, and into the kitchen. I need something to help me sleep. What I would give for a couple of beers. Can't go there. Can't have a sleeping pill. I have a few of those left over from when my father died. I think I even have a couple of Valium. Can't go there, either.

My heart still thuds in my chest. The snippets of images and sounds from the nightmare keep haunting me. I need to do something to work off all the adrenaline. Wear myself out so I can go back to sleep. Walt needs me to be strong, to take the lead if necessary. He may need some sort of surgery or rehab. I'm his partner. He's counting on me. I need to be at my best in the morning.

I pad into the entry hall and stare at the boxes. I guess unpacking a few things is as good a way as any to burn off stress. Or I could just go out and take a nice long run in the rain—except it's not just raining, it's storming. A boom crashes outside as if to confirm my assessment. I like storms but not running in them. I have no desire to test Mother Nature.

Unpacking it is.

I pick up the knife I left here the other night. A memory flashes—something sharp jabbing into my upper arm. Pain spears me. I frown and pull up the shirtsleeve on my left arm to have a look. Nothing. But then my skin on the underside seems to burn. I toss the knife aside, walk to the mirror above the hall table near the front door, and raise my arm so that I can see the back side of my upper arm—the part I can't see no matter how I twist my head around unless I have a mirror.

I stare at the small gash. It's healing. Looks days old. How the hell could I have done that and not remember? I should have felt it every time I took a shower. It's a miracle it didn't get infected. Damn. Memories of a cardboard flap slicing my arm, me rushing for something to staunch the flow, pour into my mind. I walk back to the stack of boxes and lift the flaps of the one I have opened. Sure enough, blood stains one of the corners. How in the world could I have done that and not remember? I don't even remember opening this damned box.

I shake off the suddenly very real idea that I'm losing my mind and force my attention to the task at hand. I pick up the knife and cut the tape over the flaps on another box. As I draw the flaps open, I think of the one file I didn't tell Walt about. I really should have told him.

But something about it scared the hell out of me. I can't quite label the feelings. Between that damned file and Walt's news, I came home a mess. Holding it together through dinner must have prompted the nightmare.

Last night, after I'd sifted through the files on Fanning's victims, I moved back to the one labeled "The Child." The patient was obviously female, and she was my father's patient. But the notes weren't like the usual office visit notes. These were more like notes made on visits to the patient in some sort of facility. Observations. Hypnosis therapy. Maybe the patient was in the hospital or a mental health facility.

I just need to know what my father was doing and why the files were separate from the rest of his patient files.

Unable to think about all the questions anymore, I pull a framed photograph from the box I've opened. My graduation from the police academy. I smile at the photo of my parents and me. It was the last time we were all together before my mother died. I slide my finger across the glass as if I can touch their smiling faces. It was a really happy day.

I think of my childhood growing up on the farm. I was so protected. Even as a teenager. My parents took such good care of me. Then I think of the child in that file and how horrible her childhood was.

My father's notes detailed the neglect she suffered at the hands of her biological parents. The mother overdosed when the girl was only seven. Things grew worse from there. The father was an addict and completely inept. When it became obvious he couldn't take care of himself, much less the child, he sold her to a man for money to buy drugs.

How could any father do such a thing?

But it happens, and as a cop, I know this better than most.

The truly bizarre part of the child's story was the shocking detail about to whom the father sold her: Carl Fanning. There is nothing in the case files about Fanning having a young girl with him at any time beyond his catch-and-release victims. I replay the interview with Andrea Donnelly in my head. She remembered thinking she saw Fanning drop off a girl at the theater. At the time, she had thought the girl was his daughter, which made her less afraid of him. The idea was dismissed since no other victim mentioned having seen anyone with Fanning.

Then again, he moved around the tri-county area like a gypsy, never straying too far from Nashville and never staying in one place too long. When questioning neighbors in the few places the original detectives investigating the case knew to look, they discovered very little cooperation. No one wanted to get involved. If they dared to talk about what a neighbor had been doing, perhaps his or her own secrets would be revealed. See no evil, hear no evil, speak no evil. People who live that kind of life have their own rules, and those rules rarely line up with the law. Fear is a powerful motivator.

Nothing in any case files related to Fanning suggest he kept a victim. My gut clenches at the memory of reading the depraved things he did to that poor girl.

There is no description of the child, only references to "she" and "her." At the time of my father's interviews, she appeared to be about fifteen. She wasn't sure of her actual birth date. She couldn't remember the names of her bio parents.

The final entry in the file states the child died.

It doesn't say when or where she died. I have no idea how my father even knew her or came to have her as a patient. Logic suggests that she was a patient at one of the mental health facilities around Nashville. But her file, as well as the others who were victims of Fanning, being among my father's personal files makes no sense.

How are those victims connected to my father? I'm certain it must be in relation to his work. But in what capacity?

A jab of pain spears so sharply and deeply into my brain that I grab the box to keep myself steady. The framed photograph from my graduation slips between my body and the boxes and bumps to the floor. Thankfully, no shattering of glass.

I take a breath, squeeze my eyes shut to ride out the wave of pain. What the hell is happening to me? How many headaches does this make in the past week? Half a dozen? Somehow I manage to pick up the photograph and place it back into the box.

The faces in the photo blur, and other images tumble one over the other through my mind. Me stumbling near the edge of the woods. The smell of freshly turned earth fills my nostrils, expands in my lungs. A mound near a copse of trees. A grave. Someone buried in the woods.

She is gone forever now, Liv. At peace. My father's voice whispers those words to me.

I think of my mother. But wait, we didn't bury my mother at the farm. I think of the prison guard and how he said that Fanning kept muttering the same thing over and over after the angry scene at the prison with my father.

. . . we all got bones buried somewhere.

The sound of a shovel sliding into soil cracks through my brain. The pain that follows brings me to my knees.

She's never coming back, Liv.

TWENTY-SIX

Sunday, May 6

Someone is screaming.

I feel myself drifting through the fog of sleep, rushing toward the sound. I need to wake up. He's calling my name. "Liv! Liv! What the hell happened?"

My eyes open.

Sunlight filters in through the plantation shutters. It's so bright. I close my eyes again.

"Liv!"

Hands grip my shoulders and shake me.

I open my eyes. David is staring at me, his expression clouded with fear, his eyes wide in uncertainty.

Walt. What if something has happened to Walt?

Air rushes into my lungs as if I have only now started to breathe. I sit up. "What happened?"

David blinks, stares at me as if I've lost my mind.

"What happened?" he echoes. "That's what I want to know." He waves a hand at the bed. "Where the hell did all that mud come from? I've been all around the house, and I can't figure out where this came from. Your shoes are on the side porch caked in mud. The floorboard in your Subaru is smeared with mud. Did this happen at a crime scene? What time did you leave the house?"

As the questions fire from his lips, my gaze travels down the length of me. He has pulled the covers back, and he's right, I am covered in mud from the waist down. My jeans are caked with it. My socks are muddy. I stare at my hands; they are muddy as well as bloody.

Blood? Shit. Where did the blood come from?

"Tell me what's going on, Liv? Please, baby. I can't help you if you don't talk to me. Something is very wrong."

I meet his gaze. "I was called to a crime scene. It was storming." I blink to hide the lie in my eyes. "A headache started on my way home. By the time I got here, I was out of my mind in pain. I must have come straight upstairs and climbed into the bed. I'm sorry." I look at the mess I've made. "I'll clean it up."

"No." He waves his hands back and forth. "Don't worry about that. The housekeeper will take care of it. It's you I'm worried about."

"Don't be ridiculous, David," I argue as I sit up. The room spins. "I'm fine."

He shakes his head. "Liv, you are not fine. You've had way too many headaches in the past few days. Something is very wrong," he repeats.

My heart sinks and my stomach lurches.

"I . . . I have to go to the bathroom." I stumble from the soiled linens and rush to the bathroom. There's nothing in my stomach to evacuate beyond the bitter bile that coats my throat and mouth on its way up and out. I sit on the Italian-tile floor, the cold leaching into my bones.

Finally, when I have heaved until I feel like my eyeballs will pop out of my head, the urge fades and I drag myself to the shower and turn on the water. Feeling like death, I peel off my filthy clothes and climb beneath the hot spray, allow the heat and pressure to cleanse my skin, to warm the muscles and bones beneath. My palms burn as if I've poured alcohol onto an open wound. I turn my hands up and stare. The skin is raw and red, and what looks like ruptured blisters seep blood.

The shovel. The words penetrate the cloud of disbelief still banked around my brain and images seep in. Digging. Rain pouring down on me. My hair plastered to my head. My hands burning as I kept driving the shovel into the ground.

A flash of lightning reveals the barn in the distance.

The farm. I was at the farm . . . digging?

Did I bury the files? Try to hide my father's connection to Fanning?

I shut off the water and grab a towel. As fast as I can, I scrub the high-end terry cloth over my skin and rush to the closet. Jeans, sweat shirt, socks, and sneakers. I run a comb through my hair. I should dry it, but I don't care. There's no time for that. I take my badge and service weapon from the bedside table. No phone. I glance around the floor. I check beneath the tousled covers. Nope. Dammit.

Taking the stairs as quickly as I dare, I try to think where my cell phone is. What about my wallet? I'm not big on purses, so when I'm on duty, I just carry a small credit-card-style wallet with my license and pertinent plastic. Anything else I need, I stick in my jacket pocket.

I would rather avoid the kitchen since David is probably in there and will want some sort of explanation, but my keys and fob aren't in the entry hall. They're likely in the kitchen, on the counter, since he said I left my muddy shoes on the side porch.

I push my wet hair from my face. Water from the ends seeps into the cotton of my sweatshirt.

"Coffee?" He lifts his cup as I enter the room.

"No time." I walk straight to the counter by the side door and reach for what I need to be on my way.

"You're just going to leave? Liv, you need to see a doctor. I am really worried about you."

I close my eyes and wish for a way to explain, but there is no way. I have no idea what's happening to me. How am I supposed to explain it to him?

"We'll talk when I get home," I promise the same way I've promised a dozen times before. Just this week I've made that promise several times.

He moves up behind me, and I shiver with the urge to run. He has no idea that I am falling apart—unraveling at the seams—and I don't know why. I only know that I have to go and find out what I was digging up last night. Or burying.

My mother is buried at Woodlawn in the same family plot as her parents and her brother, who died as a toddler. My father was buried next to her just a few months ago. There can't possibly be anyone buried at the farm.

"Are *we* okay, Liv? Maybe you just don't know how to tell me you don't want me anymore."

I turn to him, can't leave him feeling this way. "It isn't you, David." I stare up into his eyes and tell him as much of the truth as I can . . . as I understand. "Something is wrong with me. Something I can't comprehend. These headaches are coming with bizarre flashes of memory, and I don't know what any of it means. I have to figure this out before I can do anything else, do you understand?"

Maybe it was the sheer agony in my voice or the fear in my eyes, but he nods. "Is there anything I can do? I want to help."

I hug him tight for a moment, then I draw back. "Just let me do what I have to do. I promise I will explain everything when I know how."

He nods. "Okay. I'll be here waiting."

Then I do what I should have done minutes before. I walk out the door.

My cell phone and my wallet are in my car. The cell phone is dead, so I put it in the charging slot and drive away from the man who will thank me when this—whatever the hell it is—is over. No matter that I have no idea what any of this means, I understand with utter certainty that David is far better off without me.

The blisters on my palms burning, I grip the steering wheel more tightly and barrel out onto the street.

I drive like a bat out of hell. The sooner I get to the farm, the sooner I'll know what really happened last night.

Half an hour later, I park in front of the house. The door stands wide open.

My heart drums in my chest.

I swallow, wish I had some water.

I climb out of the car and walk toward the porch. My fingers curl around the butt of my weapon. Without making a sound, I climb the steps. The breeze whispers in my ears. I tune it out. Slowly I move across the porch and into the house. Total silence. Room by room, I go through the downstairs. All is clear, the safe room is just as I left it, with the dried vomit on the floor and files spread around like discarded life stories.

I check the library and that side of the house, then slowly climb the stairs. I go through the four rooms, including the one that was mine until recently. No one. Nothing.

The house is clear. I must have left the front door open.

Deep breath. I descend the stairs and walk back outside. The sun is warm and so bright, it hurts my eyes.

There's no mud on the porch, so I left the house open before I got muddy. Did I see something in the files that made me believe something was buried on the property? Other files my father wanted to hide? Information about Fanning?

Or was I the one doing the burying? It's possible that during some sort of crazy blackout, I decided I needed to protect my father from whatever I found. I may have buried evidence.

My body begins to shake and I feel sick to my stomach. My gaze rests on the barn. I start in that direction, but then I notice the shed door is standing open. Behind the house, there is the detached garage, and a few yards beyond that is a garden shed that belonged to my mother. It was her haven. Her gardening tools and fertilizers are still stored there.

Did I go in there? My heart thumps.

I walk toward the shed with the sensation that I am watching myself do this. It feels surreal. Not me. This can't be me. Can't be my life. The closer I get to the shed, the more certain I am that I cannot go inside.

No choice.

I rest my hand on the butt of my weapon, and I step inside. The interior is shaded from the sun; it's dark and cool inside. I reach up and pull the string. A single bare bulb flares to life overhead.

No mud. Nothing appears out of place. My gaze darts around the room. It's about fifteen by twenty feet, with a nice long worktable in the center. Shelves line three of the walls. Tools hang from pegboard along the fourth wall.

My gaze settles on a pale shadow on the pegboard. The place where a shovel once hung. My gut tightens.

Okay. There was a shovel. Apparently I did do some digging. My palms burn, reminding me that there was never really any question. I walk back outside and wander around the yard, widening my search for a chunk of mud or some muddy tracks. If I dug something up and then walked back to my car, based on the mud on my shoes and jeans, I had to have left a trail.

I see a blob of mud in the grass. Then another and another. I follow the random trail until the mud splotches become bigger, closer together. The path leads me to the tree line and then disappears into the thick undergrowth.

I have to look carefully to find the broken sprigs of greenery, the bent limbs of wild shrubs, but I locate the path I obviously took. As I wade through the brush, my clothes getting damp from the moisture clinging to the leaves, I see where larger limbs have been broken from bushes and small saplings. I couldn't have wreaked that much havoc just walking or running past. I inspect a fractured limb. This was broken off at my shoulder level. Why would I feel the need to tear off limbs and sprigs of shrubs?

I must have totally lost my mind.

Fear knots in my belly. I am, I decide, slipping over some edge that I cannot see.

About twenty yards into the woods, I find a small clearing. The missing shovel lies on a mound of dirt that has been exhumed from the center of the clearing. At the head of the open hole is a rusty metal cross that has obviously been here for some time. My knees threaten to give out on me.

The hole in the ground takes up most of the cleared space next to the mound of dirt. The shape is undeniably the proper size for burying a body.

I shake my head. This cannot be. But the cross—my gaze touches the rusty metal again. My heart thumps harder and harder and I can't breathe.

I stare into the hole, where the missing tree limbs and sprigs of brush line the bottom. My next breath is a struggle. "Just get it over with," I mutter.

Holding on to a sapling, I ease down into the waist-deep pit. Whatever else happens, I have to know what I put in this fucking hole . . . or whatever was already here. I reach for the limbs, toss the first one and then another out of the way.

I remove another handful, and there, on the ground in front of me, are bones. A skeleton. Terror lights in my chest. It appears to have been wrapped in a pink blanket. The band of slick pink nylon that served as a border is all that remains of the covering. The rest has decomposed and vanished into the earth. But the bones are there. Splattered mud is stark against the white shape that lies almost fully intact like the skeletons you see hanging in a science classroom.

I blink, take a step back. My backside hits the ground behind me as I stare at the bones. *No.* No. No. This can't be.

Not an animal. Human bones. Bones that have been buried for a very long time.

Horror burns through my veins. *I know these bones.*

Noooo reverberates around me like the wind, buffeting my being. I jerk my head up to see where the soul-shattering sound is coming from, and it is only then that I realize the screams are coming from me. I scramble out of the pit, my head spinning.

The next thing I know, I'm running . . . running toward the house. I rush inside, fly up the stairs, mud on my shoes causing me to slip. I scramble onward, toward my room. I need to be in my room—the one where I slept my whole life. The place where my history is documented from birth until just before my father died when he hung a photo of the two of us above the lamp on the bedside table.

I remember that day as clearly as if it were yesterday.

What is happening to me?

I stare at the photo, our smiling faces. This is who I am. Whatever is wrong with me, isn't about that . . . can't be about my family. I close the door, sag against it to catch my breath. When my body stops trembling, I look at the wooden doorframe to my left and the tick marks my parents posted there each time they measured my height from the time I was old enough to stand on my own. Happy laughter echoes in my head. My mother and I twirling around the room.

This is my room . . . my space. My history. My life.

I go to the bookcase above the desk where I did homework as a kid. I grab a photo album and stare at the pictures of my parents and me. My muddy fingers flip through the pages. I stare at photo after photo. It's all there. All the memories in my head are right here on these pages.

The pain shears through my head, and I stagger, close my eyes.

Not again.

The stabbing pain intensifies. I squeeze my eyes shut more tightly. Drop the photo album and stumble to my bed. I curl up on the soft, familiar comforter and pull a pillow over my head.

If I'm very, very still . . . keep my eyes closed tight . . . maybe it will pass.

TWENTY-SEVEN

The Child

"There he is."

He was practically slobbering at the mouth like a wild dog as he watched the small boy. Skinny kid, maybe nine or ten years old. Mexican, or something like that. He was kicking a ball down the sidewalk. No one else around. I figured he must have been on his way home from a friend's. Most kids had friends.

But not me.

"What do you want him for?" I asked, an uncertainty growing inside me.

I couldn't keep the resentment out of my voice. I tried. I really did. It wasn't that I gave one shit about this bastard anymore, but I guess it was about survival. This boy—this new kid—was the person who would take my place.

The bastard behind the wheel no longer wanted me. I could tell. And I was glad, sort of. I had made up my mind that he would not hurt me again. I was leaving the first chance I got. But now he wanted someone new to rut. Someone to use to make himself feel good and powerful.

He wanted this boy. A boy, I knew, couldn't get pregnant. A boy wouldn't have the blood—the girl teaching me to read called it "the rag." Having a boy would be a lot easier.

I shouldn't have cared.

But somehow I did.

"I want you to go talk to him."

I stared at him as if he had lost his mind. He'd made me play lookout plenty of times when he picked up kids, but not in a long time. Not since that one girl asked if I was his daughter. "Why do I have to talk to him?"

"Talk him into going into that house over there," he explained. "Tell him you dropped your cell phone and your arm is too fat to reach through the crack and get it. Tell him you'll pay him." He dug a five-dollar bill out of his pocket.

I stared at the money. "I can't do that."

He backhanded me, knocked me against the window. "Do it now before he's gone, or I'll make you wish you had!"

My face stinging almost as much as my pride, I scrubbed away a telltale tear. "Whatever."

I got out of the car, closed my door quietly, and then went around the bumper. Since the front door of the old house was standing open, getting in wouldn't be a problem. I hurried up the sidewalk until I was even with the house, then I shouted at the kid.

He stopped, his red-and-blue ball held tightly in his hands. He stared at me, his face full of uncertainty.

"I don't mean to bother you." I smiled real big as I hustled across the street toward him. "Can you help me a minute?"

The boy glanced around as if looking for someone to ask if it was okay to talk to me.

"Don't be afraid. I just need someone with skinnier arms to help me get my cell phone." I pointed to the house. "I've been staying in there because I have no place else to go, and my phone fell into a crack in the floor and my arm is too big to reach it. Can you get it for me?" I pulled the money out of my pocket. "I'll pay you."

He glanced at the five-dollar bill and then nodded. "Okay."

It was so easy. The stupid kid did exactly what I told him, except when we got in the house, *he* was waiting. He pressed the cloth in his hand over the boy's mouth, and the kid passed out. He told me to watch him while he got the car.

As I waited, I stared at the boy, who looked even smaller lying on the floor. "Sorry," I muttered.

We took him to our place. He cried and cried and cried. I watched the way the man, who had been my only family all this time, touched this boy. I knew he wouldn't wait long to rut him. But he was holding off for some reason. Probably prolonging the foreplay or something. The girl who was teaching me to read said some guys liked that part better than the fucking—that's what she called the rutting.

Finally, when the boy just kept whining, he got mad. He told me to watch him and that he'd be right back. I think he was going to get some liquor. I remembered he did that to me. Had me drink it so I wouldn't whine so much. He was probably going to do that to the boy.

I sat stone-still on the tattered old chair and watched him huddled in the corner, his hands and feet bound, the gag in his mouth. I remembered being tied up just like that before he started putting me in the trunk and then the box. It wasn't this place. It was somewhere else. But he had done the same thing to me. Tonight, after he got enough liquor in the boy, he would fuck him.

I would be forced to listen . . . to remember.

Then the boy would look at me with those big brown eyes, and he would blame me because I was the one who trapped him.

No.

I was not going to be a prisoner any longer, and I was not going to be the reason this boy lived the kind of life I had lived.

Hell no.

I was suddenly so angry and yet I was terrified. How would I do this? Thinking it was one thing, but where would I go? Could I really take care of myself?

I thought of my new friend, and I realized I could haunt a street corner just like her. I could survive the same way she did.

I went over to the boy. He drew away as if he feared I would hurt him.

"I'm sorry I helped him catch you."

He sobbed, snot running down his skinny face.

"I'm going to help you, but you have to promise me something first."

He stared into my eyes, the sobs fading to a hiccup.

"When he comes back, I'm going to knock him out and then cut you loose. You'll have to run for help. Tell the police what he did to you so they'll arrest him. But you can't tell them about me. Promise?"

His head bobbed up and down like one of those crazy street beggars on crack.

"Okay. But if you break that promise, I will come back in the middle of the night and . . ."

He shook his head fast.

"We have a deal, then. You just sit right there and be quiet. When he gets here, you start your whining again. I'll be ready."

I didn't have much. Two pairs of jeans. The shoes I wore. A second pair of socks and panties and one other T-shirt. I packed all of it into a plastic bag from the supermarket. Then I remembered my teddy bear. It was the one thing I'd had for as long as I could remember, so I put it with the bag. I hid them behind the ragged couch.

In the kitchen, there was no knife. He never left stuff like that lying around. But in the very back under the sink, there was one of those big old forks—the kind people used for barbecuing. I guess the people who lived there before us had a grill. I took the big fork and tucked it between the cushion and the sofa arm, and sat down to wait.

Half an hour passed with me and the kid just sitting there, waiting for him to return. I was pretty sure the kid had shit himself, since I smelled something bad. I couldn't risk helping him clean up because I needed to be in position for when the monster returned.

Finally, he unlocked the front door and came in, a paper sack in his arms. "Got you something, too," he announced, grinning at me. He pulled out a bottle of Coke and a bag of chips. "I thought you might want to go next door and watch TV."

We often heard the girl next door's television playing. He didn't know that I watched it sometimes when I went over there for my lessons.

"Okay," I said.

He put the bag down on the sofa next to me. "Me and the boy are going to bed now. He's tired." He slid the half pint of liquor into his back pocket and turned toward the boy. "Smells like you need a bath."

I watched for a moment, the racket the kid was making growing as he sobbed louder and louder. The piece of shit bent to touch him, and that's when I moved. My fingers curled around the handle of the big fork, and I rammed it into him as hard as I could.

He screamed, jerked away from me.

The fork still grasped in both hands, I jumped back as he twisted around. His eyes were big and round, and he was staring at me as if he intended to kill me.

He dove at me. I thrust the fork forward, ramming it into his gut this time. He just stood there staring at me. I pushed harder, driving the fork as deep as I could.

He crumpled to the floor, but he started to rant at me. Screaming that he was going to kill me. I had to do something!

I grabbed the old ceramic lamp from the table. Jerked its cord free of the wall and crashed it as hard as I could over his head.

He collapsed onto his back and stopped moving . . . stopped making sounds.

My heart was in my throat. I crouched next to him and reached into his pocket in search of the knife he carried. I knew he had one. I had seen it before. I dug until I found it. My hands shaking, I ran to the boy and cut him loose. I pulled the balled-up sock out of his mouth.

Before he could take off, I grabbed him by the hand and pulled him toward the monster on the floor. His feet dragged and he cried as if he feared I was going to back out on our deal.

"Shut up," I snarled. I reached down and pulled the fork out of the bastard's gut. Blood dripped from its two points. He still didn't move. He might have been dead.

I didn't care. I hoped he was.

"Take this," I ordered. The boy took hold of the bloody fork with both hands, the same way I had held it when I stabbed the bastard. "Go outside and start screaming. Throw this on the sidewalk so people see it and know something bad happened in here. Then run down the street screaming for help. Don't stop until someone calls the police. They have to call the police. Do you understand?"

He nodded frantically.

"If the police don't come, he'll get away and find you again. You have to tell them what he did to you and that you stabbed him to get away. Understand?"

He nodded again, big tears rolling down his cheeks.

"You can't tell them about me, remember?"

Another bob of his head.

I got my bag and my teddy bear from behind the couch. "Go!"

I watched for a moment as he ran out the door. He threw the big fork onto the sidewalk just like I told him and started to scream for help.

I dared to breathe, and then I turned to go.

Harsh fingers wrapped around my ankle.

My heart stuttered to a near stop. I fell face forward. My bag and teddy bear flew from my hands.

"You fucking bitch!"

I twisted around and kicked him in the face with my free foot. He howled and his fingers released me. I grabbed my shit and ran.

That was the last time I saw the monster that stole my life . . . until one week ago.

TWENTY-EIGHT

DETECTIVE WALTER DUNCAN

Liv isn't returning my calls. I'm worried as hell.

I tell myself she might be sleeping in, but my gut says something isn't right.

Thankfully, I feel way better this morning. That run to catch Melanie Hardeman messed me up but good.

I smile as I think of how Liv took care of me.

"She's a good one," I say aloud. Truth be told, sometimes I still talk to Stella. It makes me feel less lonely when I'm alone at the house like this.

Mario Sanchez arrived home at eight this morning. He and his buddies drove through the night to be home in time to rest and prepare for a birthday party this afternoon. One of his pals is turning thirty. He called and said I could come to his house whenever I'm ready.

Just as I'm loading up to head that way, my cell vibrates with an incoming call from dispatch.

"Duncan."

"Detective, this is Officer Rajas. There are six people waiting here at headquarters to see you. Reeves and Hyatt—the two in the BOLOs are among them. I've sequestered all six to the conference room."

"Keep someone watching them," I urge, my heart rate picking up. "I'm on my way."

I'll text Liv as soon as I get to headquarters and park. No time for texting now. I need to focus on driving.

Fifteen minutes later, I'm striding through the entrance and headed for the conference room. Patricia Shelby's husband, new baby in his arms, sits in the lobby. I don't slow. No time. At the conference room door, I give the officer standing by, Officer Loudon, a nod of dismissal and enter the room. I close the door behind me and look over the assembled group.

The six study me, their faces clouded with fear and exhaustion. None look as if they've slept in days.

I settle at the head of the table and say, "Who wants to start?"

Janie Hyatt raises her hand. "I guess I started this, so I should finish it."

Interesting way to put it. "All right. I'm listening." They can write their statements later. I figure it's better if I hear what they have to say before we do anything official.

"When I learned Fanning would be released on probation rather than serving the last five years of his sentence, I had to do something. I could not let him go free." She sends a pointed look around the table and then at me. "Pedophiles don't change. They can't. There is no rehabilitation. They're either carrying out their sick desires or they're dead. There is no in-between."

I say nothing. My opinion is the same.

"We—the seven of us—got together and decided to take care of him."

"Number seven being?" I ask rather than dive into the admission of planning a murder.

"Mario Sanchez."

I nod for her to go on, but then I hold up a hand. "First, I need to advise you all of your rights." When several start to argue, I interrupt, "It's the law."

I recite their rights and then motion for Hyatt to continue.

"I believe Melanie has already told you how we decided who would do what."

"She did." Anticipation and a weird kind of dread is thumping inside me. I'm having trouble feeling good about all this.

"Dana and I decided to take the final step. This was our plan, and we didn't want to put that monkey on anyone else's back. So it wasn't one of the steps that could be drawn by the others."

I suspect she means they didn't trust anyone else to do the job.

"What part did Sanchez draw?"

Hyatt and Reeves share a look before Hyatt explains. "He was supposed to help us, but then he backed out. Said he couldn't do it."

All this time, Liv and I have wondered about Sanchez. Seems he bowed out. Understandable, I guess, since he and his wife have a baby on the way. Or maybe he has another reason I don't know about yet. Like his own plan.

"We picked Fanning up," Hyatt says, "when he came home from work one night and drove him to the cabin. The one you and your partner visited."

So they had cameras.

"Trail cams," she confirms before I can ask.

"Was Fanning in the barn when you set it on fire?" I ask. No need to beat around the bush.

"He was. Our mistake was in leaving before it burned to the ground. There was no wind. It had rained like hell the night before. We weren't worried about the fire reaching the cabin or the woods. But we didn't go far. When we returned a little while later, the fire was basically nothing but smoldering embers. We hoped and prayed that meant the job was done. The ash was too hot to dig through looking for whatever was left of him, but the answer was obvious. My old blue truck—the one I kept at the cabin—was gone."

"We've stayed hidden since then," Reeves says. "We couldn't be sure what he would do. But after what happened to Patricia, and then when Melanie told us about her coming clean, we decided it was time to end the charade." She draws in a big breath before she goes on. "We would have killed him—we tried. But we failed, and we have no idea where he is now." Hyatt puts an arm around her and pulls her close.

That certainly explains a lot. No matter that both Shelby and Hardeman have spoken about this plan, it's damned mind-blowing to hear it in detail—particularly recounted in such a calm manner. "Can you tell me if he was injured in any way? Before the fire."

Apparently he was capable of driving.

"There was a big gash in his left arm, but he had that before we picked him up. I have no idea how he injured himself."

That likely explains the blood in his house. I scrub a hand over my face. "This is . . ." I'm not exactly sure what to say. In all my years as a detective, I have to admit I have never heard a story quite like this one. Damn.

"I appreciate you all coming forward." My thoughts are racing. I need to find Liv and fill her in. More importantly, we need to find that bastard. I hope to hell he drove off and died somewhere. The trouble is, nothing has come back on the BOLO for the truck. He could be any-fucking-where.

I clear away all the other thoughts and force myself to focus on the moment. "I need you all to write your statements and then sign them. I'll have an officer standing by to provide any assistance you may require. You can leave once that's done." I get to my feet. I have to get out of here and find Liv.

"Is that it?" Hyatt asks.

I survey the frazzled-looking group. "For now."

I locate Officer Loudon, who was watching the door when I arrived. "Make sure they all write their statements and sign them before they leave. Put the statements on my desk."

"Will do." Loudon gives me a confirming nod.

"And close out those BOLOs I issued for Hyatt and Reeves and their vehicles—except the one for the old Ford truck."

"Yes, sir."

Sanchez is expecting me. I need to hear his side of this. Not to mention I'd like to know his reason for dropping out of the plan. A part of me still thinks there is more to him than I know. Something about his escape all those years ago that is not in the case file.

Sanchez is waiting at the front door of his home when I arrive. I apologize for running late. He shows me to his private study. To be so young, he's earned a surprising number of awards from the firm where he works. Most of Fanning's victims have done fairly well for themselves despite the horror of their childhoods.

"So," Sanchez says once we are seated around his desk, "how can I help you with this investigation? I'm assuming since you're here that you haven't found Fanning."

I shake my head. "Not yet. You're the last of his victims we have to interview. In fact, I'm running behind because the other six showed up at headquarters to confess the plan they attempted to carry out. Sounds like you dropped out."

Sanchez nods. "I wanted to be a part of it, but I couldn't. I couldn't risk my responsibilities." He shrugs. "My friends and I had this excursion to Mexico planned already." He shakes his head. "Their plan just wasn't the right thing to do. I decided to leave justice to you."

Smart man.

He smiles then, though the expression is a sad one. "You thought I had something to do with his disappearance."

I shrug. "We considered the possibility the same as we did for the others. Taking him to Mexico and burying him seemed like an interesting option."

Sanchez laughs. "I can't say that I wouldn't have enjoyed doing just that, but no, we didn't. I haven't seen or heard from that bastard since the trial. If the world is lucky, no one will ever hear from him again."

Sanchez's wife appears with two glasses of iced tea. Her rounded belly makes me think of Liv. I hope she can work things out for the best. Whatever that might be.

"Was there anything else, Detective Duncan?" Sanchez meets my gaze again. "I get the feeling there's something more you want to ask me."

I smile. Perceptive guy. "You know, I've read over your statements repeatedly. The ones you made when you were ten years old and then your testimony at the trial. You told your story carefully, ensuring all bases were covered, but it feels like you left something out."

His eyebrows rear up. "Really. My lawyer and the district attorney seemed to think my testimony was powerful. You know, unimpeachable."

"That's true. Maybe it's just me." I look him directly in the eyes. The truth is, after Liv and I learned what the other victims were up to, I began to wonder about Sanchez all the more. Mostly because something about his original story just didn't sit right with me. "I feel like there's something else you need to tell me." I shrug. "I don't know. Maybe it's the fact that you were a skinny ten-year-old. Little for your age. And you bested a forty-something-year-old guy who was experienced in handling kids—each one of them larger than you. You not only bested him, you left him in bad shape. How did you manage to do that?"

He stares at me, unmoving, his face suddenly clear of emotion. "You read the court transcripts. The statements I made to the police. You should know the answer."

I shake my head. I am just not buying it. "You had help, didn't you?" I'm on one hell of a fishing expedition, and I'm just hoping he'll take the bait. My gut, every instinct I've got, tells me he had assistance escaping that bastard.

"Maybe I got lucky." He turns his hands up. "Maybe Fanning had a bad day. Who knows?"

"What was your relationship with Dr. Lewis Newhouse?"

His expression closes. "Detective, I think—"

"Whatever secret you're keeping, Mr. Sanchez," I cut him off, can't let him take that path, "you're not helping anyone. I need you to be straight with me. Lives depend on what happens next."

He smirks. "You mean Fanning's life?"

Anger flares. I let him see it. "Not just his. There are others who are hanging by their fingernails here. I need your help. Now. And you're wasting my time. If that bastard isn't caught, then he'll just do the same thing to some other kid that he did to you and all the others."

Silence swells between us for a moment. I see the change in his face when the tide of his emotions shifts in my direction.

"I've never told anyone this," he confesses. "She asked me not to tell and I didn't. I owed her my life, and I wasn't about to let her down. Do you understand the position I was in as a child? She literally saved my life."

"Who?" My heart is racing. "I need a name."

He shakes his head. "I have no idea. I never knew her name. When Fanning took me, he didn't just take me to some parking lot or run-down building to rape me. He took me home. He was going to keep me. He said as much."

That part is news as well. No other victim that we know of was kept. "Go on."

"He already had another kid, a girl he'd been keeping. I don't know for how long. But she was older than me. I think maybe he was done with her and wanted someone younger. She must have sensed this and decided we both needed rescuing. She is the one who put him down so we could escape. She made me promise never to tell anyone about her. I think she was afraid the police would blame her for what he'd done."

I can scarcely sit still. God dammit, I need more than that. "He never called her by name?"

Sanchez shook his head. "He called her 'it.' She had this old, ragged teddy bear." He shudders visibly. "She was pale and thin and her clothes were tattered and dirty. It was horrible. But she saved my life, and I made a promise to keep her secret."

"I understand." I make a decision quickly. "You have my word that I will keep this between the two of us, but I need more information. If I have a sketch artist come—now—do you think you could describe her in detail?"

He smiles, his dark eyes bright with emotion. "I will never forget what she looked like. She was my superhero, always will be. You don't need to call anyone. I've drawn pictures of her my whole life."

Anticipation has me stretching over his desk as he digs through a drawer. He pulls out a sketch pad and flips it open to a page.

"This is the last one I did. I was thinking of her when Fanning was released last month."

I stare at the young girl's face. She looks vaguely familiar. I mentally run down the list of Fanning's known victims. She doesn't look like any of them. "Can I keep this for a while?"

He nods. "If it will help, yes."

I meet his gaze and consider for a long moment if I really want to know the answer to my next question. "This is important. I need a straight answer. How did you know Dr. Newhouse?"

He lets out a long, low breath. "Just before the trial, he talked to me after school one day. I thought he was just another of the doctors the police insisted I see, but he said no. He came to speak to me about something different." Sanchez stares at his hands for a moment. "He told me if I stuck with my story and never told anyone about the girl that he would pay for me to go to college anywhere I wanted to go." He laughs. "I thought he was bullshitting me, but he wasn't. Even before I graduated high school, he had already made all the financial arrangements. Even sent a letter of recommendation for me. He did exactly what he said he would do. The funny thing is, he didn't have to. I would never have told anyone about her anyway. I made a promise and I intended to keep it."

"How did Dr. Newhouse know about her?" Every cell in my body is on alert. "You said you never told anyone."

"I have no idea. I never told another living soul until just now."

The realization hits me then, shakes me to the very core of my being. I draw in a hard breath. Swallow back the denial burgeoning in my throat. "Did Newhouse mention why he wanted to protect this girl? Was she a patient of his?"

Sanchez shakes his head. "He did not. Looking back, I guess that's the only reasonable explanation. She had to be a patient of his. I learned later that Newhouse was a major donor to a number of organizations that help children who are victims of abuse. I guess maybe it was personal some-how for him."

"You never heard from him again?" My pulse is tripping. I can't find my footing with the theory swelling in my brain.

Sanchez looks away for a moment before he answers. "I hadn't heard from him in all those years until he contacted me back in January. He said we needed to talk about a couple of things. First, he warned me that Fanning's release date was coming up and that I should be aware, watchful. Dr. Newhouse feared the bastard would try to seek revenge. But I figured Fanning was just a sad old man incapable of hurting anyone anymore. Just in case, I had a new security system installed at my house and sent my wife to her mother's in Memphis while I was gone to Mexico."

Whatever else Fanning said to Newhouse, this confirms the doc had reason to suspect the bastard might reach out to some of his victims. "What was the other thing he wanted to talk to you about?"

His gaze searched mine for a long moment. "He wanted to make sure our deal remained in effect. He said he'd heard I was having a kid. He insisted on setting up a college fund for my unborn child." New tears bloom in his eyes. "I know Dr. Newhouse is dead, but I feel like I am betraying him now. He was good to me. I kept my promise to her and to him until this moment. Do you see why we can never tell anyone?"

I nod. "I think I do." I push my weary body from the chair, stare at the drawing once more. "I'll get this back to you, Mr. Sanchez."

I say goodbye to his wife and walk out of the house. All that he told me—the face he has drawn—whirl in my head. As I reach my Tahoe, my cell vibrates against my side. I climb behind the wheel as I answer it. I hope it's Liv and that she had a better night last night. I called her before I came to meet with Sanchez, but her cell went straight to voicemail. I need to see her. To talk to her . . . this idea expanding in my mind can't be right.

Can't be. Can't be.

"Hey, Detective, it's Reynolds."

It might be Sunday, but cops don't have the luxury of being off duty just because it's the Lord's Sabbath.

"Hey, Reynolds. You get that other report?"

I start the engine but don't move. We've been waiting on the DNA results on the second blood type found in Fanning's house. I'm assuming that's why Reynolds has called. I'm praying it will take this damn theory nagging at me in a whole different direction.

I need it to go a different way.

"Sure did, and you are not going to believe what the lab report says. I'm thinking they got this one mixed up with that case a couple years back when all those cops got injured by that strung-out perp. You might not remember, but we had to separate out all the blood types, perform DNA tests, it was a real mess."

My heart sinks.

"Anyway," Reynolds goes on, "I'm standing here staring at the lab report on that second blood type from your crime scene, and I'm certain this can't be right. There has to be a mix-up. Some kind of wacky mistake."

But I know there's no mistake.

TWENTY-NINE

DETECTIVE OLIVIA NEWHOUSE

I woke in my childhood room. The pain is gone, but I am left unsettled.

For a long moment I stand in the kitchen with my untouched coffee and ponder all that I have found in this house. The most troubling is the file labeled "The Child." There were videos as well as the reports. I haven't looked at those yet. I haven't called David or Walt.

I set my mug aside and head back to the panic room. I sit down on the floor and pick up the file. Just skimming the pages, I am sickened by the words there. I look at the storage devices that are labeled with interviews and assessments. I pick up all of this and go to my father's office.

When all is spread out on his desk, I sit in his chair. I'm not sure watching these videos has anything to do with how we can find Fanning, but I feel as if I need to watch them.

"Just do it," I mutter. Walt will be calling to tell me it's time to go to the meeting with Sanchez. David will wonder what I'm doing. The chief will be pressing me about my father's involvement with the case. I need to get this done. I pick up the first of the memory sticks and reach to poke it into a slot.

My fingers fumble and I frown. Why won't it go in? Since his desk sits against the wall, I have to turn the monitor around to see the back side. There's already a memory stick in the port. It's not seated firmly, which is why it wasn't showing up on his desktop, I guess. Curious, I seat it more firmly, then turn the monitor around and check the display.

The icon for the storage device pops up on the screen, and I click it. The only item stored there is a video labeled "For Olivia."

My heart jumps and I double-click the file.

The file opens, and I'm looking at my father seated at this very desk.

"Olivia, I decided to make this video when I learned of Carl Fanning's impending release." He looks away, his eyes glistening.

My hands cover my mouth and I want to cry. My heart hurts just hearing his voice.

"If you're seeing this, then something has happened to me. I did not want the truth to die with me, but after your mother passed, I could never find the proper way to tell you the things you needed to know." He falls silent for a moment. "Above all else, please know how very, very much we love you. You were and are our everything. What we did was wrong in the eyes of the law, but it was the right thing to do. For you and for us. I hope you can forgive me for not telling you the truth long ago. Read the file marked 'The Child' and watch the video sessions. Then you'll know everything. I love you, Olivia."

Tears are streaming down my face. I stare down at the file spread on his desk and start to read again.

Later, I've lost track of time and my head is spinning. Part of me wants to scream and rant that these are lies. All of it. But I know it isn't. It's the truth, and some part of me recognizes this.

I stand and trudge up the stairs to my bedroom. With all that I have read and watched in "The Child" file, I have lost a part of me that I will never get back. I am confused and horrified and deeply grateful at the same time.

I have cried until I am certain there are no more tears inside me. Within the pages of the file and in those video sessions, the truth about me and who I am is crystal clear. My lips tremble, and no matter that I thought I had cried it all out, more tears brim in my eyes.

Even as I devoured the horrifying words and watched the shocking interviews, the memories of my real life tumbled one over the other into my brain. It was as if some wall fractured and then broke, allowing a past I had forgotten to burst free.

In my room, I reach down and pick up the photo album I tossed aside before. There, on every page, are my memories. Each recollection of my life burned into my brain came from these photos . . . from the stories my parents told me. From the pieces implanted using hypnosis and neuro programming.

But none of it ever happened to me before the age of fifteen.

A halting breath shudders through my chest as I lay the album aside, get to my feet, and do what I know I must.

I walk out of the house. I stare toward the big barn that once housed beautiful horses. Dr. Lewis Newhouse told me about all the graceful creatures that once grazed in the pastures surrounding his home. His wife, Corrine, was an internationally famous equestrian in American dressage. Once upon a time, her trophies lined the walls of their home. But it was their child, their beautiful, sweet daughter, they hoped to groom for Olympic competition. There was never a horseback-riding injury. I have never ridden a horse. I am not that child.

I draw in a heavy breath and consider all that I learned from that file. It's almost like some sort of science fiction movie or maybe some twisted fairy tale.

There once was a child named Olivia Newhouse. Her parents protected her so carefully from the ugliness of the world that her prestigious and lettered father experienced in his work every day. She had private tutors, never once attended school outside her home. Everywhere Olivia went, her mother or a cautiously chosen and carefully vetted nanny was sure to go. And still the child, at the tender young age of eleven, encountered her first taste of drugs. For the next two years, she sneaked behind her loving parents' backs and found a way to fulfill this new need that pulsated relentlessly inside her.

But then her parents discovered her dark secret and the real trouble began. The child was put under house arrest, not allowed to see or to communicate with anyone. One night she decided she no longer wanted to live that way, so she swallowed a whole bottle of her mother's secret stash of sleeping pills.

When she was found, unresponsive and barely breathing, she was rushed to the hospital. But the damage was done. Her heart continued to beat with assistance, but her brain was already dead. In time, Dr. and Mrs. Newhouse took their beloved brain-dead child home and made her as comfortable as possible. No matter that a machine was required to keep her breathing and that Dr. Newhouse was well versed in the science of what had occurred, they hoped and prayed that the specialists were wrong and that one day she would open her beautiful blue eyes and come back to them.

But she never did.

Each day for two long years, Corrine drew more deeply into herself. The beautiful horses were neglected and eventually sold. Dr. Newhouse gave up his practice. They sat in the quiet house day in and day out, listening to the wheeze of the machine keeping their daughter alive and waiting for a miracle that was not going to come.

Dr. Newhouse decided he had to do something or he would lose his precious Corrine as well. He thought of all the young girls who lived on the streets of the city. The ones whose parents had forsaken them . . . the ones whom society had let down. He began searching the streets until he found exactly the girl he was looking for. A girl with the blond hair and blue eyes of his precious daughter. A girl the right height, who could, with the proper grooming and education, become his sweet daughter and fulfill the life she had been destined to live. But this child had been damaged by another man—a monster—and it took time for Dr. Newhouse to convince her to trust him. Finally, she did.

She climbed into his car and allowed him to take her to the farm he had told her all about . . . to the woman waiting to be her new mother.

That was the day I, the Child who once belonged to a monster, became Olivia Newhouse.

My new father took the "it" Carl Fanning had created and polished her into the perfect daughter.

I stare toward the woods and the grave I opened last night. I know now that the real Olivia Newhouse was buried there once the machine keeping her body alive was turned off. My new father waited until my transition was complete, then he told me that it was time for the child in the bed to have peace. I remember thinking she was like Sleeping Beauty except no prince was coming to wake her. Her brain was dead and no force on this earth could bring her back.

But she could be replaced, and that is what the Newhouses did.

Of course, by then, I didn't remember my former life. During those long months of grooming and educating, I didn't understand that I was being reprogrammed. Though my father meant well and certainly saved me from a life on the streets and perhaps a horrible death, what he did was ultimately brainwashing. Using hypnosis and other techniques, he slowly replaced my bad memories with good ones—with Olivia's memories.

I swipe at my damp cheeks again and shake my head. Basically I can tell you everything about her and her parents. About this place and the lives they lived here. The vacations they took . . . everything.

But I do not know my real name. I don't remember my biological parents.

Until one month ago, I didn't recall the name Carl Fanning. I saw his face on the news during his highly publicized release from prison, but the name and image of the man barely registered in my brain. My beloved father did a very good job of scrubbing him from my memory.

I now recognize that approximately one week ago, just before Walt and I landed the Fanning case, my subconscious started trying to recreate those awful memories in an effort to prompt me to protect myself. I had no idea I was being watched by pure evil. But my most basic instincts sensed that danger hovered close by. Fanning was watching me. I saw him more than once, but he had disguised himself, and the recognition didn't click in my consciousness, only in my subconscious. The human mind is a very complex thing. It hides the details that one cannot bear to face. Denial is one of the strongest human emotions that exists. Considering my brain had been programmed to avoid any aspects of the past, the denial was even more powerful. I saw what I wanted to see and ignored all the rest.

But those deeply entrenched survival instincts from my early childhood combined with the enhanced protective hormones of pregnancy ultimately proved stronger than my denial. They kicked in, and the child I once was emerged. All those times in the past week that I crashed into the blackness of an intense migraine, went utterly unconscious into what felt like a black hole, the child I used to be resurfaced . . . did what had to be done. Even in my dreams, sometimes the memories seeped through. But each time I awoke, the carefully programmed adult me took over and the deeply ingrained denial did the rest.

Then, a few days ago during the aura—those awful minutes before a debilitating migraine kicks in—some of the memories came crashing back in spurts of ugly images and awful words, and this time a few of them lingered. The denial was fighting a losing battle. This very minute, more memories are filtering through the carefully constructed membrane of protection the only real father I have ever known helped to put in place in my damaged mind. I assume these recalls are of actual events, but I can't be certain. So much is still unclear.

Had all the elements of this perfect storm not occurred, I might still have no idea about my real past.

Even now, all that I know for certain is that I cannot remember my real name—the one given to me at birth—but I am the child Carl Fanning raped and abused for eight long years. I am the "it" whose universe was filled only by him and what he wanted.

Now all I have to do is find that son of a bitch and make sure he never does that to anyone else.

First, I need to check that in my sleep last night I didn't move the bones. They are evidence now. Everything on this farm is evidence. The files, the videos. All of it.

As I pass my mother's potting shed, I pause. I spot something blue but only a glimpse. Moving cautiously, I ease around the corner and stop stone-still in my tracks. A blue Ford pickup—an older one—is parked behind the shed.

"What the hell . . . ?"

I move closer, open the passenger side door, and look in the glove box. The registration shows the truck belongs to Janie Hyatt's riding academy. What the hell is it doing here?

I think of the cabin Walt and I visited and the barn that was burned. Fanning's neighbor stated that two women matching Hyatt's and Reeves's descriptions drove past Fanning's rented house. I consider how, according to both Patricia Shelby and Melanie Hardeman, the victims banded together to plan his demise. But why would they bring him here? They couldn't have known my secret. Even I didn't know it.

But Mario Sanchez did.

The reality hits me like a punch to the chest. He is the skinny kid I helped escape. He may know who I am . . . God knows Walt and I have been on television enough.

I was in the shed yesterday. Fanning is not in there. That leaves only the barn. I head in that direction. I think of all the times I have traveled this path with my mother or father. Some of the memories, of course, are not real, but they feel real.

I open the barn door and step inside. Even after all these years, it still smells of hay and horses. My heart quickens. I've had flashes of memories about him being chained, and after discovering the bones I dug up, more snippets of memory seeped into my head. Images of me—the other me, the one I didn't remember—torturing him. I shudder.

I find the switch for the lights, flip it, and then move deeper into the enormous structure. The tack room is on the right. My mother's trophies and ribbons as well as those of the child who's buried in the woods are neck deep in that room. All the horse gear was sold along with the horses.

At the end of the row, in the very last stall, I find him. A length of chain has been looped to the ring on the wall meant for a horse's lead rope. He is handcuffed to the chain. The smell of feces and urine and death fill my lungs. My first impulse is to see if he's still alive, but I resist. I will not go near him. I hope he's dead.

Whispers of words, flickers of images, sift through my mind. Finding the note he left on the windshield of my car while I was in the house going through my father's papers late Sunday evening. *I'm waiting in the barn.* Me walking toward the barn, agony spearing through my brain with every step I made. I haven't tended his wound, that's obvious, but I haven't killed him, either. Perhaps my dedication to the oath I took prevented me from crossing that line.

The eerie calmness I feel surprises me. I'm not sure what I should be feeling, but I'm certain this is not it. As an officer of the law, it's my duty to serve and protect, yet I cannot bring myself to do either for him.

His eyes open and the corners of his split lips lift upward. "I didn't think you were coming back this time."

"How did you get here?" The words are mine, but it's as if someone else prodded me to ask the question. I am oddly numb. Shaking inside where he can't see.

I steel my spine and force my brain to shift into cop mode. I might not know the name I was given at birth, but I am still a cop. Although I can't be sure exactly what's happened here, I have an idea. On the floor between us is a balled-up piece of paper—his note. I should pick it up; it's evidence. But that would mean moving closer to him. I don't want to be close to him. I want to run . . . to hide. The images and sounds of all the things he did to me erupt in my brain, and the anguish nearly doubles me over.

He laughs, the sound dry and rotten as if his throat is ripping apart. "Why, you brought me here at gunpoint, don't you remember?"

I steady myself and move my head from side to side. "No. You're lying." At least, I hope like hell he's lying.

If he's telling the truth, that means I have become the monster. Perhaps there wasn't a note. I remind myself that I'm a master at denial. It is a traitorous friend. I glance at the wadded-up paper again. But there it is. There was indeed a note.

"Well, maybe you did and maybe you didn't," he says on a wheeze, drawing my attention back to him. "But what do you think your friends in the police department are going to believe? You wouldn't be the first cop to crack, particularly under the circumstances. If you tell them the sad, sad story of your life, maybe they'll feel sorry for you and send you to one of those cushy mental hospitals instead of to prison. Either way, you're going down, girl."

I think of the baby I'm carrying, and my heart clutches. "I did not bring you here. You drove that blue truck, didn't you?"

He shrugs. "What else was I going to do after those two bitches tried to roast me like a fucking Christmas turkey?"

So Hyatt and Reeves did take him. I refuse to call it kidnapping no matter that I am aware of the legal term. "Why come here?"

"That's for me to know and you to figure out. But we both know what your friends are going to think when they find out," he singsongs.

Piece of shit. I tamp down my anger. I refuse to allow the bastard to goad me into doing something stupid. The image of a baby being taken from me arrows into my head, rips through my heart. I flinch. My body trembles with the need to end him.

I struggle to push the emotions aside and to focus on my training. I am a cop. A homicide detective. A damn good one. I will not allow this son of a bitch to damage another minute of my life.

I reach for some sense of calm and push a smile into place. "You were scared and wanted to hide, didn't you? Those women scared you."

Fury whips across his face. "No bitch has ever scared me," he roars. "The only thing they did besides set themselves up for a kidnapping charge was screw up my timeline." He smiles a sinister, sickening display. "But I got back on track because here we are."

And then I know. That's what the note was about. I stare at the way he's shackled. I laugh. "You know, finding the hardware store where you bought the chain and the pawn shop or wherever you picked up those police-issue handcuffs won't be that difficult. Just time consuming. You might as well tell me the truth." I shrug. "Otherwise I'm going to make sure the whole world knows what a coward you are and how your victims got the better of you—just like before."

I smile as if he—this—is all just a big joke and I am weary of it. But deep inside, the outrage pounds, desperate to be unleashed. I hold back. This baby I'm carrying is counting on me to be smart. I just need him talking. He's so full of himself, he'll have to brag about how smart he is.

He laughs then. "Newhouse took you and turned you into something you could never really be. I told him that deep down you were still mine. I branded you at seven years old. He couldn't wash that away."

Pain spears my heart as I imagine how the man who raised me—the only father who ever really loved me—felt at hearing those foul words from this bastard. "You were wrong."

"If you're so changed, what am I doing here dying like this?"

"You don't sound as if you're dying."

"Oh, I'm dying all right. But I'm taking you to hell with me."

"Obviously you aren't clever enough to make that happen." I know this scumbag. If I keep at him, he will spill his guts. "You never were very bright."

"It was so easy." He grins at me like the devil he is. "I saw you and that cowboy partner of yours on the news. I recognized you instantly, and I knew despite all the polish and highfalutin education that deep down you were still my little girl. My heart pounded so hard I lost my breath, got hard just thinking about you. Right then and there, I called my attorney. Made sense he wouldn't want nothing to do with me unless there was something in it for him, so I told him my plan. Let's just say he was intrigued. All he had to do was dig up everything he could find on Lewis and Corrine Newhouse and their lovely daughter, Olivia."

I want to vomit. To scream. But I need him to keep talking, to explain what the hell he means. What he did. I have to know what happened during all those blackouts I experienced this week. I'm guessing I came out here. Saw him. Talked to him. Judging by all the bruises, maybe tortured him. The chip bags and empty water bottles on the floor indicate someone was keeping him alive.

But I need to be sure. "You see," I taunt, "I knew you weren't smart enough to plot all this on your own. The lawyer helped you, didn't he?"

He attempts to laugh but coughs instead. "He gave me the lowdown on you and the Newhouses. I figured out all the rest from there. Planned every last detail, and I knew that once we spent some time together, you would want to hurt me. All I had to do was set things in motion. Those other idiots thought they could take me down. All they did was make it easier for me. The police were too worried about finding me—the victim—to wonder if I was up to something."

I lift my chin and stare directly into his beady eyes. "I guess you weren't expecting that I'd forgotten all about you and the life we shared."

Another of those dry laughs rips from his throat. "Yeah, right. You're lying just like he did. Newhouse told me you weren't that child anymore, that you didn't remember anything from the past. He begged me to let you go. He was so sincere, so worried that I would hurt you again, that he just kept upping the ante. So I took the money he offered for my silence. He turned it over to my attorney, and I put him right to work on what I wanted. By the time Newhouse came back to the prison for a final meeting, I knew all his secrets. I knew his wife was dead and that you weren't this Olivia you were strutting around claiming to be. I guess that chat kind of tore him up, because he dropped dead of a heart attack a few days later."

I roar with outrage and rush toward him, determined to finish off what is left of his pathetic, shitty existence. "That man was my father—nothing you have done or can say will change that. I loved him and he loved me. You took that from me, and I want to tear your fucking head off."

He just laughs and laughs until he can't breathe, and then he coughs and coughs. I wish an artery would rupture and send blood spewing out of his sadistic mouth.

"The minute I got out"—he clears his throat—"I started watching you. Went through your trash. That's how I got your blood. That night you cut yourself—you really should close the blinds in that swanky house—I watched you take the mess out to the trash. I took it, not sure exactly what I'd do with it, but a plan was coming together."

I think of the second blood type found at the scene in his rental house. "You planted my DNA in that shithole you call home. You couldn't think of anything more original?"

"Pretty fucking brilliant for a not-so-bright nothing like me."

"Too bad you just confessed to a police detective." Too bad I didn't have my cell phone recording this conversation. I have no idea where the damned thing even is.

"They'll never believe you. Not after all the bizarre shit you've done this week. I'm sure your hotshot fiancé thinks you're crazy as hell already. You told me that yourself. I don't think you meant to. You came in here muttering and talking to yourself. I swear, you even had me convinced you'd lost it. Between me and Newhouse, we done mind-fucked you up good, girl."

I ignore his crude words. What he thinks is irrelevant to me. "I know what you're up to, Fanning. You want me to take the fall for your murder. That's your way of exacting revenge, isn't it?"

"Now you're getting the picture." He smirks.

I want to beat that smirk off his twisted face. He's right. I want to make his heart stop beating. I want him not to exist any longer. I want to scream at the injustice of it all. He stole my life not once, but twice.

Now I am no one . . . I have nothing . . .

Defeat straddles my shoulders like an elephant. Tears spill past my lashes, and I curse the weakness.

"I had a different plan at first," he says, as if I give one shit. "You wouldn't have liked it any better, trust me. But you see, right after I was released from prison, I found out I have AIDS. Full-blown. Hell, that damn prison hospital probably knew it but didn't tell me just to keep from having to take care of me. I was so close to my release date, I guess they just decided to keep that little secret to themselves and let me find out all on my own. The clinic says I can't take the medicine I need because of all the other shit that's wrong with me. Heart issues. Rotten liver. Kidney troubles. It's all falling apart on me. So, you see, I'm a dead man anyway. Even if this"—he tugs at his restraint—"is cutting my time a little short, it's worth it to have sweet revenge before I go."

Now I understand what my father was doing looking up information on the victims and visiting this sick psycho in prison. He was worried *this* would happen. A new wave of fury twists inside me. My fists clench with the effort of holding back the building rage. I want so desperately to end this . . . to end him.

"Making you angry, am I? Too bad. You're the reason I went to prison. If I hadn't gone, I wouldn't have contracted this shit. All these years you've had it made. Been treated like a princess. Now, you're going to pay for what you did to me."

I charge forward, put my face in his. "No, I'm not." My words are ice cold and as hard as stone. The rage simmers, but I am in control. "I'm going to walk away and let you sit here in your own shit and piss until help comes. And then you're going back to jail for the rest of your fucking pathetic life. While I live and do all the things you can't even dream of." I spit in his face.

As I start to draw away, he grabs me around the neck with his free arm. The move is so abrupt, I lose my balance and fall against him. *Fuck!*

Psychotic laughter pierces my ear as I try to twist away, but I'm not quick enough. He yanks me closer and presses his nasty mouth against my throat. I feel his teeth close on my flesh. *No! No! No!*

Pulse pounding, I pull his hair, poke at his eyes. Try to stretch my head out of his reach. He won't let go. *Shit!* How can he be this strong?

My heart lunges into my throat. *Have. To. Get. Loose.*

I plow my elbow into his gut. Claw at his injured arm. He screeches in pain. I yank away from him. Land on my butt and scramble out of his reach.

His howls of misery shift to laughter, then to a coughing jag that puts him on his hands and knees, gagging and puking.

Die, you bastard. I get to my feet and back fully out of the stall. I touch my neck with the top of my hand—the only clean part. Fear that he broke the skin rushing through me.

He starts to laugh as he collapses onto his side. "I almost got you."

Red-hot rage washes over me, but I shake it off and square my shoulders. "But you didn't."

Then I turn and walk away. He screams and rants, but I don't look back.

I am never looking back again.

THIRTY

Detective Walter Duncan

The tires squeal as I slam to a stop in front of Preston's house. I jump out of my Tahoe and rush to the front door and start pounding. I need to find Liv. She isn't answering her cell. I'm worried. Worried sick.

This whole idea is wrong. Not possible. I can't fathom how to explain it, and yet I know there is no other reasonable explanation.

It was Liv's blood found with Fanning's in his damned kitchen. Liv is the young girl who helped Mario Sanchez, a skinny ten-year-old kid, escape that bastard. Liv is the mystery child that Andrea Donnelly thought was Fanning's daughter.

My heart breaks for her. I cannot imagine what this is going to do to her. My God, what she has been through.

A sob catches in my throat. The idea of what that bastard likely did to her tears me apart. I don't understand how it all came about or what role the Newhouses played in this mess, but I know I have to help her. I have to make this okay somehow, no matter what it takes.

The rattle of the lock and the swing of the door opening send renewed tension through my muscles. Preston stares at me. "If you're looking for Liv, she's not here."

"Do you know where she is?"

"She left in a hurry." He steps back, leaving the door open.

It's not until then that I notice the box cutter in his hand. A frown nags at my brow. The stack of boxes I helped Liv move from her place still stands to one side in the entry hall. Preston zips the box cutter along the taped edges of the box closest to him and starts prowling through it.

Since he left the door open, I take it as an invitation. I don't have time for him to find his manners. "Are you saying you haven't seen her today?"

"Look"—he glances at me—"you're with her more than I am. Haven't you noticed that something is wrong?" He puts the potential weapon aside and reaches for the flaps of the box. "I woke up in bed with a woman covered in mud from the waist down. She said she was at some crime scene last night and got muddy. Was she?"

I'm not going to try to explain. I wonder whether he knows she's carrying his child. The urge to shake the shit out of him is nearly overpowering. Instead, I take a breath and follow my cop instincts. "What exactly did she say when she was leaving?"

"She said there was something she had to do and that she would tell me everything as soon as she could." He shakes his head. "I have no idea what's going on."

The sheen of emotion in his eyes, his voice, tells me he means it. So maybe I was wrong about him. Maybe he isn't a total asshole.

I take another deep breath. "Okay. How long ago did she leave?"

I figure she's at the farm. Whatever is happening, it's rooted there.

"Maybe two, two and a half, hours ago." He pauses and looks at the grandfather clock in the corner. "It's eleven now. I got up at seven thirty. Saw the mud and freaked out. She showered and left. I'm pretty sure she was out of here by eight thirty, maybe quarter of nine." He shakes his head again. "I honestly don't know what to do. I told her I'd be waiting for her. That I could help if she would just talk to me."

The claws of worry dig deeper. "She probably went to the farm?"

He nods. "She's been going there a lot lately. I'm not sure she wants to be here anymore." He reaches into the box and pulls out an object. A frown scrunches his face. "What is this?"

He holds up a ragged old teddy bear.

Another knot twists in my gut. It's hers . . . "We should go now," I urge. "Olivia is in trouble."

A lot more trouble than either of us know.

Driving like a crazy man, it takes the longest twenty-five minutes of my life to reach the farm. Liv's car is there. So are three Williamson County Sheriff's Office cruisers and an ambulance. The tight band around my chest loosens a fraction. Preston and I are out of the Tahoe before it quits rocking. I check her car. Her wallet and cell phone are on the console. I frown at the mud. Preston was right. Mud on the floorboard and some in the driver's seat.

He's already through the front door of the house, calling her name.

I rush in behind him and do the same.

The house is dead silent.

Preston turns to me, and I say, "The barn."

We head outside. I spot a uniform coming out of the barn. That's when I start running. Preston is right beside me.

I reach the barn, my chest wheezing, pain radiating through me like an electrical current.

Two paramedics are coming out with a gurney. Fanning, the scumbag, is strapped on it, bellowing about how she tried to kill him.

My face twists with disgust. *What goes around, comes around, you piece of shit.*

"Olivia!"

Preston sees her before I do and is running toward her. Uniforms are spread out inside the barn, going over the place.

That's when I realize I've been holding my breath. The air pours into my aching lungs as I walk toward Liv and Preston, who is holding her tight against him. I want to grab her and hug her, to promise her everything will be all right, but it won't be. Not for a while. At the moment, the reassurance she needs has to come from Preston. Everything else will have to wait.

I will do whatever necessary to find a way to protect her from all the official stuff.

I muster up a calm face and join the two of them. "You okay?"

She nods. "I will be eventually."

The thousand knots in my gut loosen a little.

She looks to her fiancé then. "There's so much I have to tell you."

He hugs her again. "We're going to be fine," he promises, his voice breaking.

Liv's right. She will be, and I'll do all in my power to help make that happen. Sounds like Preston intends to do his part as well.

We're all, I realize, going to be okay.

THIRTY-ONE

Four months later

"It's a boy!"

David and I stare at the ultrasound screen. Tears slip from my eyes even as I try to blink them back.

"Olivia"—David stares at me, his own eyes wide and filled with wonder, his hand squeezing mine—"we're having a boy."

I can't speak. I can only smile and let the tears flow.

The evening after I found Fanning in the barn at the farm, I told David the whole story. All of it. Since then, I have been amazed every day by how kind and caring he has been about every single thing. He has gone above and beyond to help me through each day, and there have been some tough ones. I am truly grateful that he is the man I fell in love with. That never changed. He was only reacting to what was happening to me. I was the one pushing him away, because subconsciously I felt I didn't deserve him and that I couldn't make him happy. I had to find my way through all that. The man tells me every morning when we wake up how much he loves me, how thankful he is for me. How he can't wait to be a father to our children. I am so very happy.

Not to mention, his family has been incredible as well. Everyone is thrilled about the baby. It's just all so wonderful. Sometimes I worry that it won't last. But then I remind myself that I know it will.

Once we've seen Dr. Raiford and she has assured us that all looks just as it should, we drive home.

As he navigates into the garage, he says, "There's something I should tell you."

I groan. I can only imagine what he is up to. He's so on top of everything. The nursery is complete except for the final bits of decor related to gender. Those will be going up next. He has already decided to take an extended leave when the baby is born. Just days ago, he informed me that he's even planning a babymoon. He is so excited. It makes me very happy.

I, on the other hand, am still somewhere in the neighborhood of somewhat terrified. I'm having a baby, and I have no idea how to do that or how to be a mother. David insists we will figure it all out together.

I'm counting on him.

He shuts off the engine. "Don't be mad."

I turn to him. Have no clue what he means. "How could I be?"

David really has proven over the past few months how he intends to be there for me and our child through whatever comes our way. I can count on him, and that means so much. If he has some big surprise planned, how can I be upset?

"I know we promised each other there wouldn't be any more sur-prises, but I couldn't help myself." His face tells me he really wants me to understand.

Whatever this is, he's thrilled about it. Obviously. "Okay, so what's going down?"

He grins. "The family is inside. They wanted to throw a little gen-der-reveal party."

I roll my eyes and groan again. "You haven't told them yet, have you?" I can't see how, since we've been together every second since the ultrasound. Well, except for when I went to the bathroom. Man, if he told . . .

"I haven't. I swear." He releases his seat belt and gets out, then rushes around to my side of the car and opens the door.

I release my seat belt and climb out. "I didn't see any cars. Are you sure they're coming?"

He escorts me out of the garage. "We have to go through the front door."

I look up and down the street just in case I missed something, but I still see no sign of the vehicles his family drives.

"They parked the next street over so you would be surprised."

"I see." I loop my arm around his. "I guess you weren't supposed to warn me in advance."

He shoots me another lopsided grin. I do love that face. I hope our little boy looks just like him.

"Thanks." I lean my head on his shoulder as we pause at the front door.

He unlocks and opens it, and we walk in. The house is utterly silent. I can just imagine the whole Preston crew all hidden behind curtains and hovering behind the sofa, waiting to surprise me. We share a secret smile and head deeper inside.

The boxes that once crowded the foyer have been unpacked. I am fully moved in. I decided the best way for me to show my love and respect for the man and woman who gave me their love and security was to donate the farm to an organization that will turn it into a safe haven for abused children. The money the Newhouses left me will fund the transformation of the property as well as the operation for years to come. No matter that what they did was wrong—divisive, even—their intent and the relationship that developed between us as the years passed was loving and generous. I will always love them as if they were the family I was born into.

I saw to it that their daughter, the other Olivia, was given a proper burial next to them.

As for me, I'm working with a brilliant therapist who is helping me get used to what my history actually is versus what I've believed for the past sixteen years. Lots more memories have seeped in—none good, sadly. But I deal with them. I remind myself that none of it can touch me now. It's in the past. This is my life now.

"Surprise!" an array of voices shout as we enter the great room.

I put my hands to my chest in faux surprise. "What is all this?"

David's entire family is here, all wearing either pink or blue. I can't blink fast enough to stop the tears. I do a lot of that these days. His family really has embraced me in a way I only dreamed of.

It's the tallest of the guests who draws my lingering attention. Walt is wearing a blue tee that looks a tad too small. He winks at me. I glance at David, so very grateful that he included Walt. The man is family, too. I can't imagine my life without him.

I'm suddenly surrounded by people trying to give me hugs and begging to know whether we're having a boy or a girl.

David pulls me away from the others, and we move to the long table that stands in the center of the room, where all sorts of food and decorations wait. My goodness, the whole room is full of streamers and baby decorations. In front of the table, two good-size boxes with question marks on them wait for us. One question mark is pink and one is blue.

"You ready?" he asks me.

I nod. We lean down and take hold of the box lid that has the blue question mark and lift. The moment we do, dozens and dozens of blue balloons float up.

The cheering and clapping goes on and on. Suddenly, I am swallowed up in more hugs and teary congratulations.

I hear the popping of champagne corks and more cheering.

"This is quite the celebration, kid."

I turn to Walt and savor a big hug from him. When I draw back, I narrow my gaze at him. "And you didn't say a word."

He puts a hand to his chest. "Hey, I was sworn to secrecy."

He leans down and we hug again. "Thank you," I murmur against his ear. "I could not have gotten through the past few months without you."

"You"—he draws back—"have got this."

I swipe more silly tears away. He's right. I have got this. It wasn't easy in the beginning, but I'm getting there. Walt has been an amazing source of strength. I will forever be grateful for him.

We eat and drink and laugh, and I am so very happy. I look from one guest to the next. All are smiling and teasing David. His parents look so proud. This will be their first grandson.

I think of my other son. The one that was taken from me when I was just shy of fifteen. I wanted to find him, and I did. Actually, Fanning did. When my father gave the bastard's attorney all that money, one of the things that Fanning asked him to do was to locate the boy. Fanning intended to use him to hurt me. But his plan backfired. My son is a happy and healthy fifteen-year-old who lives in Chattanooga. I met with his parents and explained everything. They are wonderful people. Looking at all the photos of him, hearing about his life, was amazing. Not having the chance to hug him or be a part of his life is hard for sure. But allowing him to go on with the really good life he has is the least I can give him. If and when they need me or he wants to meet me, they know where I am. They have raised a great kid. I can only hope to do so well.

As for my career, that is on hold for now. The investigation confirmed that the now-deceased Carl Fanning did indeed set out to frame me for his own murder. An unexpected and surprising new way, in my opinion, to leave this world via suicide by cop. The bastard died two days after he was taken from my barn. A bad case of pneumonia and complications related to his other health issues took him out. During those final two days, he refused to give a statement about how he ended up in my barn or anything else. It was as if he understood he had lost, and he just shut down. Based on the testimony of Fanning's attorney, Alexander Cagle, and that of Walt as well as Janie Hyatt, no evidence of criminal behavior on my part was discovered.

The psychiatric evaluation concluded that I was not aware of my interactions with Fanning after he imprisoned himself on my property, and, therefore, I was not criminally liable for whatever events occurred during that time. However, that same conclusion called to question my mental fitness for duty. Completely understandable. I love being a cop, so maybe one day I will get back to it.

Though Olivia Newhouse is my legal name, I am not Olivia Newhouse. Olivia Newhouse died at home when she was fifteen years old after being in a coma for two years. I have no idea what my real name is or who my biological parents were. Given the situation, I have chosen to keep the name Olivia, but I am a Preston now.

I smile at my husband as he and Walt laugh over glasses of champagne. Walt has been assigned to desk duty due to his heart condition. No more going into the field for him. His cardiologist is certain he will continue to do well as long as he sticks to his meds, a strict diet, and exercise. I am making sure he does exactly that.

As for the victims who banded together in the hope of ending Fanning, Walt tossed their signed statements. No one else had seen them except for the officer who left them on Walt's desk, and he didn't read them. Their confessions were never added to the case file. Walt and I decided they had suffered enough. Thankfully, the DA decided not to go after them for harassment or any other charges. Hyatt's burned barn and stolen truck was all Fanning. At least, that's how the report was written, and no one is questioning it. All involved can go on with their lives.

Case closed.

Is any part of what we did wrong? Maybe. But we're not looking back on that one, either.

David ushers me over to where the cake is being sliced and served. I lean close and inhale the scent of him, so very grateful that I didn't ruin our relationship with my secrets. My therapist also helped me to see that David's attempts to stop our relationship from falling apart triggered the child I once was to fight against the perceived domination. Poor guy.

He really was getting the worst of me. I smile as he passes me a slice of cake. Just watching how happy he is makes me happy.

In addition to all the psychiatric testing and therapy I've endured the past few months, I've also dealt with the other necessary tests, including for HIV, since I was in close contact with Fanning. I am good. No worries about that.

This is just the beginning of my new life.

The life I've led until now belonged to someone else. In truth, I suppose you could say I've died twice and been resurrected. This time, this life will be all mine. My goal is to figure out the motherhood thing so I can be the best mother possible for my child. I don't really know how normal people take care of normal children. I've never really been normal; certainly none of the people involved with the first three decades of my life could be labeled as normal.

I want this child to have a real normal . . . whatever that is.

Lucky for me, I have a big, loving family. I look from David to Walt and the other people gathered in this room. Who could ask for more?

Life is good, and I am looking only forward.

About the Author

Photo © 2019 Jenni M Photography LLC

Debra Webb is the *USA Today* bestselling author of more than 180 novels. She is the recipient of the prestigious *Romantic Times* Career Achievement Award for Romantic Suspense, as well as numerous Reviewers' Choice Awards, and was the first recipient of the esteemed L. A. Banks Warrior Woman Award for her courage, strength, and grace in the face of adversity. She was also awarded the distinguished RWA Centennial Award for having published her hundredth novel. Debra has sold more than ten million books in many languages and countries. The author's love of storytelling goes back to her childhood, when her mother bought her an old typewriter at a tag sale. Born in Alabama, Debra grew up on a farm and spent every available hour exploring the world around her and creating stories. For more information, visit www.debrawebb.com.